PAST TENTS

TEACHERS' LOUNGE
BOOK 4

STACY TRAVIS

COPYRIGHT

This book is a work of fiction. Names, characters, places, rants, facts, contrivances, and incidents are either the product of the author's questionable imagination or are used factitiously. Any resemblance to actual persons, living or dead or undead, events, locales is entirely coincidental if not somewhat disturbing/concerning.

Copyright © 2024 by Smartypants Romance; All rights reserved.

No part of this book may be reproduced, scanned, photographed, instagrammed, tweeted, twittered, twatted, tumbled, or distributed in any printed or electronic form without explicit written permission from the author.

NO AI TRAINING: Without in any way limiting the author's and publisher's exclusive rights under copyright, any use of this publication to "train" generative artificial intelligence (AI) technologies to generate text is expressly prohibited. The author reserves all rights to license uses of this work for generative AI training and development of machine learning language models.

Made in the United States of America

Print Edition

ISBN: 978-1-959097-88-4

"Another one down." John Witty's voice hung in the teachers' lounge like a cloud of perfume. Witty always spoke in a scandalized stage whisper, even if he was just commenting on the weather. Always with his round wire glasses slipped down his nose, so his fierce blue eyes made direct contact.

I just wanted to eat my salad in peace, but instead, the lettuce and cherry tomato hung suspended just outside my mouth while I waited to hear what had Witty's boxer briefs so utterly twisted.

Rubbing a hand over his dark beard Sherlock Holmes–style, Witty shook his head like the end of planet Earth might be near.

I wasn't worried. Yet.

Witty had a flair for the dramatic, appropriate since he was the drama teacher, but he sounded like the town crier warning that the sky was falling. Last week, the cafeteria substituted brownies for layer cake, and he made it sound like nuclear winter.

"Another one? Another what?"

"Diamond's home with the stomach bug." Witty tilted in his stiff-backed chair, patted his rounded stomach, and adjusted his bowtie. He wore a neat little clip-on every day, and today's featured tiny rubber ducks on a blue background. The wispy brown hair on top of his head blew gently with the overhead air-conditioning.

Meanwhile, I felt sorry for Loretta Diamond, who'd worked as the school nurse for almost two decades. After a few years on the job, most teachers develop a hardy resistance to any and all vermin that students hurl our way. I hadn't been sick in two years, despite having one-on-one sessions with several kids who didn't tell me they had budding colds and flus.

Loretta, however, was the opposite. Anything that even hinted at infecting a student at Green Valley High ended up felling Loretta like a beetle-infested tree.

Unfortunately, a spate of stomach bugs had been sweeping through the school ever since we all enjoyed a faculty lunch a couple days ago. There were rumors —and there were always rumors at Green Valley High—that patient zero wasn't actually a patient, but instead, a tainted batch of chicken salad.

"Oh, no. Poor thing." I cast a futile look around the teachers' lounge. Clara and Nick were the only other teachers there. Sitting in stiff-backed chairs, they chatted away at one end of the table and shared a bag of salt-and-vinegar potato chips. It would have been way more comfortable for them to sit on the couch, but *no one* sat on the green couch against the wall.

Not ever.

Not since it was rumored that two faculty members had sex on it. One was further rumored to be our principal, and that was too much information for me.

Clara and Nick were so besotted, they didn't seem to register Witty's dire news. I could see Nick's index finger curled around Clara's underneath the table, and it gave me a warm feeling to think about those early days of budding love. The early days that were nothing but rainbow skies and cartoon hearts floating all around. Steamy late nights that plastered a satisfied grin on a girl's face for days.

I'd had days like those. Or hours . . . or . . . moments?

The point was that I'd had my cartoon hearts—however brief—and however clouded by revisionist history, dreams, and embellishment. And however ripped off from whatever Regency romance novel I was reading. If my friends accused me of confusing my life with those in my books, they were most certainly . . . probably correct.

It didn't mean I'd lost touch with reality. It just meant I had healthy romantic dreams that would most certainly . . . not become reality.

Sigh. Yeah, who needed reality?

I mean, it's not like I spent a lot of time worrying about turning my life into a novel. That was impossible. Obviously. I knew Mr. Darcy wasn't going to rock up to Green Valley on his horse and declare his undying love for me. Still, I could fantasize about the kind of swoony, possessive men whose words dripped with passion and masculinity: "I won't allow another man to kiss you. You belong to me. You have since the day we met."

These men had locks of hair that fell roguishly over their foreheads, abs visible through winter-weight cotton shirts, and jawlines that could carve facets into diamonds. Their voices came out in growly rumbles that sent a thrill of awareness right down to my . . .

"I didn't see if Diamond ate the chicken salad, but I really hope not because I had two helpings," Witty whispered loudly, sending a spray of pineapple Fanta in my direction.

The record scratch that brought me back to reality was men like Witty—kind, dependable co-workers who'd married good women and made the happily ever after look easy. Witty served as a father figure to me, doling out hopeful advice from time to time when he sensed I was giving up on romance. "There's a lid for every pot," he was fond of saying.

What he didn't understand was that the men who I fantasized about in my novels did not exist. I knew this. It had been drilled into me by my mother, and then I'd learned it the hard way. Twice. Two budding relationships, two cases of heartbreak I should have seen coming.

Now I relied on myself. I was happy teaching high school art and yearbook design and going home to a small, spotless house. Happy and single.

I stood up to reheat my coffee and noticed the assortment of ceramic coffee mugs with sayings like "Don't make me use my teacher voice" and "Teaching is a work of heart." No one ever washed those mugs, so there they sat, week after week, growing ten colors of mold.

I popped my lukewarm coffee into the microwave, watched the inner carousel spin slowly, and wondered for not the first time how microwaves work.

"It's all about moving the molecules. Exciting them." I didn't need to turn to identify the voice over my shoulder. Just like I didn't have to ask my question out loud for Clay Meadows to know I was wondering about the microwave.

Reading my mind was just something he did. Quietly, unobtrusively. Always serious and stoic, always leaning in to say things just to me, as though he and I shared a secret, and leaning away just as quickly to go about his business.

The problem was that he moved *my* molecules all over the place when he spoke and he excited them just by walking into the room.

I willed the chills that prickled across the back of my neck to abate along with the flush I felt creeping across my cheeks. I hated that my body reacted to Clay, heart rate speeding to a faster clip, even as my brain gave it firm instructions to chill.

Clay was standing close enough that I could smell the woodsy, fresh scent of whatever soap or aftershave he used. I swallowed hard and popped the door on the microwave open, even though my coffee still had twelve seconds to go. "All yours," I said, taking a generous step aside.

He slid a tray of something into the microwave and started it with the quiet press of a button. I tried not to notice every small movement Clay Meadows made, but it was impossible. Not when his six feet, three inches of muscle took up residence in a room.

Today, Clay wore a tan blazer over a gray tee and a pair of dark jeans which hugged his runner's thighs. His hair had the rumpled perfection of a mad scientist mixed with a sexy surf-wear model.

He shoved a hand through it whenever he was thinking, which was often. Add the tortoiseshell reading glasses, and he ticked every box on the how-to-look-hot-and-nerdy checklist.

He and I had known each other since we were teenagers. He was—and still is—my older brother Jefferson's closest friend. During our teen years, Clay spent half his waking hours at our house, but he was always on the go, moving in and out of our kitchen, upstairs and back down again, into the hallway and out the door. Never stopped long enough for a conversation with me, which was just as well since I was fifteen, two years younger, and tongue-tied around guys other than my brother. I was awkward and shy, he was tall and handsome, and his constant proximity made him the object of all my fantasies.

A lot had changed in nearly two decades. Now, I was confident and outgoing, and my teenage dreams of Clay Meadows had long since faded, replaced by dreams of fictional men. We'd worked together for going on ten years, and other than conversations that involved Green Valley High, we rarely talked outside of the teachers' lounge.

Clay was still fast moving, stoic, and evasive, brow always furrowed with a permanent crease, hazel eyes always darting around as though his mind was elsewhere. Students loved him. He taught a senior honors seminar and a Shakespeare elective, and he coached the track team.

He kept his circle of friends small, and as one of Green Valley's most notorious bachelors, he didn't let in many women either. Not that they didn't try. Not that every match-making auntie countywide hadn't given it a go as well.

But according to the rumor mill, first dates with Clay Meadows rarely led to second ones. Ever discerning, he always explained, "It's not you, it's me," and moved on. Clay was as commitment-phobic as Mr. Darcy was swoony. And as my mother would warn, "Leopards don't change their spots."

I inhaled deeply as a melted cheese aroma filled the room. At least it distracted me from the soap smell and the man emitting it.

"Wow, that smells amazing."

Glancing at my wilting salad, Clay nodded. "Mac and cheese. Leftovers."

"Even better. Where are they left over from? Restaurant or did you work your magic on some Kraft noodles at home?"

Clay tipped his head toward the microwave and inhaled a whiff of a smell that made me want to throw my salad in the trash. Or at him. "It's from that new place outside of Knoxville. They Know What to Do with Pasta."

"Smells like it."

"No, that's the name of the place. Guess that's the point, to make people talk about it. Now you won't forget the name, right?"

"True. But I'll birth a platypus before I drive to Knoxville for mac and cheese."

I heard what sounded like a grunt or possibly a laugh, but when I looked, Clay's face had regained composure. I didn't ask why he'd driven so far. Clay never discussed his personal life, which required nothing short of a papal oath of silence, at work, but if Clay had taken a date to a pasta place, I'd hear about it from six different people by fifth period. The faculty around here were more up in each other's business than a fat hive of bees.

As soon as the buzzer sounded on his mac and cheese, Clay whisked it out of the microwave, gave me a fist bump, and left the teachers' lounge. "Catch y'all later."

"Bye," I called, turning to watch him go. Which meant I was looking right at our principal, Curt Pindich, when he came into the teachers' lounge.

"Oh good. Ally. I need a favor." He tapped a long yellow pencil against his lip. It looked freshly sharpened. Like a weapon.

Pindich and I didn't have the best relationship, mainly because he was always one poorly worded sentence away from sexual harassment. He always hinted at the two of us spending time together outside of work, which gave me the *ick* big-time.

Spray-tanned and perfectly coiffed, Pindich looked like he'd just gotten back from vacation. He was charming enough around the female parents to make them giggle and sporty enough around the men to seem like a bro.

Only the teachers saw his evil side. If he didn't get his way, punitive busywork and budget cuts came our way. I'd long ago learned that where he was concerned, the best strategy was to keep it brief. "Principal Pin Dick, what's up?"

"It's Pindeech," he enunciated, as he always did when other teachers were in the room. And I always somehow *forgot* how to pronounce his name. Just like the rest of the faculty did. Behind his back.

With the spreading chicken salad bug, I figured he needed me to substitute for a class this week. I did a quick inventory in my mind of the teachers I hadn't seen today, but since I'd rushed in late, it didn't tell me much.

"Sure. How can I help?" I got to work finishing my salad.

"I'd like you to go on the senior English class retreat to the Smoky Mountains. Green Valley Outfitters has made all the arrangements for gear and there will be a ranger at the campsite. We just need another teacher's eyes and ears on the kids."

"Yeah, that's funny," I said through a bite, not bothering to look up from my salad. It didn't matter that growing up in Green Valley gave me an appreciation for the changing color of the fall leaves and the dampness of the evening air. I loved the purpling of the lakes right before dusk, when the last rays of sun hung in the air. But I enjoyed those things from afar.

I preferred a down comforter on my bed and a soft rug under my feet. I didn't even care for the fancy pre-pitched tents, barbecue grills, and bedding that went along with glamor camping—glamping. And anyone who knew me— and that included Principal Pindich—understood that the great outdoors and I were hardly on good terms.

This discussion would end as soon as Principal Pindich delivered the punch line, weird as his sense of humor may have been.

"Funny how?"

My topknot mess of a bun left my face feeling exposed. I'd inherited my pale blue eyes from my dad, and I'd long ago learned that people mistook their gentle color for innocence. Principal Pindich had the steely gaze of a puma sizing up a meal, and I willed my eyes to fight back.

"Um, me and wilderness activities don't mix." It was a joke, right? For the good of the student body, I would not—could not—chaperone.

"Loretta Diamond was supposed to go, but sadly, she's in no shape to consider it. I can't chance that she'll be healthy by the time of the retreat."

"It's more than two weeks from now."

If Pindich had a mustache, he'd have been twirling it. That was how pleased he looked as he leveled the blow. "You're the backup nurse. You took the first aid course. We need someone with your considerable skills. There's extra pay involved. I'm doing you a solid here. You should be thanking me." He had the nerve to wink.

I felt the color drain from my cheeks. Of course he thought I made sense in the wilderness—I'd completed an extensive first aid and medical training course over the summer and had the poor judgment to announce that I could put anyone's leg in traction using only the limb of a tree.

We'd been at a party before the start of school. A margarita had been involved.

Several margaritas. Witty's doing. He was no good as a mixologist because he never measured—he chatted while he poured, and that led to very strong drinks.

"So . . . there's no one else who can do it?" I asked hopefully.

Pindich shook his head. "You're a team player, Ally. I'll have Clay get you the details. He's the lead on the trip. Or if you'd prefer, I'll buy you lunch one day and catch you up." His smarmy smile left no question about what I'd do.

"Clay knows about this?" My voice was a defeated squeak.

"Not yet. I just decided on it when I saw you in here. Would you mind letting him know?"

Of course Clay had been born to bound happily from river rock to fallen log in pounding rain without a jacket. He was always off climbing rocks or hiking in the forest. Or running like a greyhound. He earned rave reviews every year after chaperoning the small group of seniors who attended.

And now he'd get the results of Witty's margaritas. A glampfire girl as his co-chaperone.

I could only imagine how fast that greyhound would run away when he heard the news.

My last two English classes of the day flew by, fueled by the seven bites of mac and cheese I'd chomped through at my desk while grading a pop quiz from earlier in the day.

By the time the seniors filed out of my Shakespeare elective, I felt the familiar twinge of anticipation. I wanted to get outside. I needed to breathe real air.

I had one of the best jobs on the planet, but the one downside to teaching English was the practical need to do it indoors. Students learned best in an orderly, structured environment. I knew this. I just always felt myself agitating to do things differently.

On days with nice weather, I often took my students outside and created a sort of outdoor classroom. The fresh air helped them think. But if nothing else, my students got ample opportunities to write descriptively about nature. Even if it wasn't strictly part of the Green Valley High curriculum, I thought it should be.

Shedding the restrictive blazer, I stretched my arms behind me before putting the jacket on a hanger in my truck. I wasn't so much fastidious about my clothes as I was lazy—I didn't want to have to iron the jacket the next time I wanted to wear it, so I shouldn't toss it in a heap.

I threw my gym bag over my shoulder and slammed the door to Blue Eye, as my pickup truck was casually named. No one questioned it when I explained it was an homage to Toni Morrison. An English teacher quirk, people figured.

In reality, my truck could have no other possible name once I saw the paint color. There'd only been one person with eyes paler than the summer sky, and it made me happy to name my truck in honor of Ally Dalbotten. Even if I was the only one who knew it.

Especially then.

Especially when Ally was the sister of my good friend Jefferson, and a guy doesn't go around naming his truck after his friend's sister. Or her eyes.

I needed to get over her. I knew this, and I'd tried. I'd gone on plenty of dates, but I wasn't interested in any of them.

Just her.

Even if I knew Ally and I were impossible.

It helped to get outside in the fresh air on a run or a hike, so I changed into my shorts and running shoes in the bathroom and headed out to the track that encircled the football field. Running helped my state of mind and elevated my mood, always had. If I was lucky, I could get a mile in before the track team came out for practice. Maybe two.

The students seemed to have the same reaction as I did to being inside all day, but it generally took them twice as long to socialize, change into their gear, and make their way outside.

Usually, it took a good twenty minutes for high schoolers to get their *shpilkes* out after class, *shpilkes* being a Yiddish term that means full of energy, impatience, and general restlessness. I found the term satisfying.

I taught my students that they should search for the most appropriate words when they wrote, even if the words came from a different culture or language. It also gave them awareness and respect when borrowing words from other cultures. Today, I was the one with *shpilkes*.

Inhaling the warm afternoon air, I felt my lungs relax, grateful for the fresh air and whatever amount of time I had to myself on the track. I started at a jog, taking one of the outside lanes out of habit.

I'd made it two laps around the track before I heard the steady crunch of shoes hitting the track behind me. There had been talk for years of replacing the classic track with modern tartan composite in the school's colors, blue and gold, but the district hadn't approved the budget. So we ran on dirt.

"Clay, hey." Jefferson's footsteps drew up behind me, plodding heavily like they always did.

"You sound like a hippopotamus."

"Only to you, twinkle toes."

At least twice a week, Jefferson took an afternoon break from running his construction business to show up and run some laps on the track.

"What's good, man?" I kept up my pace, knowing he'd catch up in seconds. His feet fell in step with mine and I readied myself for an update on his current construction project.

"Well, you didn't hear it from me, but Shane's kitchen is a train wreck." Jefferson was a mild gossip, always blabbing and warning that the news didn't come from him.

I laughed because Shane, my younger brother, had told me that the kitchen remodel was going swimmingly. "Of course, I didn't hear it from you. You never spill tea."

"Cabinets were supposed to go in next week," Jefferson said, breathing heavier as our pace increased. "'Course we're still waiting on a shipment of wood, and it's stuck on a freighter in the Gulf, so it's not happening next week."

"I won't tell him, if that's what you're worried about." Shane, my only sibling, was a bread maker at Donner Bakery and had gotten engaged last year to his high school crush. They'd been remodeling her grandmother's family home together. "I'm off on a school retreat the weekend after next, and he won't be at the jam session this week." Shane had professional French horn–playing chops, so he often skipped the local jam sessions when the Nashville Symphony needed him.

"It's his fiancée who scares the dickens out of me. She wants us on more of a schedule. She can't understand why construction goes in fits and starts and doesn't happen when she's ready."

I laughed again, imagining Julia reading him the riot act when he veered off schedule—she liked schedules. Also a baker, she'd moved back to Green Valley after a decade of running a bread empire in California. With the slower pace around here, she'd taken her type A personality out on the construction workers at the house.

"Don't let it get to you."

"Yeah, yeah. I know."

We rounded the bend and passed by the hurdles. I felt a twitch, my body daring me to jump over one. Just one.

"Don't do it," Jefferson warned.

"Don't do what?"

"Break your ass jumping over something that's too high for an old man." He pointed behind us at the hurdles, all raised to the men's racing height, daring me to clear them with an easy stride.

"It's not called jumping. It's hurdling. And I *could* do it without breaking my ass, but I'm choosing not to."

"Good thinking, grampa. You're getting smart in your old age."

"Younger than you."

"By a month."

Back in high school, I'd been the odd combination of long-distance runner during the fall cross-country season and short-distance hurdler during the spring track season. It didn't make sense to my coaches. By all accounts, I should have run the mile or the two-mile races. But the hurdles called to me, and I learned how to get over them in quick, neat bursts of energy.

Even now, coming out to the track sent a ripple of adrenaline through my veins, as though someone was hiding with a starting gun and I just might have to sprint. At thirty-six, I didn't want to believe that anything had changed. Didn't want to admit that I might not be able to keep up with my old pace or, worse still, that I might not get over a hurdle without catching an edge and knocking it down. Better to stay in the outer lanes.

"Damn wind," I grumbled at the gust that kicked up when we rounded the curve and started down the back straightaway. My runners would complain for the entirety of practice that the wind was responsible for their slower times. Any chance to beg for forgiveness. What they didn't understand was that I knew the wind was a hindrance, but I liked giving them a little obstacle. It made for a better workout.

"A little headwind never hurt anyone." Jefferson knew how I thought about these things. "Gives you something to work against."

"Exactly. How long are you staying?" I could hear voices of students crossing the grass field, which meant I might not get a full two miles in. Depended on how long it took them to change clothes. I picked up my pace a tiny bit. Jefferson kept stride.

"I'll probably run three. Can't do more than a dozen or so laps without getting batty from running in circles."

"It's an ellipse, not a circle."

"Great."

I ran beside him in silence. We'd known each other for long enough that we didn't always need to talk in order to communicate. I didn't have many friendships like that. Actually, I only had one.

"So I heard a rumor." His words came in ragged breaths as he ran, our pace faster now than either one of us would have liked.

"Explain," I huffed. One-word answers were better.

"About your grandmother."

"Yeah?" That was odd, given that she'd died seven years ago, but Jefferson was like a bloodhound when gossip was afoot.

We rounded the curve, and with the wind at our backs, started running even faster. We were still shy of an all-out sprint, but I was sucking wind. So was he. But being just as stubborn a son of a bitch as me, he wasn't about to tell me to slow down.

"Could be nothing," he panted.

"Yet you're here."

"To run."

"So run."

For a full lap, neither of us said anything, our mutual pulling in air and exhaling substituting for conversation.

Eventually, curiosity got the better of me and I gave Jefferson a nudge. I'd regained control of my breath enough to talk. "Let's hear it."

He cocked his head, and I got only a bit more than a side-eye, but it was enough for me to see the discomfort. He wanted to tell me something, but he also didn't want to tell me.

"Out with it," I insisted. Not knowing was making it worse.

"Heard a new rumor about why Principal Pindich left that law firm in Knoxville."

Rumors had been flying about the principal since he took over the job after Kip Sylvester. We'd all figured the new guy couldn't possibly be worse than Kip, but those two were cut from the same cloth. Principal Pindich was just as vindictive as Kip, but he managed to come off like a smooth, polished gentleman whenever it mattered.

"Hart Law." I knew the place. They'd handled my grandmother's affairs before she died.

There were always rumors about Pindich, and he only fanned their flames, saying things like, "When I was at the law firm . . ." or "You know, I worked at a law firm . . ." But Pindich wasn't licensed to practice law in the state of Tennessee. Apparently, he'd finished law school and never taken the bar. Never worked in the field again after leaving Hart Law. Moved to Green Valley.

"Yeah."

"Fired for being a douchebag, probably."

"If only that were a reason to fire a guy."

"So tell me . . ." I had to catch my breath before continuing. "What's the rumor this time?"

"I just went on a date with a woman, Sadie, who worked at the firm when he did."

"And?"

Jefferson didn't answer, his huffing breath taking the place of words. "Her hot take was that Pindich tried to date a wealthy client. Someone geriatric."

My ensuing bark of laugher made it hard to catch my breath, but the image of Pindich romancing the elderly was worth it.

"Thought maybe it was your grandmother," Jefferson added, chuckling beside me.

My laughter abruptly halted. I wanted nothing to do with *that* image. "You just had to go there," I muttered, picking up my pace until Jefferson was panting louder than me, trying to keep up.

"I mean, she did have a house on Bandit Lake, after all. Maybe he thought he could woo it out of her." The guy didn't know when to give up. My grandmother did have a house there. And she left it to me, not to Curt Pindich. End of discussion.

"Heard something else," Jefferson panted.

"Wow, you read the *National Enquirer* while you were getting your hair done or something?" It cost me some oxygen to get the words out, but someone had to let Jefferson know he sounded like his own personal hen party.

He didn't say anything, so I picked up my pace. If he was going to torture me, I'd torture him back. In seconds, I heard the pounding of his feet on the track as he gained on me.

"Blithe . . . Tanner." His words came out like a curse as he chased after me. I did this kind of ridiculous running every day of the week and therefore had an unfair advantage. Plus, the hurdling, back in the day.

"Yeah?" I couldn't slow down now. There was only fast or faster. I gave it a little more gas. We'd already done almost a mile, and I was determined to get to two in the next six minutes.

"Her friend . . . has a niece. Wants to . . ." His voice trailed off as he inhaled a mammoth breath. Then another. We were going too fast for a conversation, running around the track at top speed, each of us pouring on the gas for his own reasons.

He gasped and started to finish his explanation, but I waved a hand to cut him off. I already knew what he was going to say. If Blithe Tanner wanted to get me to date her friend's niece, the conversation could wait until we'd finished running. This felt too good.

My lungs craved the air that I was delivering in large, satisfying breaths. I needed the endorphins, plain and simple, always had.

Running had started as a sport. I'd done decently well, and it allowed me to be a competitive athlete all through high school. I played soccer in the winter, but fall and spring were when I exceled at racing sports. In the summer, I entered local five- and ten-kilometer runs, and most of the time, I outran nearly everyone.

Part of it was good racing habits—like I tell my team, train the way you race, race the way you train—but most of it was that I could get lost in my head on a run, which meant I'd put in far more miles than were required to train for a 5K. That meant that race days were easy by comparison.

My body craved the endorphins, that runner's high that left me feeling blissful and centered. So I kept doing it. I had no idea why my body needed those endorphins so badly. I didn't know I was different from anyone else.

That came later—the bouts of depression, the clinical explanation for my moods. Back in my early twenties, I'd really struggled when it settled over me like a cloud I couldn't shake.

Right when I should have been dealing with it, I'd pushed away the signs that my mental health was deteriorating because I'd finally met a woman I thought I could love. Okay, maybe it wasn't love. But I'd convinced myself that being with her would make me happy enough that it would send my depressed feelings into hiding. Of course, mental health doesn't work like that. And our breakup sent me over the edge and into an abyss.

I was so down, felt so worthless. On some days, I didn't get out of bed, didn't eat. I didn't care about anything, felt like my family and friends would be better off without me dragging them down.

I couldn't separate rational from irrational thoughts, and my parents couldn't help me through it. They didn't understand why I couldn't just "man up and get over it." Not that they were callous; they just couldn't relate.

Back then, I didn't know what I didn't know. I didn't see myself with any sort of objectivity. I only felt what I felt, an unshakeable mood of despair. I withdrew from my group of friends, went to work like a robot, and didn't expect to feel any differently. I didn't think I deserved anything else because I thought somehow it was my fault that I felt the way I did—worthless.

Jefferson Dalbotten was the one person who'd leaned in, rather than getting scared off. He followed me down to the bottom of the mental pit and insisted I seek help. He resisted my excuses and found me a psychiatrist who came up with a treatment plan. The antidepressant I now took every morning kept me on more level ground. I still had highs and lows, but they existed on an elevated plane compared to where I'd been.

But even Jefferson didn't know the reason I stayed away from relationships after that—out of fear of falling into the same abyss again. Safer to go out once or twice with the women who were pushed my way and call it a day. And never consider someone like Ally Dalbotten who'd make me want the kind of relationship that would put my heart in jeopardy.

After two more driving laps around the track, I slowed to a jog for the final four hundred meters that would get me to two miles. As our breathing came back toward conversational, I elbowed Jefferson in the ribs. "Jeff, did you come for the workout? Or are you here to meddle in my dating life?"

He threw up his arms in protest. "Not meddling at all. I'm not telling you to date Blithe's friend's niece. Just letting you know a missile is headed your way in case you want to duck. Or . . . maybe put on a baseball glove and catch the damn thing for once."

I laughed at that. Ducking was more like it. That's how dating felt these days. When I'd turned thirty-four, everyone and their sister had somehow emerged from the countryside, all convinced they needed to find me a wife.

But I didn't want a wife. I wanted Ally.

For years, I'd told myself that it was better never to start anything with Ally because I couldn't risk how I'd feel if a relationship with her ended. I couldn't risk falling back into the abyss. Better to admire her from afar and never pause too long when she was nearby.

Grabbing on to a rail by the bleachers, I held my foot and stretched my quad. I hoped that signaling the end of my little run would cue the end of the conversation. But Jefferson never could take a hint.

"Maybe one of these days it'll be the right one. Couldn't hurt to keep an open mind."

I wasn't about to tell him the only person who fit that bill was his sister. And I didn't want to go into why I'd never take a chance on letting something happen.

But I imagined that on some level he knew.

"You doing okay?" The hint of quiet gravity in his voice let me know he was asking about my mental health.

"I'm fine. Thanks. The meds are working. All good."

"So why not consider the possibility this niece of Blithe's friend could be smokin' hot?"

"Just not interested."

I jogged in place. I knew he was antsy to keep running, so I hoped he'd eventually give up on this discussion so we could get moving. "Asking one more time, are you okay?"

"Yup. It's under control."

"Okay, good. Just checking."

Sometimes it annoyed me that he knew. It gave him license to ask about my feelings and that bugged the crap out of me.

"Yeah, I know. Thanks. It's not about that."

It was always about that. A little bit.

"Just go on the date," Jefferson said, starting to jog away from me, facing backward so he could watch me grimace at the suggestion. "Do it for me. I want to hear stories. You always have the best stories," he said, retreating and nearly tripping over his own feet. If he did, he'd deserve it.

"Look where you're going!" I urged.

Turning himself around, he picked up the pace again and I looked down at my watch. Sure enough, we'd hit a mile in under six minutes. I hadn't done that anytime recently, and judging by the rush of endorphins I felt, my body approved.

I contemplated whether I could take another few laps around the track before my students sorted themselves out and made it to practice.

Almost on cue, the first group of runners ducked under the bleachers and stepped out onto the track. Moving slowly, they were doing more talking than warming up, even though I'd tried to drill them with my ethos—the workout starts the minute your feet hit the track. It was a mental thing, a changeover from whatever was happening in life beforehand.

I waved the kids over. "This is track practice. How about a little running around the track?" Most of them ignored me and continued walking. Only one or two grudgingly picked up their pace to a jog and headed my way.

"Fine, fine. Walk. That'll earn you an extra lap during cooldown."

That did it. All the kids broke into a jog. The ones just entering the track did the same.

Good. I needed them to make their way over to me as quickly as possible so I could focus on them. And stop thinking about how to get out of a blind date with Blithe Tanner's friend's niece.

CHAPTER
THREE

ALLY

I could hear Clay shouting at his runners from halfway across the grass field that separated the school building from the stadium. The gruff rumble of his voice sent a blissful shiver across the surface of my skin—I wished it didn't, but it did. Hard to fight biology.

I could still remember the day when I noticed that puberty had dressed up my older brother's best friend in a full bodysuit that screamed *man*. I swear, puberty hit him on a Friday night, and he showed up at our house on a Saturday, the only threadbare shirt that still fit him clinging to his torso. His legs had grown several inches longer, accompanied by muscles that filled out his jeans and left no question of their strength.

Clay outran everyone on the cross-country team, looking like a greyhound as he dashed down the ruddy trails toward finish lines countywide. It wasn't effortless. I remembered seeing his cheeks puffing and his chest heaving as he passed by the crowd on the way up a set of switchbacks that went further up a hill before winding down to an open straightaway.

The image returned as I neared the track, and my heart rate inexplicably kicked up a notch. I had no intention of running with the team—perish the thought—but I'd changed into workout clothes anyhow.

"C'mon, Joe, kick it now. Last fifty. You've got this!" Clay's deep baritone didn't require a megaphone to resonate across the field. I could picture him crouched on the grass waving his arm to Joe as he finished his mile. Stopwatch in hand, Clay treated every workout like a race.

"Train like you race, race like you train," he explained to his team, instructing them to fuel themselves the same way whether they had a track meet or just a workout.

I slipped underneath the bleachers and entered the track on the opposite straightaway from where Clay was timing his runners. After the milers finished, they walked in a circle, hands clasped on top of their heads, chests heaving, while Clay gave them feedback and fed them their stats he tracked on a clipboard.

While he was distracted with the team, I slipped onto the track and started jogging around the ellipse, heading toward the team. I planned to speed up the closer I got to Clay and leap across his field of vision like a gazelle.

Then I'd deliver the news about my unlikely supporting role on the retreat, and we'd have a good laugh.

Best-laid plans.

I pictured myself like the gazelle I wanted to be, picking up my pace as I rounded the bend on the track, feeling an ache in my legs as they woke up after I'd spent the day standing up and teaching. Despite my general grumblings about running for sport, it felt good to move my legs. Maybe there was something to it after all.

Glancing at the grass field in the middle of the track, I noticed how the carpet of green shone under the afternoon sunlight. No wonder Clay liked coming out here. While I usually spent extra time in the classroom after school, helping the yearbook committee with page layouts, Clay came out here every day, put on running gear, and got some exercise. It seemed healthier than my after-school routine. It didn't take a medical professional to see that.

Maybe I'd invest in a better pair of shoes since the ones on my feet were the heavier white leather type that wouldn't leave a mark on tennis courts. I wasn't getting any kind of a speed advantage as the heavy soles slapped the dirt track.

Slap, slap, slap.

I channeled more big gazelle energy and pumped my arms, willing them to help me glide more swiftly down the straightaway of the track.

As I neared the team huddle, I heard Clay giving instructions for the next drill. His back faced me, so he didn't see me coming. A couple of the students in the group watched as I drew closer, easily distracted from their coach by a moving object.

When I spied the hurdles set up in several lanes of the track, I pictured myself in the Olympics, running strong in the red, white, and blue. The voices of Clay and his students morphed into crowd noises, and I pictured myself easily clearing hurdle after hurdle, pitching one leg in front and bending my other knee to the side like I'd seen runners do on TV. It looked so artful, and here I was, tap-dancing down the straightaway, a graceful gazelle.

The image in my head propelled me forward, and I picked up my pace a tiny bit, ignoring the protest from my lungs. I ran a little faster, the huffing of breath now audible enough that a few more students turned their heads to find out its source, but Clay stayed focused on whatever inspiring instructions he hadn't finished giving.

As I passed by the team huddle, I planned to leap into the air, legs extended in both directions in my best estimate of a ballerina's jeté. I'd clear the hurdle and land with a hand-waving flourish.

Ta-da.

I extended my arms to both sides as I got ready to leave the ground, intent on flying past Clay's field of vision at exactly the right moment, giving him a chuckle. Then I'd spring the chaperoning news. He'd blanch and convince Pindich to choose a less wilderness-phobic chaperone. If I went back to Pindich, he'd try to make me go to lunch with him, but if Clay asked, the odds were better for success.

The only problem was the hurdle was a lot higher than it had looked a few seconds earlier. I did my best leap, but I came nowhere close to clearing it.

Instead, I knocked it over, tripping as it fell.

My body continued its forward motion, even though my feet were only partially on the ground. I was more flying than running. Then stumbling, gaining air, careening downward and to the side.

As it was happening, I was aware enough of my surroundings to see mouths agape and hands held up in hopeless attempts to shield faces from the accident about to happen.

Clay turned his head just in time for me to see his eyes larger and rounder than I'd ever seen them, even through the magnifying lenses of his glasses. He wasn't wearing them now, so I knew it was no mirage. He looked simultaneously terrified and confused. Which terrified me because Clay never looked confused.

Confident, yes. Cocky, yes. Confused . . . never.

But I was confusing. Still stumbling, still in motion despite my knees hitting the sandy track and my hands reaching down to arrest my movement. That put me semi-upright, careening forward, moving as if by hidden motor. But the worst of it was over.

Or so I thought.

With the team splayed out around Clay and the way students tended to fidget when they were wound up waiting to run around a track, they had blocked my field of vision.

Which meant I didn't see the metal starting blocks sitting on three lanes of the track right beside the team huddle. Didn't need to see them, it turned out, in order to trip on them as well and go flying even further.

My grand jeté looked more like a wagon wheel with electrocuted blond hair, cartwheeling to her certain death in front of the entire track team.

Hitting the ground, I skidded a few feet, thanks to all my momentum. I felt a dozen pairs of eyes on me and heard a chorus of gasps. Every tiny kernel of dirt from the sandy track attacked at once, and I felt the sting on my forearms and shins.

Willing myself to stop skidding, I could do nothing except wait for gravity to do its best to swallow me. I felt the mortification set in before I'd even stopped moving, and a part of me wanted to keep on sliding, farther and farther away from all the peering eyes.

Someone shouted my name—probably Clay, but in my kerfuffle, I was in no state to discern pitch and tone.

I may have kicked myself in the head with my heavy shoes. I definitely had a gallon of gritty dirt jammed down the front of my workout tights, which were not nearly tight enough to prevent it. On the plus side, the exploding pain briefly drowned out my mortification. But only briefly.

When I finally came to a stop, I was flat on my stomach. Dust from the track swirled in the air around me, my ego waved a big white flag, and everything went silent.

CHAPTER
FOUR

CLAY

"**I**'m fine. Really."

Ally was not fine, as evidenced by the fact that her words came out like, "Fie. Rull," as she tried to form them around a tissue held against her lip, which hadn't stopped bleeding.

I'd looked down at her prone body in horror after she finally came to rest in a heap on the track. Her black workout pants were covered in brown dust, her knee bent to one side, the other leg bent so her foot stuck up in the air. One of her brand-new white tennis shoes had a dangling shoelace which was probably the culprit for her fall.

"Alexandra!" I'd dashed over as soon as she hit the ground, mostly to shield her from what I knew would be embarrassment. No adult wanted to eat dirt in front of a bunch of teenagers, let alone the ones she had to teach the next morning.

Between us, we did our best to downplay her fall and get the kids moving off to start a drill. But that didn't mean I took her fall lightly. As soon as I'd handed off the practice to the team captain, I helped Ally to a sitting position. Fearing the worst, I bent down to check her for scrapes.

Track dirt was no friend to bare skin, and I'd gotten my share of road rash over the years, mostly from falling off my mountain bike. Other than the fat lip, she didn't look like she'd taken a blow to the face, but she had abrasions up and down her arms. Those would hurt like hell in the morning.

I'd been about to ask who I could call to drive her to a doctor's office when she shooed me away and said I was being silly. Then she wobbled to standing, like a drunken sailor on stormy seas.

A drop of blood from her lip hit the track, and she dabbed her lip with a finger. "Jussa Sue." Somehow, I translated that as her needing a tissue, and I grabbed a few from my workout bag, along with the first aid kit we brought to meets. Cracking one of the ice packs, I got the cold flowing into the bag and handed it to her.

She winced when the cold hit her lip. And then she started walking away.

"I'm fine," she insisted again.

"Hold on. Let's get some bandages." I gestured in the direction of the main school building because there was nowhere near enough gauze in my little kit.

"I don't need. It. I'm fiiine," she enunciated.

She was so *not* fine that she actually thought she could walk away from the track, get into her car, and drive home. There was no way I could let that happen without bandaging her up and making sure she hadn't done damage someplace where I couldn't see it.

"Stop. Saying. That." I may have sounded like a bossy jerk, but after she protested for the tenth time, I could see she wasn't listening to my kinder words. Words like, "Come on, let me help you." And, "Let's just check out these scrapes."

Finally, my words sunk in enough to earn me a glare. That was better. I'd take a glare from her over stubborn insistence that I mind my own business. There was no way in hell I planned to do that, not when she was listing to one side as she walked with a streak of blood dripping down her chin and a dazed look in her eyes.

"We should run concussion protocols," I said as we took slow steps around the track toward the school nurse's office.

"I don't need that."

I huffed my disapproval at her. "You can protest all you want, but if you don't get checked out here, I'll drive you to the hospital instead."

"Geez, you're annoying when you're being re-thponsible," she griped. She shook her head, but I saw the tiniest hint of a smile in her scowl. Along with some dirt from the track.

Loretta was out with the stomach bug, and the school didn't have a backup nurse—budget cuts did away with that—but we did have someone trained in first aid who could pop in and out of the nurse's office when needed. Unfortunately, that person was limping along next to me.

Slowing my pace a bit, I watched her stride ahead of me and checked out her gait. No, I was not checking out her ass.

Yes, I was also doing that. The tight yoga pants made my hands flicker with the urge to wrap them around her ass and squeeze the perfect, round cheeks.

I forced my eyes lower, just as she whipped her head over her shoulder, eyeing me accusingly. "You having trouble keeping up?"

I rolled my eyes. "I'm watching your stride. It seemed like you were favoring your right side, and now it seems like you're favoring your left. What hurts?"

We still had to cross the large grass field before we made it to the administrative building, and at the slow pace she was limping along, we'd make it a little before sunrise. She stopped walking and turned to face me.

I saw the feisty sparkle in her eyes as she readied herself to lob a sarcastic jab my way. She put her hands on her hips but cringed once they got there. Lowering them, she shifted from one foot to the other. Her forearms were scraped from wrist to elbow, and as she gingerly dropped them to her sides, I noticed how she held them slightly away from her body.

Grudgingly, her face fell, and seeing the fight leave her nearly crushed me. "Everything," she muttered. "At least, my whole front side."

Nodding, I reached her in two strides and slipped an arm beneath her knees. She yelped when I drew her up, carefully sliding my hand around her back and balancing her weight against my chest. "What are you doing?" Her hands flailed about, looking for purchase. She finally settled on resting her fingertips against her stomach while I easily shouldered her weight and trudged across the grass.

"If it hurts to walk, you shouldn't walk."

"I need to walk. Walking is part of my daily life."

"You don't need to walk right *now*."

Dammit, this woman was stubborn. I'd known this for most of my adult life, given that we'd been friendly for years. Mostly we passed each other in the hallways and said our hellos and goodbyes without extensive interaction, but I'd seen her dig in her heels at a faculty meeting when she advocated for healthier school lunches even though they cost more. "We'll fundraise. I'm sure the folks in Green Valley would be happy to contribute to the good health of their young residents." No one dared shoot down an idea of hers after that.

I respected her enormously for championing what she thought was right and staying at the table until she saw results. Who wouldn't love that kind of grit and determination?

But I didn't love it when it was directed at me.

She wriggled against my chest, and I fought against the feeling that I liked carrying her more than I should. The warm weight of her grazing my chest was making me imagine doing this again—shirtless, with her in only the lacy pink bra I could see peeking out at the neck of her tank top.

Stop looking.

I snapped my gaze upward and walked a little faster. The sooner we made it to the nurse's office, the sooner I could put her down before I had full-on wood, which would be pretty hard to hide in my track pants.

"What's the rush, cowboy? Those brawny biceps getting sore?" she teased as I practically ran across the last few yards of the field and kicked open the auditorium door with my foot. She must have been half-loopy from the fall because she never talked about my body. At all.

Scooting up the auditorium aisle would get us to the nurse's office in half the time it would take to walk down the hallways of the main building.

"Not at all. You weigh less than the bowl of oatmeal I ate for breakfast."

Her laughter vibrated from her body, and it warmed the blood in my veins like she'd wrapped her arms around my heart. I pushed away how good it felt. What was the point? This was the first and last time I'd hold her like this. No sense getting attached to a feeling that couldn't last.

Shifting her in my grip, I held her a little farther away from my body and strode up the aisle between padded wooden chairs.

Flyers from last night's production of *Annie Get Your Gun* littered the floor. Fortunately, no one was rehearsing. I hadn't thought through the optics of racing through the auditorium carrying the art teacher like a new bride. But the place was vacant, and another kick with my foot got us through the back door, right near the teachers' lounge and the main office.

The staff hightailed it away from campus as soon as the bell rang, so we had the place to ourselves. Gingerly, I set her down on the cot in the nurse's office and surveyed the room. I didn't normally spend much time in here, so I didn't know what the place had in the way of bandages, but I felt sure it had something.

As I started rifling through drawers and pulling out gauze pads, I heard Ally chuckling behind me. "Is something funny? Or do you have more comments on my workout routine?"

"Oh, I always have comments on it. You know that." It was true. She liked to give me shit about how runners, and therefore track coaches, don't acquire the bicep and shoulder strength I have from running. Ergo, I must be a gym rat. Ergo, she must make fun of me.

"I do." I searched another drawer but found only more gauze and no tape. "How's a person supposed to secure gauze without any tape?"

Before I opened another drawer, she slipped off the table and came to stand next to me. I felt the temperature in the room rise with her proximity.

"Here, let me help. I stocked the place, so I know where everything is." She opened a mirrored cabinet I hadn't noticed and removed some antibacterial wipes and a box of some kind of bandages.

I pointed at the cot. "You're the one who's injured. Sit. Tell me where stuff is, and I'll get it."

Blowing out a frustrated breath, she limped back to the cot and pointed at a cabinet across the room. "In there is a basic first aid kit. It has pretty much everything. I don't think I need all that much bandaging."

I turned and looked at her, dabbing at her split lip with a tissue and contemplating me so seriously I felt like I was the one with dire-seeming injuries. "Yeah," I said, crossing the room to where she sat. "You don't think so because we haven't really looked." Giving her a once-over, I noticed that her pants were torn at the knee. An angry-looking gash contained a combination of blood and dirt. She followed my gaze and seemed to notice her knee for the first time.

"Oh. That."

"Yeah. Where else does it hurt?" Gently, I ran the pads of my fingers over her hip bones and watched as she winced and pointed.

"Just this side. I think I fell on one of the starting blocks."

Those things are hard metal with awkward pieces that wouldn't make for a soft landing. "Ouch. Okay, so could be a deep bone bruise. That's why you were limping."

"Plus this knee hurts."

"Yeah. Not surprised."

She bit the part of her bottom lip that wasn't bleeding and looked concerned. Then she nodded and slipped off the table. "You know what? I can deal with all of this when I get home. Really. I have supplies and I can clean everything off in the shower. You've done more than enough." In three seconds she'd scooted past me and was halfway out the door.

"Hey."

She stopped moving but didn't turn. "Yeah?"

"Let me run the concussion protocols before you get into a car and drive."

Her shoulders slumped, and she shook her head before turning around. Stubborn or not, she knew I was right.

"Fine. But I'm pretty certain I don't have a concussion."

"Uh-huh. Well, 'pretty certain' isn't one of the boxes you're allowed to check. You either do or you don't. So get your ass back on the table, Alexandra."

She pressed her lips together and sulked back to the cot but didn't sit. A test of wills. I moved closer, taking all of her in now.

I hated seeing her hurt, bleeding and disheveled. Gently, I lifted her onto the cot. Her eyes went to where my hands wrapped around her hips, which looked small beneath my large palms.

Legs parted and dangling off the side of the cot, she looked dazed. Our bodies were nearly flush against each other as I moved my hands to her head, checking for lumps. I heard her take a sharp inhale as the sleeve of my shirt brushed against her skin.

"Did I hurt you?" The last thing I wanted was to make it worse.

"N-no." She choked out the word, then swallowed hard.

"Tell me if I do." My eyes bored into hers, searching for signs of concussion, but her gaze followed mine steadily as I moved. I felt a small measure of relief.

"You could have really hurt yourself. Promise me you won't try anything like that again." I couldn't keep the anger from my voice, and seeing her hurt made my blood boil.

She let out an exaggerated exhale. "Yes, Sir Snarlypants."

"Thank you." I meant it sincerely, and I caught a hint of a smile as she nodded. As her lips pulled to the side, it was like the sun moving from behind a cloud, lighting up her pretty heart-shaped face.

"Now let's rinse this track dirt off your arms." She nodded and didn't push back as I ran through the various tests and concluded she likely had a mild concussion. Not serious enough to warrant a trip to the hospital but enough to force her to take it easy for the next twenty-four hours. I wasn't sure she was capable of doing that.

"You know the danger is if you get hit a second time. That's where you're at a real risk of brain damage," I reminded her.

She snickered. "You gunning for my job as fill-in nurse? I won't go quietly, you know."

"Hardly."

"You just happen to know about concussion protocols?"

"I'm a track coach, remember?"

"Exactly," she shot back. "I could see if it was soccer or football, where concussions are more common, but how many two-hundred-meter-dash runners end up with concussions?"

I bit down hard on my bottom lip to tame my laugh into submission, but I couldn't stifle it as I tipped my head and waited for her to see my point.

"Oh, fine. Laugh. But I never said I was a runner, so it still doesn't make sense for you to know concussion stuff." She searched around her but didn't seem to find what she was looking for. "Did I have a bag with me?"

"What kind of bag?"

She looked behind her on the cot, but it sat just as empty as it was a minute ago. "My gym bag. It has my purse in it. Did we leave it on the field?"

I studied her face for signs I missed something. Maybe it wasn't such a mild concussion after all, because she wasn't making sense. "I never saw a bag. Do you remember holding a gym bag while you were sprinting around the track?"

She blinked as though shuffling off the confusion and scooted off the cot, rising to her feet. "Right. Of course not. I left it in my car. That's what I meant."

"Are you sure you feel okay? Do you have someone who can keep an eye on you tonight, make sure you don't need anything?"

She waved a hand. "I'm *fine*. I told you I was fine. You just scrambled my brains with all your inappropriate concussion knowledge." She started again for the door.

"Alexandra."

She stopped. Turned. "You don't need to use my full name. 'Ally' will do just fine."

I liked saying her full name. I knew she didn't use it, and I'd always thought of her as Ally, but seeing her injured had brought out a stern, possessive side of me that wanted to lay claim to her well-being by hearing her gorgeous given name on my tongue.

"What was that, anyway?" In all the hubbub of getting Ally onto her feet and sending my track team captain off with instructions to finish up training for the day, I hadn't asked why she'd hurdled past my team in the first place. Sometimes faculty members used the track to work out, but generally not during team practices. And Ally was never among them.

"What?"

I pointed in the direction of the track. "You out there trying to leap tall buildings in a single bound."

"I'm Wonder Woman. Didn't you get the memo?" she said dryly.

"Wonder Woman had an invisible plane. And a lasso."

She shrugged. "I heard you were having tryouts."

"Uh-huh. You didn't make the cut."

She stared back at me with her large blue doe eyes and offended pout. "Wow. Give a girl a chance."

It was my turn to stare back. I could wait her out. I taught high schoolers, for fuck's sake—I was made of patience. Finally, she rolled her eyes.

"Fine. I was trying to make a big entrance before telling you some stupendous news."

"Stupendous? This sounds serious. Did someone tell you I'm being fired or something? Stupendous like that?"

"Clay, of course not." She glanced around the room, thinking. "Though it would be a good new tradition to sneak up on people when they are being fired."

"Yeah, except I can't remember the last time anyone was fired around here."

"Exactly, so why was that your go-to thought about why I'd come dashing around the track to find you? Glass half empty, are we?"

She had no idea. We'd known each other for half our lives but we didn't really *know* each other. There had always been parts of myself I didn't share with the people closest to me, and she and I were more colleagues than friends. I never saw us as anything more than that. At least, that was the lie I'd had playing on repeat in my head. And it would continue playing until the end of days.

It was how things had to be. I was broken in ways I didn't want Ally to understand. I felt certain there were pieces of me that would never be fully mended. Any fantasies I harbored about the two of us were simply that—fantasies.

"I'm a closet optimist."

"Ha. I think you can do better. Your life looks pretty rosy."

Again, she knew nothing about my life. That's why we remained colleagues rather than crossing the barrier into friends. Friends would ask questions and expect answers from other friends. I wasn't willing to go there with her.

"So your grand entrance was supposed to be more like a bucket of water dumping on my head when I walked into a room?"

She held up a finger as though an idea had been hatched. "That would have been a much better plan." Looking down at the abrasions on her arms, she winced. "And saved me an evening extracting bits of dirt from my various parts with tweezers."

It felt wrong to let her tend to her wounds herself, but there was a limit to how pushy I could be without seeming overbearing. She was better trained than I was at knowing how to treat abrasions. Maybe that's why she was so eager to get away from me.

"I'd like to help you," I offered. "If you tell me you have someone to look after you, I'll leave you alone, but otherwise, I'd like to follow you home, or better yet, drive you." I didn't want to do these things at all. The longer I spent playing nursemaid to her, the harder it would be to stop.

"Drive me?" She stared at me aghast as though this were a fate worse than death.

"Yes. Someone with a mild concussion shouldn't get behind the wheel of a car."

"I'll Uber."

"No you won't. I'll drive you," I fired back at her.

"I need my car," she insisted.

"For what?"

"To get back here in the morning."

"I'll come pick you up." This was not the insurmountable problem she was pretending it was.

"No you won't."

"Why are you so stubborn?"

"Why are you?" Her voice went up an octave as she vented her frustration at me. Her shoulders drew up near her ears and she blew out a breath that did nothing to reduce the tension in her body. I had no idea why she felt so resistant to having someone help her, but the more she resisted, the more I needed to understand why.

I took a step back, sensing I needed to give her some physical space or she'd just back up and go for the door again. Her shoulders dropped a few millimeters, but that was it. Then I took a second step back.

She exhaled. The scowl on her face melted away, and her glaring eyes returned to their normal blue innocence. But her cheeks stayed pink, the combination of her creamy pale skin and her fiery disposition.

There was no disputing Ally's beauty. Shorter than me by nearly a foot, she had curves that I'd tried to ignore when I carried her from the field. Tried and failed.

Her blond hair, golden in the sun, offset the deep pink of her plump lips and a light dusting of freckles across her cheeks. My hands itched to reach out and trace a finger along the round contours of her face, the apples of her cheeks, the dip of her chin that gave her face its heart shape.

Blinking a few times, Ally swallowed hard. I stuffed my hands into my pockets.

"I don't know why I'm stubborn. I just am," she admitted quietly as though it cost her something she held dear.

Leaning toward her without taking a step closer, I tried to comfort her without triggering the fight-or-flight response I could see running hot in her veins. I wanted to understand this too.

"I don't think that it's necessarily a bad thing," I reassured her.

She almost laughed. I saw the muscles in her cheeks twitch and pull upward, but she schooled her expression immediately. Like it had betrayed her by almost giving something away.

I wanted to push that button again. Something in me was hooked in getting a response, like a rat pressing a button in order to get a treat. I knew in that moment that I'd do it over and over again, even if it was unhealthy for me.

"Ha. Spoken like someone who's either equally stubborn or who just isn't afraid to lose a grudge match."

"Maybe there's a third option." Slowly, I'd nudged her to turn around and move with me toward the door of the office. She didn't resist, so I continued our walk down the hall.

She was still limping, which made me double down on my theory about a deep bone bruise. If I was right, the initial pain would go away in a few days, but it would still hurt if she tried to run around the track. Probably a good thing if she had any designs on making another grand entrance.

"Yeah, what's that?"

Making our way toward the teachers' lounge, we walked slowly. Ally blotted a fresh tissue against her lip a few times and saw that it remained dry, so she tossed it in a trash can.

"I don't consider being stubborn a bad thing because often it's how people accomplish great things. By not taking no for an answer, even when the odds are stacked against them," I told her.

I watched her process my words with the hint of a smile. It's a good thing we were walking slowly because I wasn't watching where we were going, not when I had the choice of looking at her instead.

"I often feel like I'm bucking the odds. And you're right, it motivates me. I'll take Door Three, if you're offering."

We each grabbed a cup of water from the teachers' lounge and then went out to the parking lot. "My purse is in there," she protested when I walked past her car. She popped the lock and retrieved her purse while I opened the passenger door of my truck. "I'm glad you're giving in to reason."

"You're right about driving. But I'm not going to the hospital for a few scrapes and bruises. Let's not be crazy." She surveyed the step up to the bench seat and hesitated. Without further thought, I scooped her up and placed her on the seat. Once again, our faced were inches apart as I reached across her body to fasten her seat belt. I expected pushback—insistence that she could buckle her own seat belt—but her gaze met mine and stayed there, those blue eyes watching my every move.

For a moment, it looked like she'd stopped breathing. Only the fluttering pulse at her neck offered the proof that settled my nerves.

The scent of her tickled my nose, and I fought the urge to close my eyes and inhale more deeply. Instead, I closed the car door and clenched my fists, taking a deep breath of reality before making my way to the driver's side.

"I'll only let you drive me if you promise not to tell the rest of the faculty about my big splat."

"I won't say a thing, but I can't promise half the teachers don't already know. Word spreads fast." I chuckled at her constant pushback. "You missed your calling. You'd make a great negotiator."

She nodded, head resting back against the seat. "Not the first time I've heard that. Or just that I'm stubborn." An odd feeling of possessiveness set in as I wondered who else had said it. I quickly tamped down the surge of jealousy. I had no claim on her. The rogue feeling was absurd.

I closed my door and focused on putting the key into the ignition. Feelings had no place here. I was a colleague offering her a ride because it was the right thing to do.

Nothing more.

CHAPTER
FIVE

ALLY

Clay was quiet on the drive to my house once I gave him my address, which was just south of town. The faculty socialized outside of school on occasion, but he'd never been to my house, nor I his.

"I just realized I have no idea where you live," I said, recalling that Clay gave Witty a ride to school when the Winstons were fixing his car a few weeks ago. Maybe they lived near each other.

I studied his profile as he stopped at the four-way stop a few blocks from my house. Clearly, we weren't neighbors because no one who lived near me ever stopped at that stop sign. We all just slowed and rolled through it.

A muscle in his jaw flexed like he was clenching his teeth. Maybe I was being too nosy. "You don't have to tell me. Whatever. I was just making conversation."

"No, I don't mind people knowing where I live. I'm up near Bandit."

I couldn't have heard him correctly. Surely, he didn't mean Bandit Lake. The houses there weren't for sale. They were sitting on private parkland that was handed down through families. Specific families. And even though I hadn't known Clay well growing up, I was pretty sure I'd have known if his family lived on the lake.

"You live . . . on the lake?"

He tore his gaze from the road to hit me with the first smile I'd seen since I splatted in front of the track team. "You seem surprised."

"Oh. It's just . . . not many people do."

He shrugged and turned back to the road, making me inexplicably sad. I didn't realize how much I liked seeing his smile until it faded from his face, and he returned to his Teacher Clay disposition, thoughtful and serious. "I was the favorite grandkid. So I was deeded a lake house with instructions to find love and be happy there. Talk about a recipe for guilt."

"Why would you feel guilty?"

"Because I didn't do anything in particular to deserve it, other than having a health condition in common with my grandmother. She felt a kinship, and now I have lakefront property. And as to the love part, maybe it's good she isn't around to see that I haven't made good on that."

My brain focused on the part where he mentioned a health condition. I snuck a glance in his direction. He looked okay, as strong and fit as ever, and I chastised myself for not knowing something was wrong. A pang of worry sliced through me. Was he sick?

"Are you . . . okay? Healthwise?"

His eyes shot to mine before returning to the road. I saw my look of concern mirrored in his.

"Yeah. Basically."

It wasn't the reassurance I was hoping for. "Basically?"

He tipped his head from side to side as if considering whether to continue the conversation. "Yeah."

"As in, you eat all the dessert today because of it?" I was trying to be chill, but he was freaking me out.

"No, more like I don't do relationships because of it."

Um, okay.

This was my longest conversation with Clay that didn't involve students or curriculum and I found myself lapping up details like vital nutrients. So that was why none of the dating rumors ever turned into the real thing. He was staying away. Running. Like a greyhound. Like I'd always thought of him as.

And my mind was teeming with other questions. What kind of health condition? Was that the thing he was struggling with? My own malfunctioning hormone center wanted to know.

"Things you want to talk about?" I knew I was being nosy, but I was interested and he could always shut me down. I expected him to shut me down.

"Not particularly."

I should have left it alone, but the mixture of concern for his well-being and guilt over never looking beyond the surface made me keep pushing.

"It's just . . . if you're sick, I'd, um, like to help you. I mean, if you have a condition that requires hospitals and tests and drugs, I'd want to, you know . . . I'd want to make things better." I was spiraling, unsure what I could offer that would make any difference, but I needed him to know I'd try to help.

"Thank you." His hand moved to cover mine for a brief moment of reassurance before returning to the steering wheel. But I didn't feel reassured.

"Is it fatal?"

"No." I was studying his profile and saw a heavy blink. A muscle in his jaw twitched. "At least, not when managed properly."

"Clay . . . that sounds bad."

He blinked rapidly a few times, opened his mouth, and closed it again. I sat motionless, watching him. Then he started talking, haltingly at first. "I . . . it's, um, depression."

He waited, and I nodded. "That's . . . I'm sure that's hard."

"I figured you were going to say I don't seem depressed."

"No. Do people say that?"

He raked a hand through his hair. A piece fell over his forehead and he flicked it away. "I don't tell many people. Or anyone, really."

"Why not?" I wasn't trying to be nosy, but I wanted to understand him better. I knew how so many of our high school kids were struggling with mental health issues, how it took time for them to open up about it. But hearing him say he kept it to himself broke my heart. To feel so isolated, so alone, unable to talk to people about this weight pressing in on him. *What must it be like?*

Eyes narrowed, Clay glanced at me as though gauging my interest. I returned his look with a wide-eyed stare, and he shrugged.

"I guess it was impressed upon me that feeling sad is no big deal. Everyone feels blue sometimes and they just handle it. You know . . . that depression is just someone being lazy and not trying hard enough to be happy. That it isn't a real condition."

I felt the need to shake my head as though that might dislodge such a crazy notion. "What? Of course it's real. What does that even mean?"

"Nothing. Bottom line is that I struggle with it, and my therapist wants to change my dosage but I already have side effects and I don't want more. The meds make me feel like I'm not myself. If I could, I'd stop taking them altogether."

"That's ridiculous. Depression is serious. If your doctor thinks you need meds, take the meds."

"I am. I do." He sounded exasperated, and I sensed that he was done talking. I waited for a moment, but he pressed his lips together and said nothing. I couldn't help feeling foolish for not being more observant and somehow knowing this about Clay. And it touched me in a deep place that he trusted me enough to tell me now.

I couldn't get over the idea that he'd struggled with his mental health under the false narrative that it wasn't real. And he held all of it in, only letting people see his outward strength. It broke my heart. And made me want to gather him up like a baby chick and smooth his feathers until he felt loved.

My stomach chose this moment to let out a loud rumble. "Guess I should've eaten more than just a salad all day."

I was so caught up in my confession, I didn't notice Clay signaling and pulling his truck over until we'd stopped on the side of the road, right in front of Donner Bakery. He unlatched his seat belt and turned his whole body to face me. He brought one knee up, rested his elbow on it, and leaned his forehead on his hand.

"Alexandra."

"Yes?"

"That's not good. You should have mentioned that."

"I just did."

He blew out a breath and rubbed his hand over his face. "I mean before, when we were assessing your injuries. Do you need a doughnut? Or a chocolate bar? Is your blood sugar low?"

"I don't think so. Sometimes I just forget to eat."

"You forget . . ." Shaking his head, Clay tipped the back of his hand against my forehead as if checking for a fever. He really didn't know much about first aid if he thought I had a fever from falling over a hurdle. "Alexandra, I was already concerned about leaving you alone with a possible concussion and now you're telling me you forget to eat. Are you sure you can handle this yourself?"

"Oh, definitely. I'm fine."

He stared at me for another few seconds, blinking at me as if in disbelief. This was the longest drive from school to a person's house in the history of time.

Well, it wouldn't be if he turned the car back into the lane and stepped on the gas.

"Anyway, as to the other thing, people don't will things to their loved ones unless they want to. Unless you swindled your grandmother, I don't know why you should feel guilty about receiving a gift."

"Yeah. I guess."

"Did you?"

"Did I, what?"

"Scheme and plot to trick your grandmother into leaving you her house on the lake?"

"I did not. I didn't do anything good *or* bad. She struggled with depression for most of her life and that was her big reason for choosing me. She wanted me to be happy, and I guess she thought Bandit Lake might be good medicine. It seemed rather random."

His eyes passed over my face and down my chest, where my breasts were split by the seat belt, then down to where my hands fidgeted in my lap. Finally, his gaze moved back up to my face where it settled on my swollen, cracked lip before meeting my eyes again. "So your blood sugar isn't low now," he confirmed, as though his once-over proved it.

Plowing through my overstuffed purse, I produced a tube of Mentos and popped one in my mouth. "There. Better?"

I watched Clay chew on his bottom lip, noticing how the week's worth of scruff highlighted his sharp jawline, how his Adam's apple rose and fell when he swallowed. In all the years we'd known each other, I'd never spent this much time in one place with him alone. He was always moving, always had one foot out the door and a plan.

Slowly, with an exaggerated effort, Clay turned back toward the steering wheel and popped on his seat belt. "You don't make it easy, do you?" he muttered, almost like he didn't mean for me to hear it.

But since it was a question and I had an answer, I responded, "Guess not."

As we drove, I wondered what his house was like. Even back when he and Jefferson spent most of high school together, I'd never been to Clay's family home. I had no occasion to be invited. I was the little sister, not a part of their social circle. But back then, he didn't live at Bandit Lake. That I knew for sure.

A left turn just past Daisy's Nut House brought us to my neighborhood, and a few more turns had us heading down my street.

The truck stopped in front of my house, and Clay jumped out. Before I could take my seat belt off, he'd come around to my side and flung open the passenger door of the baby-blue truck. Without asking, he slung my purse and workout bag over his shoulder, scooped me up just as he had earlier, and carried me down the walkway to my front door.

My head whipped around to make sure none of my neighbors were around to see this. There would be questions for sure.

The coast appeared clear, and Clay deposited me on my feet at my front door, where I noticed my twin pink geraniums looked wilted and in need of water. It was strange because they'd been fine this morning, and I'd only planted them in the matching terra-cotta pots because they were extremely hardy. I regularly missed a week of watering at a time and had never seen them lose their vigor.

Clay didn't seem inclined to hand over my purse, so I cleared my throat and gestured with a nod of my head. He stood with his arms crossed, leaning against my green-painted banister. He'd shoved the sleeves of his workout shirt up to his elbows, so the bulge of his forearms nearly assaulted me with the sudden need to purchase a block of marble and sculpt them.

"Don't get that from running," I said weakly, trying to harness some sass and failing. Maybe my blood sugar was low. Maybe I did have a concussion. Or maybe it was just that Clay had been exceedingly kind to me over the past hour, and I wasn't used to it. But suddenly, the normal banter I counted on didn't come.

"Sorry?" Clay towered over me normally, but the strange confusion I felt around him now made me slump, so he was even taller. Taller and wrapped in layers of muscle.

"Nothing. I meant thank you. For carrying me all over the place and getting me home."

He nodded but he didn't smile. His hazel eyes heated until they looked like twin discs of coal. The way he was studying me made me feel naked. And slightly unnerved. I glanced down to be sure I hadn't shed my clothes without realizing it. Not that it would have mattered. Clay looked like he might incinerate anything flammable simply by looking at it. And looking at him, I wanted that superpower for myself.

"So, you deflected earlier. Why were you leaping over hurdles earlier?"

"Oh. Right. I planned to tell you Pin Dick wants me to chaperone the retreat with you."

I waited for him to groan. Or grimace. Or look for a parachute on his back that could whisk him out of here. Instead, he looked . . . pleased?

"Okay, works for me."

I waved my hands like erasers. "No, no. Not okay. I know nothing about camping. That's the ridiculous part of the whole thing. I'm the last person you'd want in the woods, trust me."

He pressed his lips together and I felt his eyes rake over my face. It made me blush, which had never happened in his presence in all the years we'd worked together. I shouldn't be reacting to him that way just because he'd carried me in his muscular arms like a stray kitten.

"Let's agree to disagree on that one. Assuming you're healed by the weekend after next, we should figure out a time to go over things."

He seemed so calm. So innocent.

A laugh barked from my chest. Or more like an unhinged cackle. "No. I'm not going."

His eyes narrowed. "What?"

I gestured between us. "Me. The retreat. Not happening."

He held up a hand and dropped down onto my porch swing. I'd been ambivalent about installing it a year ago because, although it looked cute, I couldn't imagine anyone sitting on it. My house was small. It didn't take me so long to come to the door that a person would need to sit and wait, take a load off. But right now I felt grateful for it because Clay looked as unsteady as I felt.

"I mustn't have heard you right. You went to all the trouble of making a big *Swan Lake* entrance during my track practice in order to taunt me about chaperoning and now you're not going?"

Pacing in front of my door, I nodded and prattled on, making sure he understood exactly why choosing another chaperone made sense. "I did it to *tell* you about the chaperoning and seek your help getting me out of it. This is just Pindich trying to torture us both. I'm not a wilderness girl. I'm scared and inexperienced out there. Trust me, you don't want to be alone on the side of a mountain with me."

"Try me."

My mouth opened but no sound came out. The last thing I expected was that Clay Meadows might *want* me on the retreat. No. I must have misinterpreted him. I regained my ability to prattle. "It was a momentary case of poor judgment on behalf of Principal Pin Dick. You can convince him as much, and you and your students will be spared another great embarrassment of having to scrape me up off a mountain trail when I step on a log and trip."

"You shouldn't step on a log."

Squinting at him, I took a step forward, bringing us toe to toe and stopping the swaying of the porch swing. "What?"

"You step *over* the log, but use a walking stick to check the other side for snakes hidden in the grass. If you step *on* the log, you could get hurt if it's slippery or rotten."

I waved my hands in his face. "See? This is what I'm talking about. This is why I don't belong on this trip."

"But you're trained in wilderness first aid."

"So what? Anyone could do that."

"Anyone *could*. You *did*. And no one else will have time to get certified before that weekend. With half the faculty out with food poisoning, we don't have a lot of options."

I cursed under my breath, hoping Clay wouldn't be able to make it out. Because it was very unladylike.

"What's that?" The corner of his mouth tipped up into the hint of a smile. He was toying with me. That's what this was. He didn't want me on his rugged retreat any more than I wanted to be there.

On this, surely, we could agree.

"I'm not a wilderness girl. I don't like bugs. Bears will want to eat me. And I don't know anything about tents or campfires or snakes hiding beneath logs."

"Now you know about the logs. The rest I'll teach you."

"Ha. Even if we had all the time in the world, it wouldn't be enough."

He stood up from the swing. Somehow even taller now.

Confident. Towering. Smug.

Hot.

"I can teach you in one weekend everything you'll need to know to be a top-notch co-chaperone."

"But why? Why would you want to do that?" I was genuinely confused by his willingness to help.

He shrugged. "Sounds like a fun challenge."

"No, it's an awful challenge, an impossible challenge. You could convince anyone else on the faculty to go with you. And Pin Dick would probably agree."

"You call him that to his face. I think you're the only one he'd let get away with it," he observed. I wondered if he'd been wanting to ask me about this for a while.

"I'm also the only one he makes come to unnecessary after-hours meetings in his office."

Clay's eyes went big and his hands flexed. "He ever cross a line?"

"Nothing that would stand up as an overt hostile work environment. He's sneaky like that."

"I want to pound him into the asphalt." Clay's voice dropped an octave, deep with anger. He was usually so restrained and affable that it took me aback to see his dark expression, jaw locked and tense. His protectiveness stunned me.

I placed a hand on his forearm. "Don't do that. Just do me a solid and ask him for another co-chaperone." Then I let my hand linger for an extra couple of seconds because, holy hot-for-teacher, his forearms were firm and roped with muscle. Reluctantly, I let it drop and felt a shiver roll down my spine.

"He'll never go for it. We need someone there who knows first aid. There will be a ranger with us at the campsite, so you'll mainly be wrangling the kids, and you know all of them, so it's actually perfect."

"Perfect except for my whole fear-of-the-woods thing." I was doubly glad to have a porch swing as I dropped onto the bench where Clay had sat moments before. I knew I was cooked.

He pointed at me. Decision made.

"Here's what we're gonna do. I have a closet full of camping supplies at my house, so we're going to have a little dry run at camping."

"What's that mean?"

"We'll camp out in my yard. Twenty feet from the house, if anything spooks you. But the terrain will be similar, so we'll pitch some tents, build some fires, and do some hiking. By the time the retreat rolls around, you'll know everything you need to know, and you just might enjoy yourself in the great outdoors."

I held up a hand to push away the crazy idea, but he stepped closer at the same time, so I ended up pushing against his chest. His rock-hard chest. "Let's not get carried away with the *enjoying* part," I said, swallowing thickly.

"You can do this, Alexandra. I promise." He held up a finger and wagged it. "But only if you're okay. You're not hiking anywhere until a doctor clears you. Much as I'd like you on the trip, you're not going if you have a concussion."

He tapped two fingers against my temple and the contact sent a zing of electricity coursing through my veins. Suddenly, the concussion escape route didn't feel as enticing.

"I think I'm probably okay, but, yes, I'll get checked out."

Watching me, Clay nodded slowly. He took a couple of careful steps backward before turning to jog down my front steps toward his truck. "Take it easy tonight. And if you need anything, call me. Okay?" he called.

I nodded weakly, unaccustomed to this side of him, a side that was the polar opposite of the stoic, hurried professorial guy I knew at school. Hot heartthrob Clay Meadows was actually kind of a softie. Which made no difference whatsoever because he was staying away from relationships.

And that was just as well, because so was I.

CHAPTER
SIX

CLAY

I'd always surmised that I was in danger of falling hard and fast for Ally Dalbotten if I ever stopped moving long enough to get to know the woman she is now. Which was why I never stopped moving. Knowing her better would only do destructive things to my heart.

Turned out I was right.

I liked this woman. After less than an hour in the nurse's office, tending to her wounds and trying not to devour her soft skin with my eyes, I knew I was in trouble. Then she got me talking about my depression, which I never did, and it felt surprisingly okay. She didn't change my mind about the risk of a relationship—let's not be foolhardy—but she had tested my resolve.

I was looking forward to being tested again a little too much.

My brain churned, trying to come up with reasons why the two of us couldn't and shouldn't chaperone the retreat together. Conflict of interest? Sure, when my interest in her created a conflict with my dick. Didn't think I could go to the principal and tell him that was why I'd need a new co-chaperone.

I hadn't finished clenching my jaw over that when I saw my brother's truck parked in front of my house at the end of the long drive. Whenever I made the final right turn into the private neighborhood around Bandit Lake, whatever tension I still carried from my day slipped away like an unwanted cape.

Shane sat on my back porch, which was really more of a side porch because it wrapped around half the house. He and I had restored and refinished it together last year, giving him permanent rights to drink a beer there whenever he wanted, according to him.

The truth was I never minded coming home to company, not that I'd ever give him the satisfaction of telling him that.

At first, after our grandmother deeded the property to me, my parents, Shane, and I assumed she'd made a mistake. She'd lived to ninety years old, most of those years spent hosting family gatherings at this house, and it seemed like the natural order of things would be for my mother to inherit it. Line of succession, Green Valley style.

But my grandmother had other plans. Without mentioning it, she put the house in my name and left her money and other worldly possessions to the rest of my family.

"She always was quirky," my brother had reasoned when he read the terms of the will. He left it at that, but my parents felt the burn of being snubbed. They were solid folk, raised to work hard in life and have few things given to them that they didn't earn. They weren't fussy, which meant they didn't expect their children to be that way either.

Little surprise, they felt like depression was just a case of mind over matter. If I wasn't happy, it was because I wasn't trying hard enough. Then, I inherited the house.

Feeling undeserving and a little guilty, I'd instituted an open-door policy so Shane and my parents could use the place whenever they wanted. It only seemed fair.

Everyone had their own lives to attend to, so most of the time I spent nights and weekends here alone. Hence I didn't mind it at all when I found Shane sipping one of my beers on my side porch.

"You get lost on your way home?" Shane chided, opening the outside fridge and handing me a beer without asking if I wanted one. After spending over an hour with Ally, I wanted ten, just to cool the heat in my veins.

"Something like that." I explained Ally's incident on the hurdles and filled my brother in on the upcoming retreat and my new co-chaperone. He raised an eyebrow when I mentioned Ally's name, so I neglected to tell him I'd offered her a private camping lesson in my yard. I kept it simple—no big deal. "How long have you been here?"

Shane stretched his long legs out and put his feet, clad in hiking boots, up on the porch railing. He ran his left hand over the beard he'd let grow longer, and which he'd grown fond of stroking. Give him a pipe and he'd look downright thoughtful.

He used his smaller right hand to balance his beer bottle on one thigh. My brother had been born with symbrachydactyly, a rare condition that gave him a little hand with only a hint of fingers. He'd never let it stop him from doing anything though, and I admired him for that. If anything, he seemed to get more power from that hand when he kneaded dough, so good on him for making lemonade from what God gave him.

One more reason for my parents to scoff at an "invisible affliction," which was how they saw my depression diagnosis when I sought therapy after college.

"About a half hour. Thought we could barbecue if you don't have any plans."

I looked at the time, which was unnecessary since the sun had just begun to set over the lake and that put the hour at about seven in the evening. "Barbecue sounds good. I've got a couple steaks in the fridge, but I don't have much to go with 'em."

Shane reached down and picked up a bag of russet potatoes and a grocery bag. "Saw the steaks when I was here last time," he admitted. "Also saw that you didn't have much else in your fridge."

I took the proffered bag and shuffled through the items, glad to see he'd picked up a roll of paper towels for the kitchen in addition to sour cream, chives, broccoli, and a quart of orange sherbet. It was moments like this when I wondered if I'd ever let a woman get to know me well enough that she'd show up with the perfect array of foods. Wondered if I'd ever let anyone get to know me well enough.

And, as usual, I realized I was the problem in that scenario.

———

I flipped the steaks one final time to sear them with a crosshatch pattern. Even though it was just the two of us eating, I still wanted them to look worthy of a restaurant meal.

Shane came outside with the potatoes, baked in the kitchen oven and topped with chopped chives and sour cream. He'd sauteed the broccoli in chili oil and garlic, making me once again grateful to have a brother who could cook. It reminded me I needed to plan the meals for the retreat, so we didn't end up eating trail mix for three days straight. That wouldn't do.

After we'd divvied the side dishes up on plates and cracked open another two beers, Shane and I sat in chairs facing the lake under the darkening sky and waited for the steaks. "What's Julia up to?" Since they'd started dating last year, Shane didn't come for dinner nearly as often.

"Out with Joy. Girls' night."

"Gonna be a late one?"

He shrugged. "Who knows."

We were no closer to Shane telling me the real reason for his visit than we'd been an hour ago, and I knew there was a reason. My brother didn't just show up for dinner unless he had something to get off his chest. "To what do I owe the visit, Shane?"

His beer was halfway to his mouth and he froze. Grimacing at the fact that I knew him better than he usually realized, he slowly raised the bottle the remaining two inches, took a long sip, and put it on the table. "Mom and Dad want you to come to dinner," he said, not meeting my eye. I hadn't been to their house in over a month.

"They sent you over as emissary? Couldn't ask me themselves?" My parents and I weren't on the best terms, but sometimes they at least pretended. Guess today wasn't one of those times.

He shrugged. "I might've offered. C'mon, Clay. Just come. It won't be like last time."

A laugh exploded from me at his naivete. "Why the hell not?"

"Because I made them promise not to do it again." At the last family dinner, they'd surprised me by inviting their neighbors along with their twenty-five-year-old daughter. The worst part was that she didn't seem to feel nearly as awkward as I did, and Shane got wrangled into a discussion in the kitchen about sourdough starters, leaving us alone for nearly an hour.

"Sorry if I don't exactly trust y'all."

"Hey, don't lump me in with them. I didn't know she'd be there. And at least this time, I already addressed it with Mom and Dad."

"Yeah," I groused.

He held up his beer again and watched me over the rim of the bottle before taking a sip. I knew he was thinking something, and most of me wished he'd keep it to himself, whatever it was.

But the rest of me was curious. "What?"

He shrugged. "Just that you have this opportunity to spend time with Ally Dalbotten and I'm just wondering if you're finally planning on doing something about her. Finally." Shane asked as though he was talking about a slight chance of showers during a morning hike. When, in fact, he was talking about a torrential downpour that would likely flood my entire world.

My brother remembered how bad I had it for Ally Dalbotten, but I didn't feel like going there.

"Not gonna do anything except go camping." I pulled the steaks off the grill and watched them sizzle on the plate, pink juices oozing from the sides. "Hey, can you grab the steak sauce from inside? I made a fresh batch."

I assumed the conversation would be over at that point. It was my intention, anyway, which was why I sent Shane into the house for the sauce. By the time he returned, we'd be onto another subject.

But my brother had never done what I expected back when we were kids, and it seemed he didn't plan to deviate now. He returned with a mason jar filled with a mahogany mixture of caramelized onions, brown sugar, and balsamic vinegar, all reduced down to a thick sauce. "Conversation not over."

"Seemed over to me."

"It'll be over when you ask her out, finally."

"Not happening." I handed him his steak and watched his eyes water at the delicious smoky smell. "And now the conversation's over."

CHAPTER
SEVEN

ALLY

After Clay had convinced me to spend one night this weekend camping in his backyard, I'd sent him on his way, stripped off my clothes, and spent an hour soaking in my bathtub. I had abrasions on my stomach where my shirt had slid upward, and that nasty scrape on my knee had taken a painful scrubbing with a washcloth to clean up.

Then I'd slept like the dead and hobbled out to Clay's truck in the morning when he came to pick me up. Opening the passenger door and helping me up the step, he was freshly showered, and all too perky for seven in the morning.

"I feel bad that you had to come early. You don't teach sunrise."

"I'll do a morning workout, then shower before second block." He pointed to his track pants and fresh long-sleeved T-shirt, which hugged his chest and might have been tight enough to reveal his six-pack right through the fabric. If a person was looking.

Me. I was that person.

I ignored the abs when he handed me a hot cup of coffee. "You are speaking my love language with this," I said.

"Wasn't sure if you had coffee already. No pressure to drink it." He went around to the driver's side and slid into the seat without using the step. I took note of his sinewy forearms. I watched his right arm flex as he turned the key in the ignition.

I scolded myself for noticing how his track pants hugged the curve of his tight ass and how his muscles moved under the fabric. This was way past my usual idle appreciation of Clay as an art form. I certainly should not have been sneaking looks at how the crinkles around his eyes proved that he did indeed smile sometimes. Those times when his face broke open like clouds letting in the sun. Like he was doing right now.

Staring at me and smiling. Because I was staring at him and smiling like a loon.

"You okay there?" he asked. It's a fair question because I was gaping at him like an art patron examining brushstrokes on an impressionist painting.

"Um, sure. Yes. Fine."

He drummed his fingers on the steering wheel but continued staring at me. Waiting. For what?

"The coffee? Is it okay? It's a vanilla latte. I wasn't sure what you liked, and this is how I make mine." Only then did I realize I hadn't answered his question.

"Oh, yes, thank you. This is awesome. I usually drink whatever's in the teachers' lounge, so it's a treat to have this on the way to work."

He turned off the car engine and spun in his seat, looking like I'd hocked a wad of spit into his cup. "What?"

"*What* what?"

"Please tell me you're joking. You do not drink the swill at school."

"It's not swill, it's coffee."

"It's swill."

I laughed as he started the truck again. "You are a coffee snob. I had no idea. All this time I've been giving you shit about your workouts, and I could've been razzing you for being a coffee elitist." It felt good to get back on our normal terms of workplace banter. I needed to stop distracting myself with how nice he was being to me because it was throwing off my mojo. And those biceps . . .

I reached over and yanked his sleeve down to his wrist. Eyeing me suspiciously, he pulled the other one down.

He shrugged. "I'm not apologizing for liking real coffee. You know they don't clean the urn out before they make a new batch, right? It's just watered-down swill on top of yesterday's swill."

Feeling a small surge of bile, I took another healthy sip of coffee and swallowed. It was a hundred times better than what they had at school. "This is delicious. Thank you again."

"So that garbage you're always heating in the microwave . . ." He pointed an accusing finger at me after backing out of my driveway. "Not only is it old coffee, it's old shitty coffee."

"It's coffee." Frankly, I was surprised he noticed what I was doing with the microwave. He moved in and out of the teachers' lounge so quickly, it always seemed like he had somewhere pressing to be.

"Coffee. Snob. I like this new bit of information." Settling back, I shimmied against my seat, satisfied. Then I scooted a little closer to the cool window because he must have turned the heat on in the truck. That was the only explanation for why I was sweating.

He turned to face me, pointing two fingers between his face and mine to indicate he'd be watching me. "Drink your coffee. If I catch you heating it up later at lunch, we'll have words."

"Yes, sir."

Clay's eyes narrowed on me, his breathing suddenly deeper, those hands clenching the steering wheel tightly. But he turned his head to glare out the windshield, muttering something under his breath before pulling out onto the main road.

The day went by as usual, only Clay didn't come into the teachers' lounge during lunch. I doubted that anyone noticed. Anyone but me. A lot of teachers ate in their classrooms or ran errands during the forty-five-minute break, and we hadn't exactly said we'd meet up. Just because he mentioned checking to make sure I didn't reheat this morning's latte didn't mean we had a set plan. I was being ridiculous.

So why did I keep looking up every time the door opened?

No. Reason.

I didn't see Clay again until after school, when he was standing on the track with a whistle. His team had finished their warmup laps and were dropped down to the grass in front of him to stretch. Head bent over his clipboard, Clay didn't see me. The last thing I planned to do was go anywhere near the runners. Or the hurdles. Or the track.

Turning toward the teachers' parking lot, I said a silent goodbye to Clay, found my car where I'd left it the day before, and drove home. Another soak in the tub, and I felt almost human again. A microwaved plate of lasagna and a Netflix binge, and I felt a little lonely. This was the reason I'd convinced my best friend, Lucy, to meet me at Genie's Country Western Bar, and here we were. Lost in a crowd.

A group of guys drinking beers in a corner made me think of Clay, and it bugged me. The whole point of going out was not to think. Or to think in the company of good friends.

Genie's was packed for a weeknight, every table full and two deep at the bar. Someone had turned up the music so it could be heard over the cacophony of voices, which only made people talk louder. But Carrie Underwood was going to take a baseball bat to her ex's car, if anyone bothered to listen.

"Why's it so busy?" I asked Lucy, who'd been my best friend since ninth grade when we'd bonded talking about our older brothers who didn't want us following them around to parties.

She shrugged. "Always happy hour somewhere."

Too focused on my current dilemma to question her analysis, I dug right in. "Lu, I need some advice."

She'd been studying the screen above the bar where a Nashville Predators hockey game had the attention of half the folks in the place. As soon as she heard my words, her eyes snapped to mine. Sweeping her dark hair over one shoulder, she scooted her chair closer in order to hear me over the voices.

"Ooh, sounds juicy. I'm here to help, you know that." I did know. It was the best part of our friendship.

I debated how much to tell her. Word traveled faster than a boll weevil in a cotton field around here and I didn't want anything getting back to Clay. I bit my lip and reconsidered saying anything at all.

Lucy swatted my shoulder. "Oh, spill it. I can already tell it's about a man, so why don't I just keep guessing and you can nod or blush or whatever until I get it right."

"Fine, if you put it that way, I'll just tell you." I inhaled a cleansing breath, checked the score of the game—three to one, Predators—and took a long swig of my beer. "I have to spend not one but two weekends camping with Clay Meadows."

She whistled. "Not exactly shooting fish in a barrel, that one. Good luck."

"I'm not trying to shoot him. Or kiss him, to be clear."

"Okay, good. Because I was about to talk you down."

"I'm already down, thanks."

I felt my face fall at her low opinion of my odds, and she immediately corrected. "Oh, honey, it's not you. You're the biggest catch around. Any guy in this place . . ." She spread her arms wide and looked around. "And I don't mean Genie's, I mean Green Valley. Any of these guys would be blessed by the angels to have you. But Clay? You know he's notorious for short, meaningless relationships."

Other than a very dedicated hermit, everyone knew.

My dating record didn't look much better.

Just to prove my lack of prospects, I looked around Genie's. At one table, a group of guys barely old enough to drink knocked back beers and played a drinking game with dice. One of them caught me looking his way and tipped his cowboy hat at me with a wink. His auburn beard had that patchy look of a guy just this side of puberty. I couldn't see myself as a cougar at thirty-four.

The several other tables that were filled with couples made me sigh. I'd always imagined myself as part of a couple. Heck, I'd been part of a couple for five years. Five years ago.

I didn't need to look at the date to know it had been nearly five years to the day that Johnny Culpepper and I parted ways. Dating Johnny had felt like a good solid plan when we met right out of college. And I was a planner.

I was also a reader of every Regency romance novel from Jane Austen right on through Tessa Dare's latest. More than once Lucy had accused me of being lost in an earlier era, and maybe she was right.

Thanks to the dukes and the viscounts who could woo better than anyone, I had myself a model for how my love life would be—it would be swoony and romantic. Full stop.

My plan was I'd date a series of roguish bachelors in my early twenties, settle for one at twenty-five, marry at twenty-seven, have three moppets by my mid-thirties. Teaching would be the perfect job that would give me school breaks off to coincide with my kids' schedules.

So I graduated from college and dated the roguish bachelors, most of them variations on Clay Meadows—tall, rakish, muscular men with chiseled good looks. The best of the bunch was Johnny Culpepper, the son of a Nashville seafood importer who dazzled me with his ready smile and his ability to lead on the dance floor. We met at a wedding, began dating a week later, and by the time I was twenty-four I was ready to put my plan in place.

Johnny Culpepper seemed on board with the plan. We'd talked about my romantic aspirations and my love for formal wooing. A man who liked a challenge, he jumped at the chance to woo like the best of 'em.

He brought flowers to me after my last class when I was getting my teaching credential. He held doors open for me when we entered a restaurant and remembered my mother's birthday. He serenaded me with classical music from his phone when he told me he loved me under a moonlit sky.

So I didn't see it coming when night turned to day and the magic wore off.

Johnny explained it in such simple terms I kicked myself for not recognizing the charade. "I got caught up in the wooing. I liked doing all the stuff. It was romantic, and I loved the chase. But I never wanted a forever relationship. I just wanted the chase."

How had I not seen this coming?

It was a blow to the ego and an anvil on my tender heart.

He'd mastered all the trappings of courtship so well that I didn't really notice that Johnny Culpepper was really just a greyhound. In other words, he ran as fast as he could when the starting gun went off, pulled out all his best wooing moves when the object of his affections had yet to commit. Then, once I signed on for good, he lost his motivation.

Once a greyhound wins the race, it doesn't keep running. It stops and basks in the win.

Then it waits for the next opportunity to chase something new.

Johnny Culpepper was the first man I ever dated who was only in it for the chase, but he wasn't the last.

I kept doing it, kept falling for guys who wooed my pants off, only to put theirs right back on after they got what they wanted. Sometimes it was after one week. Sometimes after three months.

My mother thought men were unreliable, and she'd done her best to warn me. Eventually, I started to believe she was right and decided I'd never fall for that kind of man again because it wasn't good for me. There was no point in chasing after a greyhound and having him chase me back because we both knew that there was a finish line in sight.

That was why I could look at Clay with his sculpted arms, pretty face, and melted-chocolate eyes and feel like I knew something important about him. Clay screamed greyhound, and that simple fact made it easy to convince myself to feel nothing.

The past couple of days were a weird blip. I'd chalked it up to concussion brain and the seductive properties of good coffee. Nothing more. And certainly nothing that meant I'd mistake spending a night in his yard pitching a tent for anything more.

"I know. I've been immune to him for years, and then he had to go and be uncharacteristically sweet. It just . . . threw me off." I explained my crash and burn on the track, and Lucy nodded sympathetically until I got to the part about spending a night faux-camping in Clay's backyard. Then she practically knocked the drink out of my hand.

"No, that's simply not going to work."

"Because . . . ?" I knew why it wasn't going to work for me—bugs, flimsy tents, woodland creatures—but I remained confounded as to why Lucy thought it sounded so awful.

"Because it's way too much time to spend alone with that perfectly shaped hunk of Clay. If you're feeling things now, hoo-boy, you're going to be feeling things after that."

She wasn't wrong. That was my other concern. Maybe the bigger concern.

"I don't think I can get out of chaperoning the retreat, so I do need some help if I'm going to be at one with the woods. What do you suggest?"

Lucy tapped a finger against her pink-lipped smile, and I watched her eyes dart about as though looking for a place to land on an answer. Her mouth popped open, and she clapped her hands. "I'm cock-blocking you." Her voice was so sugary sweet as she smiled at me in her knowing way that I felt certain I'd misheard her.

"Excuse me?"

"I'm going to make it impossible for you to notice Clay because you'll be pining over someone else. There's a guy." Lucy's eyes gleamed with a mad scientist's glee, and I wondered what kind of Frankenstein she had in mind.

"What kind of guy?"

"Louie. He's an architect."

Lucy had never once brought up Louis the architect before, and I wondered why. "Does Louis actually exist, or are you making up a fictitious perfect guy to keep me in rapt anticipation through the weekend and therefore distracted from Clay's biceps? Then you'll tell me Louie was all a lie?"

Her eyes went wide. Then she took a sip of her beer. Then another. I felt certain I'd nailed it until she started shaking her head slowly. Very slowly.

"Nooo . . ." She drew the word out so long it seemed to have three syllables. "But that's a great idea and I will be stashing it in my bag of wing-woman tricks for later. Louie is real."

I studied Lucy. The way she met my eyes made her look serious and truthful, but there was something she wasn't saying.

"But . . . ," I prompted.

Lucy took two more sips from her glass before slamming it on the table so hard that the liquid sloshed over the side. She mopped the beer up with a red bar napkin and pushed the glass away. "Fine. He's maybe a tiny bit boring. But not in a bad way."

I couldn't suppress a laugh. "How is boring ever good?"

"When it's a relief, that's when. What you see is what you get with Louie. He's not sarcastic or jokey."

"So, no sense of humor."

She made a face of distaste. "He's straightforward. Has a stable career. He'll pay for your dinner and engage you in tasteful conversation about uncontroversial subjects."

"How do you know this man?" I found it hard to believe he and Lucy were good friends, partly because I'd never heard of him and partly because this was Lucy, just about the farthest thing from boring I'd ever known—she'd been brave enough to leave Green Valley for a big city and become a physician's assistant when no one we knew had heard of that job. She was ahead of her time, and she did not do boring.

"We were standing in the checkout line at the library and apparently he was a former student of my mom's." Lucy's mother, Frieda, was a Green Valley institution, a grammar school teacher who remembered every former student's name, even a dozen or more years after she had them in class.

"Say no more."

She nodded. "He was nice enough. Gave me his card because I told him I was looking for volunteers for the church yard sale, and he said he's free most weekends. Made a point of telling me he doesn't have anyone in his life to take care of, definitely no animals. He emphasized that."

"What does he have against animals?" I almost wanted to meet this Louie just to confirm that such a person actually existed.

And more than that, maybe Lucy had a point. If I kept my mind busy thinking about a future date with a kind, boring architect, then maybe it would distract me enough that I could be in close quarters with Clay and feel nothing.

"Yeah, the animal thing threw me a little bit, but he admitted he was bitten by a sheep as a kid and is scared of anything wearing a fur coat."

A kind, boring architect who was a little bit weird. I could work with that.

"Sounds like a dream, Lu. Set me up."

CHAPTER
EIGHT

CLAY

"Hey, feels like you've been avoiding me." Ally bumped me with her hip in the teachers' lounge on Friday morning while I was toasting a bagel. I'd arrived at school at seven to grade papers because sometimes the harsh fluorescent lighting in the classroom made it easier to focus.

It was not because I was hoping to avoid bumping into any of the faculty members who taught sunrise classes and would reliably arrive at seven thirty. And it wasn't because anything had changed in my casual friendship with Ally. But a man could only take so much, and after spending more time in the same room with her than I had in a decade, I needed some space.

Feeling the softness of her skin and the warmth of her body when I carried her against my chest had thrown me for a loop. I liked it all just a bit too much. So my overeager libido needed an Ally break. I needed to show it who was boss.

"Me? No, of course not." I continued watching my bagel brown in the toaster oven like it was the most fascinating thing in the world.

"And observe, the leopard bagel basking in the morning sun, blissfully unaware of predators waiting nearby with cream cheese . . . ," Ally intoned in a deep announcer's voice.

Grudgingly letting out a chuckle, I turned to face her. "Sorry. Zoned out there."

"Need some good heart-accelerating coffee." She held up a large, full tumbler with steam wafting from the top.

"Mmm, yeah. I didn't sleep too well, and I stumbled in here without making a pot. I'm so tired that even the high school swill smells good," I teased.

Reaching for a cup on the shelf, she corrected me. "It's not the school swill. You made me see the error of my ways, and I dug out my French press and made coffee myself." Turning the cup in her hand, she read, "'I'm just here for the coffee.' Sounds about right." She tipped the tumbler, poured half the coffee into the empty cup, and handed it to me.

"I don't want to take your coffee."

"Please. I emptied the whole French press into this thing. It's more than any one person should be drinking, greyhound."

"What?"

Her cheeks bloomed pink and I couldn't help but stare.

"*What* what?"

"Greyhound? What's that?"

She looked away and waved a hand dismissively. "Sorry. I sort of call you that in my head because you're always running around." She met my eyes apologetically and I knew if I made a big deal about it, she'd get more uncomfortable. But I kind of loved that she had a nickname for me.

"Fitting, I suppose." I reached for the cup and smelled the aroma before taking a sip. "Vanilla latte?"

She shrugged. "You got me kinda hooked. I used vanilla-flavored soy milk, so it was kind of a cheat. Anyhow, are we still on for tomorrow? I stocked up on bear spray." She made a gesture of spraying perfume into the air and walking through it.

"Hang on. What kind of bear spray?"

She shrugged. "Whatever they had at the bait and tackle place."

Guiding her to the empty plank table in the middle of the room, I pulled out a chair and faced it toward me, motioning for her to take a seat. Once she sat, I tried to explain the error of her ways. "The bait and tackle place," I confirmed.

She tilted her head as though it was obvious why a person would buy bear spray at a fishing supply store.

"If you don't see any bears, can you use it to catch fish?" I asked.

Tilting the chair back, she scoffed, "Maybe. Would that be so bad? Are you a bear spray elitist *and* a coffee elitist?"

"First of all, I see you agree with me about the coffee. And second, did you keep your receipt?"

"I guess. Why are you hovering over me like you're getting ready to give me a lecture?" she asked, just as I realized I was indeed hovering. I took a step back.

"Because I'm giving you a lecture. Return the bear spray. We're not going to be spraying bears." The image of Ally on a hiking trail spritzing a bear with an atomizer was too good not to lock away in my mind.

Pressing her lips together, she looked up at me like a student who didn't understand a word of Shakespeare despite reading it for the tenth time. I wanted to reach over and hug the confusion right out of her. Instead, I pulled a chair into the middle of the room, flipped it around, and straddled it, too far from her now for any hugging.

"What's wrong with bear spray? The guy at the store said it's effective for warding off bears."

"Of course he did. He wanted to sell you bear spray."

"Yeah, probably. And I wanted to keep bears away, so it seems like a win-win to me. Do you own stock in an animal repellant company or something? I'll buy your brand, just say so."

"I do not."

"So what's the problem? I wasn't going to make you carry it, if that's what you were worried about. I wouldn't want you to tax your muscles and mess up your workout schedule."

"Alexandra . . ."

"Yes?" She blinked her big blue eyes up at me.

"We're not going to see any bears."

"Ha. That's what the last guy said, and he's not here to say 'I told you so' because the bear ate him."

I assumed she was joking. Most people would be joking.

For now, I told myself the retreat would be fine. I wasn't worried about having Ally as my sidekick for three days because we'd be distracted by the students the entire time. We'd be lucky to string five words together at a time with each other. It would be like school. Normal.

I was a little more concerned about the little campout in my yard that I'd insisted on. Mainly, I'd done it because she seemed so ill at ease, and I wanted to make that crease in her forehead disappear. I wanted to allay her fears.

But with that came more time alone with her and that terrified me. Not because I didn't trust myself to keep my hands to myself. I was a grown man. A grown, hot-for-teacher, horny-as-hell man who was half-hard just thinking about being alone in my yard with her. Two days of ignoring her had done nothing to get rid of those urges. If anything, I'd made it worse because now I couldn't stop looking at the milky skin at the hollow of her throat and noticing how it curved to meet her collarbones. I couldn't stop thinking about how it felt to hold her against my chest and feel the flutter of her heartbeat keeping time with mine.

But I had to stop. So I would.

"We won't see bears, most likely. And if we do, I promise we won't get eaten. That doesn't really happen."

She started to laugh, a carefree sound like tiny glass wind chimes in the breeze. After setting her coffee down, she leaned back so far the chair almost tipped over. I lurched off my seat to stop her from falling, but she righted herself before I reached her.

The accusing, puzzled look on her face told me she thought I was crazy, and maybe I was. She'd unleashed something in me earlier in the week that I'd kept buried for so long I'd left it for dead. Big mistake. Apparently feelings like mine don't die.

"What's wrong?" I asked.

"I just wanted you to think I was pulling my weight and being prepared."

"I'm not worried about that. You've got my back on the first aid stuff. That's helpful enough. Let me handle the camping part. And the teaching of camping."

"So . . . we're really doing this? The dry run? Because I thought maybe I could just read a book or look at the internet or something and take a virtual camping trip this weekend. I'll watch episodes of *Naked and Afraid* or *Alone* and then I'll know more than even you."

I'd watch you naked in the woods.

I shook that errant thought from my brain before Ally saw evidence of it all over my face. "Don't watch those."

"Why not?"

If she watched either one of those shows, she'd never agree to set foot in the wilderness. I'd seen both and the people on them were survivalists. She'd take one look at someone losing a toe to frostbite or ice fishing with a stick and run for the nearest beach chair with an umbrella drink.

"Those shows won't teach you what you need to know for a school retreat. I've got this. I promise."

Voices down the hallway reminded me we'd been here talking for far too long. Ally seemed to realize it at the same time, checking the time on her phone. "I need to get to class. Yearbook's in shambles because we're using a new company this year, and their page templates are all different. As in, we can't just plug in new photos—we have to redesign everything."

"Whose idea was it to change companies?"

Ally waves a hand. "That would be me. It's cheaper, and the money the school saved allowed us to keep more in the budget for our special ed teacher, which we need."

"Got it. Okay, don't want to hold you up." Ally grabbed her coffee and moved toward the door just as Witty came in with a muffin on a paper plate. Hijacking the toaster, he pulled out my bagel, which I'd forgotten about.

"This yours?" He held it up with two fingers.

"Don't touch people's food," Ally scolded. "We've talked about that, Witty."

He shrugged, tossed my bagel on a paper towel, and went ahead warming his muffin.

"Don't watch those shows!" I called after Ally.

"Yes, sir!" she called back.

I dropped into a chair and took a bite of my now-cold toasted bagel, devoid of cream cheese. It tasted how I felt.

CHAPTER
NINE

CLAY

Ally ignored my advice.

"This guy was in his tent—or not even a tent, it was more like a tarp hanging from a tree branch—and some animal starts heavy breathing right next to him, and then touches him through the tarp!"

I shook my head, accepting the steep pitch that lay ahead of me: convincing her we'd be safe on a two-mile trail to a campsite tended by park rangers.

"Which one did you watch?" It didn't matter. One episode of either wilderness survival show would have terrified anyone planning to go camping for the first time.

"Both of them."

I held my face in my hands. This woman . . . so stubborn. "Ally, why?"

She shrugged and dropped her overnight bag at my feet. "I don't know. Curiosity, I guess." To her credit, she'd packed in a nylon duffel, not some roller bag that would be impractical on a camping trip. I'd told her I'd lend her a backpack for the retreat, and she didn't seem put off by the idea of carrying everything on her back.

"They ate beetles. Lots of them. And one guy was trying to catch a fish and ended up eating leeches. We're not eating beetles, are we?" Ally stood on my front porch, arms crossed, crease between her brows. At first, I was delighted that she'd shown up fifteen minutes early because I mistook it for enthusiasm. But it was something else.

"We won't be eating beetles. These are high school kids, remember? We'll be eating things like GORP."

"What the hell's that? Is it a type of insect? A weird plant?" She looked legitimately terrified, and I fought the urge to pull her against my chest and wrap her in my arms. Her fear was kind of adorable, mainly because I had years of camping experience that made me feel like sleeping outside was no big deal.

She was a puzzle. So capable and badass in every way—unwilling to back down when it came to refusing Pindich and his smarmy lunch invitations, feisty as hell when it came to creating an art program that none of the other public schools had, and giving me a hard time about . . . everything. But this one thing scared the hell out of her.

I needed to understand why. And my ego wanted to be the superhero that got her over her fears. Not to mention that I loved the outdoors, and we happened to live in one of the most beautiful parts of the country. It would be a shame for Ally to live here and not get to experience all the wonders in nature.

Escorting her into my house, I tried to talk her down. "It's an acronym. Good old raisins and peanuts. GORP is basically trail mix, though we don't actually use peanuts because kids are allergic."

She exhaled a breath I didn't know she was holding and looked around my kitchen, where I'd gathered our food supplies for the night. "Here, let's bring these out back and I'll show you the setup."

We wouldn't have a cooler on the camping trip because we'd be hiking a couple miles with backpacks, but for tonight's purposes, there was no need to rough it.

"You sure you wouldn't rather cook in here? This is a pretty nice kitchen setup you've got." She ran a hand over the dark gray stone countertop and admired the cabinets. I felt a sense of pride as she looked around. "Did you do a lot of work when you moved in?"

"I did a few things recently. Mostly in here." I pointed to where a big center island separated the kitchen from the den. I'd painted the cabinets a deep shade of green that matched the trees visible beyond the deck. It wasn't fancy, but the rustic charm suited me.

Other than the island marking the division between kitchen and den, it was one large room leading out to the deck. "It was two smaller spaces, but the wall between these rooms wasn't weight-bearing so we were able to take it out. And Shane and I worked on the deck a bit, installed those sliders." I pointed to the floor-to-ceiling glass windows that overlapped each other when they slid open, giving the room an indoor-outdoor feeling.

"And in answer to your question, yes, it would be nice to eat in here, but we're going camping. Come." I grabbed the cooler and beckoned her to follow me outside. She looked wistfully at the comfy blue couch in the den, touched the soft gray throw blanket on the end, and wordlessly followed me to the sliding door. When her large blue eyes landed on me, I gave in and went back for the throw blanket, handing it to her to carry.

"Fine. This is not an officially sanctioned camping blanket, but I suppose it won't kill us to have a few comforts while we're in the wilderness."

"The wilderness?"

"The yard. My yard. Nothing scary out there, except maybe an overly sharp blade of grass."

She swatted my shoulder. "Don't make fun of me. I'm here, aren't I?" She wrapped the blanket around her shoulders and shivered.

"You cold?"

"Tiny bit. I brought jackets though." She pointed at the overstuffed duffle bag which I was carrying over my shoulder along with the cooler.

"Jackets?" I emphasized the plural. We were only going to be out here for one night, and I'd promised a roaring campfire.

"Four or five, just in case."

I surveyed her large duffel. The size made more sense now. I wondered what else she'd packed. It wouldn't have surprised me if she had an inflatable mattress in there, though I sensed the issue with camping wasn't so much the lack of creature comforts as more a fear of the wilderness. Whichever it turned out to be, I'd get her past it. I was determined.

My yard was a small flat patch of grass overlooked by my back porch. In the early spring weather, cool air blew off the lake, and the trees exploded with young green leaves. The dahlia bulbs that had lain dormant all winter long had sprouted tall stems and leaves beneath tight purple buds ready to burst. Twin wooden feeders hung from low branches, where the birds would land in the morning and peck at the piles of seed.

"Wow. This is so pretty," Ally said, taking in the herb garden sprouting with purple chive blossoms, low-growing oregano, and some hardy winter lettuces.

"Thanks. It's fun to experiment."

I'd spent my childhood visiting my grandparents here, hiking in the surrounding woods, and messing around on the lake. I hadn't shared this place with people outside of my family, never invited friends over for parties. That wasn't the point of the place. I understood the good fortune of having a house on undisturbed parkland. Bandit Lake had some of the cleanest water in the state due to the restrictions over who could use it. Not taking the responsibility lightly, I felt more like a steward of a borrowed treasure than an outright owner. I was a tenant until the house moved into the next person's hands, and I wanted to leave it better than I'd found it.

Ally inhaled a deep, satisfying breath. "Mmm, I love that smell. If you can transport this to wherever we're going next weekend, I just might get on board." Ally blinked up at the cloudless blue sky and inhaled another large breath. She held it in her lungs before closing her eyes and blowing it out slowly.

"Great, isn't it? The lake has its own little microclimate." I took my own deep breath, envious of someone experiencing it for the first time.

The patch of grass was just large enough to give us space to practice putting up the tents in a row of three, just like what we'd do at the campsite. I had them laid out, along with wood for the fire we'd build and the camping supplies we'd need for some other camping practice activities.

Ally inhaled another deep breath, and I watched her shoulders drop an inch. "I've only known one other person who lived on the lake, so it's been years since I've been up here. How did I not know you had a place here?"

I shrugged. "I inherited it seven years ago when my grandmother passed. We don't exactly talk at school," I reminded her, guiding her over to the three tents. "How could you have known?" She followed me but didn't look down or acknowledge the tents in any way.

"Sure we do. I rib you about your pristine leftovers and you tell me to stop teaching my students to memorize facts about master painters."

"I've never said that. Kids don't memorize enough facts these days. They ask Siri for everything and don't have to recall anything they've learned. It's a travesty." Finally, she glanced down and squinted at the neat beige and orange nylon sacks.

"Mini parachutes?" she guessed.

"No, but that would be fun."

"It *would* be fun. Have you ever jumped out of a plane?" Her eyes danced, casting toward the sky as though looking for parachutes.

"Let me get this straight. You're afraid to spend a night in my yard, but you'd jump out of a plane at fourteen thousand feet?" Mind blown. But mind also confused.

Her eyebrows bounced, and she shed the blanket from around her shoulders, looking for a place to put it. She settled on a pair of camp chairs I'd set up near where I'd planned to make our firepit. "Sounds like someone knows exactly how high the planes fly before they let you jump out."

"I may have done some research. Then I came to my senses and realized I was not meant to free-fall through the sky while having a panic attack."

She laughed and picked up the orange tent, then twirled it from its string. "Yeah, kind of the same conclusion I came to." She watched the tent spin from her fingers. "If I ever decide to do it though, I'll be sure and call you. We can panic together."

I felt a wellspring of hope at the idea of plummeting to the earth with her if it meant spending more time together outside of school. But I dismissed the idea and the feeling just as quickly because she and I couldn't happen.

"These are tents, since you asked." I picked up the darker of the beige bundles and slipped the fastener up the string so I could take the folded tent and poles out. "These are two-person tents just like the ones the kids will use on the retreat."

"Okay," she said, opening the tent in her hands and taking out the folded nylon before the poles clattered to the ground in a noisy heap. She looked down at them accusingly, then up at me. "You made that look easier."

Tossing my bundle aside, I helped her unfurl the orange tent and turn it, so its zippered opening faced the lake. Two tarps sat on top of the mass of nylon, and I handed them to Ally to inspect.

"What are these, capes?" She waved them open to their full size.

"Yes. Once you put up your tent, you put on the cape and fly around a bit to make sure it looks okay from above."

Pressing her lips together in a smirk, she flicked my shoulder. "You're just lucky I like your magical little campground, or you'd be wearing your cape alone, greyhound."

It *was* magical. To a lot of people, my square of grass wouldn't look like much. Patchy with clusters of clovers that intermingled with the rye and fescue. The occasional dandelion. Stone flies swirling in the air, crickets singing in the distance. But I sensed she understood it on a deeper level. My heart tugged in my chest, wanting more from her than I had a right to expect.

"Okay, let's get these tents put up and build that fire. Then we can eat," I said, nearly shoving her aside to grab the folded poles from where I'd tossed them on the ground. "These are easy. They unfold and snap to full size."

I demonstrated lengthening one tent pole and let Ally straighten the other one. Then I showed her how to thread them through the clips and bend them into a bow shape to lift up the roof of the tent.

"That's it?" she asked, holding the ends of two poles in her hands. We had the tent stretched to its full size and height, but the tricky part was inserting the pole ends into the pockets where they always seemed too stubborn to fit.

"Not quite. Every kid on this trip is going to claim there's something wrong with their tent because they can't fit their poles in the holes."

"Sounds like a humblebrag to me." She smirked. Despite my attempt to ignore the innuendo, my body responded with a flare of heat across my skin, rushing straight down to my dick.

"Alexandra . . . ," I warned, my voice gravelly and strained like I'd run up a desert mountain.

"Sorry." Her clear blue eyes flashed with mischief and those pretty plump lips twisted into a grin.

I leaned my forehead on my fingertips and shook my head. She was going to test every last strand of my self-restraint until it frayed into dust. And a part of me wanted to reciprocate, to tease and provoke, to see if she was held back by those same flimsy, self-imposed ties.

Handing her the tent pole, I went around to the other side and held the other end. "Give it a good bend and do the thing."

She chuckled at my words and grunted as she tried to bend the pole. "It's stubborn." She pulled the nylon pocket as close to the end of the pole as she could, but they weren't anywhere near each other. "Why is this so hard?"

"There's a trick. Walk toward me." She did as instructed, causing the pole to bend. Coming a little closer, she bent it enough to slip it into the pocket. "Voila, we have ourselves a tent."

It listed to the side but we secured the second pole and righted it. Then we put the rain fly on top and began hammering in the stakes that anchored the tent in place. As we crouched side by side over the task, Ally's arm brushed against my down puffer jacket. A ripple of electricity surged under my skin, even though it was impossible for me to feel her touch through two layers of clothing.

I stretched one of the nylon strings taut and Ally used a rubber mallet to tap the stake into the grass. When she looked over at me and smiled, I had a split second to warn, "Careful," before she missed the stake entirely and smacked my fingers with the mallet.

"Oh, no! Clay, I'm so sorry!"

It was more of a thump than anything dire, but the look of horror on her face made me feel so much worse than any pain in my fingers. "It's fine. You barely touched me."

She raised my hand to her face, placing a soft, barely there kiss on my knuckles where the mallet struck. Almost like she was kissing away the hurt. Followed by a dawning look of embarrassment that flashed across her face before she dropped my hand and backed up.

But all I could think about was how it felt to have her breath dancing over the skin of my hand. I wanted to feel it along the skin of my neck. Her breath teasing my ear. Coming in shaky exhales as I worked over every inch of her body with my hands.

My chest ached at the feel of Ally rubbing circles on the skin of my wounded hand. I wanted so much more from her, and it was getting harder to deny it.

Ally backed up to admire our work. "Looks like a tent. Mission accomplished." Then her smile faded. "But it's pretty small for two people. Are we . . . sharing this tent?"

Her eyes wandered to the other two tents and her expression clouded. I hated her look of consternation because it confirmed what I feared—she didn't want to share a tent or anything else with me. Why should she?

I quickly reassured her, "Yeah, you'd be glad for the body heat of another person in the winter, trust me. But I planned to give you your own tent tonight, don't worry."

Her expression relaxed and she sighed. "Okay. Let me put up these other tents by myself, make sure I'm a pro now."

"You sure? It's much faster with two people."

"Nah." She ushered me toward one of the two camp chairs and gestured to it with a gameshow host's flourish. "Take a load off and watch your teaching skills at work."

The well-mannered, hat-tipping gentleman in me wanted to argue some more, insist on helping. But the enthusiastic little devil on my shoulder overrode my desire to fight her on it when she unwrapped the fleece pullover she'd had tied around her waist and bent over to pick up the first beige tent. My eyes stayed riveted to her curves under a snug long-sleeved shirt. Then they roamed lower, appreciating the nip of her waist, the sway of her hips, and the seductive roundness of her ass, which was in full, perfect view and clad only in yoga pants.

My mind spun wild, a kaleidoscope of thoughts that coalesced into a line from Shakespeare: "And this our life, exempt from public haunt, finds tongues in trees, books in the running brooks, sermons in stones, and good in everything."

Her movements halted, and she looked over her shoulder at me. "What?"

Her sparkling blue eyes seemed to see right through me, caressing even the most shadowed corners I kept locked down tight. A long, curling strand of blond had escaped her hair tie, catching the light of the afternoon sun. Springy, golden, and so soft. I swore I could feel the strands falling through my hands. She was the perfect contrast of light to all the dark I held inside.

"Um, Shakespeare. From *As You Like It*. We're reading it now in my honors seminar. It's nothing. Just the ramblings of a guy with his head in a book," I stammered, my brain still fixated on her physical form, which only became more beautiful when her eyes caressed my face with inquisitive delight.

She stared at me a moment too long for it to feel comfortable, and I felt the prickle of heat on the back of my neck. Here was where it would begin, the realization that the odd products of my brain didn't match my packaging.

Then she nodded. "It's perfect. And . . . so true."

Exhaling a shaky breath, I realized she wasn't repelled by where my mind naturally drifted. Most people accepted my propensity to quote novels or poetry as a quaint personality quirk, something to be endured or ignored. Not appreciated.

Did Ally actually find my Shakespearean blunder acceptable? Even . . . endearing?

I didn't get more time to ponder because Ally had moved on to tent assembly in earnest. She shook the nylon fabric into a billowing cloud of beige and placed it on the ground, then began unfolding the sticks and snapping them into full size. So far, so good.

But I wasn't lying when I said it was a two-person job. As soon as she slipped the pole into one side of the tent and went around to insert the other, the first side popped out. She tried it several times, moving back and forth as her frustration mounted.

A few more strands of hair slipped from her tangle of a bun and fell into her eyes. My muscles fired and I bounced on my toes, wanting to step closer so I could tuck the wayward curls behind her ear and free up her line of sight. Before I could move, she shoved a lock of hair out of her face and glared at the tent.

Cheeks flushed, eyes like shipwrecking seas, teeth sinking into her bottom lip. I couldn't stop staring. But she remained oblivious, refusing to give up without a fight.

"This infernal thing . . . ," she muttered, devising a weight from a rock she found beneath the deck and using it to anchor the pole on one side. But as soon as she started bending the other side to fit the end into the pocket, the first side popped out and the rock rolled away. "Seriously?" she spat at the tent.

"Two-person tent, two-person job. I'm here to help. Why fight it?"

"Guess I wanted to prove something."

"You already did."

Her eyes closed for a beat longer than necessary, enough to tell me she appreciated the compliment. She gestured to the loose end of the tent pole, and I held it in place while she anchored the other side.

In under a minute, we had the second tent pitched, and in under five, the third stood next to its brethren.

Ally and I stood shoulder to shoulder and observed the little family of tents like proud parents.

"Good work," I told her. "Now let's cook dinner."

TEN

ALLY

The sun had dropped behind the mountain and the sky took on a dusky blue. I returned from the kiddie pool Clay had filled by his side door to serve as our fake lake and proudly held up the pot of water I'd filtered with a hand pump. It was practice for filtering mountain lake water so we could drink it without needing to boil it first. "Ta-da. Water."

"Nicely done," Clay said, taking the pot from me and pouring off some of the water into a bottle for drinking.

What I did not tell him was that I'd gotten into a wrestling match with his portable pump and almost ended up taking a bath in the kiddie pool. As it was, my shirt sleeves were soaked and my hands wet.

"So, tell me about the wilderness thing," Clay said, poking at the fire with a stick. Tiny sparks danced into the air as the logs slid into a slightly different position, making the flames climb a bit higher. As I sat next to Clay, I immediately felt the increase in heat warm my face and hands, which I had fanned out over the fire.

"What wilderness thing?"

"Why do you hate it? Did you watch the black bear movie?"

"No. It's the dirt and bugs . . . I don't know. I've just always avoided camping." I balled my hands into fists and stuffed them under my chin. Before I even realized I'd taken such a protective stance, Clay was leaning over and gently lowering my fists into my lap. "What black bear movie?" Did I even want to know?

The feel of his hands on my skin both calmed me and sent a warning flare blazing through my chest—I shouldn't have liked the feeling as much as I did. At this point, I needed to give in and accept that I'd keep feeling these little twinges and pangs for the duration of our camping exercise, but I needed to ignore them. Just like I always did at work.

Scooting his chair closer, Clay uncurled my balled-up fists. "Holy hell, your hands are freezing."

"I know, that's why I was warming them over the fire."

"But they're not getting any warmer." He turned my hands over, looking at the way my fingers had gone white at the tips. "You have Raynaud's."

"Yeah." Raynaud's was a fancy name for poor circulation. The first time my hands had gone numb and white like this had been on a sixty-five-degree day after I'd come out of a hot yoga class and run an errand for my mom before going home and showering. The effect of my rapid cooldown and my not-great circulation was hands that felt ice cold to the touch and needed to be submerged in warm water at my mom's house in order to get the blood flowing again.

"Does it happen often?"

I shrugged. "Mostly it happens if my hands get wet and then I get cold."

Or if I get nervous around a hot guy and all my blood rushes to the muscles in my chest.

"I'm sorry. I should have offered you gloves."

"Not your job. I'm learning to be a self-sufficient camper, remember? Note to self: always bring gloves."

But I didn't want gloves, not when his hands were rubbing mine to warm them. Massaging the ends of my fingers, his calloused hands were creating friction along the smoothness of mine. His palms dwarfed mine, and the gentle touch of his large hands infused my skin with warmth. The friction sent heat to parts of me I hadn't known were cold.

I couldn't help thinking about how those rough hands would feel gliding down other parts of my body. It was dangerous territory.

My body was begging me to give in and believe these hints of feeling could lead to more. My heart wanted the romance I'd only read about in well-crafted novels. Every surge of electricity across my skin, each flutter in my heart, all the heightened senses felt like something real.

And yet, my brain maintained a firm hold on reality. This man was not my reality.

He couldn't be. Not when he only did temporary relationships, if you could even call them relationships. If I was going to dip a toe back into believing in love, thereby giving up on my self-sufficiency principles—my principles!—it wasn't going to be for a man who all but guaranteed heartbreak. No. Not him.

I pulled my hands back, rubbing them together myself because I didn't need a man to do that for me. Even if it felt amazing.

"Tell me about the bear movie."

He chuckled and leaned back in his camp chair, which sat so close to mine that our knees were touching. Even leaning away, he still overwhelmed my senses —muscled forearms resting on his thighs, sexy stubble on his jaw, that heady scent of masculine woodsman mixed with fresh soap. I inhaled a shaky breath and hoped he didn't notice.

"It's a movie they make people watch if they're first-time campers in the Smoky Mountains and they've never used a bear cannister before. It's maybe a bit over the top in its focus on bears. The reality is people are much more likely to get food stolen right out of a daypack by a squirrel or marmot. But bears are scary to most people, so they play up all the cautionary tales of people getting their tents mauled because they stashed granola bars in them."

I felt like he was trying to protect me by downplaying the threat. Even if I hadn't seen "the bear movie," I'd grown up in Green Valley, which meant I had a healthy appreciation for the damage a black bear could do. "One of these times, a bear will show up."

He studied me for a moment, and I allowed myself to gaze at him uninhibited. All masculine energy, stubble on a firm jaw, mouth turned up almost enough to look like a smirk. But it was his eyes that drew me in, the hazel tipping into chocolate territory, like they'd been melted by the fire and produced their own heat. I felt it down to my bones.

We kept getting caught like this, eyes locked, words unspoken, emotions coiled tight below the surface.

Right now it was new. Interesting enough that I let myself have this moment without forcing myself to look away. I let myself enjoy the sight of him without worrying about whether it meant anything.

It didn't. It couldn't. I'd keep telling myself that because it was the only safe option. I knew what happened when I allowed fantasies to unfurl. I got hurt, every time.

"Not tonight." The quiet gruffness of his voice startled me.

Was he answering my thoughts?

No, he was still talking about bears. I tried not to let myself think he meant anything else.

"Alexandra." When he said my name, I realized I hadn't heard half of what he'd just said.

"Sorry. Yes?" I refocused my gaze on him. His expression was soft, eyes roaming over my face like a delicate touch. I felt a rolling wave through my body.

"I'd throw myself into the jaws of a bear before I'd let it hurt you." The quiet rumble of his voice stirred something deep inside me. I felt my jaw go slack.

"I . . ." I should have thanked him for having my back. Or just left the moment alone. Instead I blurted out a nonsensical story I'd never planned to tell another soul. "My mom used to say a bear ate my dad."

That did it.

Any romantic tension was blown away with Clay's sharp exhale. "Come again?"

"It was a story my mom told us after our dad left. Of course, we knew he'd moved out, but my mom insisted that wasn't the case. She had . . . some issues handling reality."

"Huh," Clay said, nodding.

"Yeah. Jefferson must've given you the impression she was a little batshit crazy. She moved to an all-female commune in California. We haven't seen her in years."

"I guess, sure, he told me some odd stories now and then, but I never heard this one."

Didn't surprise me. I hadn't told anyone either. Because it was nuts. But despite the number of times I tried to suggest a different scenario, my mom stuck to her version of events, even if it didn't explain why my mother seemed to distrust men more than bears.

My mom tried hard to pound the message into my brain: men were never going to stick around, and I needed to rely on myself to get through life. Unfortunately, my brain had other ideas, preferring to be stuffed full of swoony suitors from Regency romance novels.

Each time I went into a new relationship with an open heart, I promptly got it crushed. "Told you so," she'd say. "Men are like that. Best you learn that now while there's still time to get your priorities straight." My mom was there to pat my head and tend to my wounded heart, her message now proven, her work now done.

After my most recent relationship ended, I relented and acknowledged that my mom was right—I'd been looking for a happily ever after instead of relying on myself for my happiness. So I doubled down on being self-sufficient and capable, strong with an impenetrable heart. This independence had served me well.

And men like Clay Meadows, they were exactly the type my mom had warned me about—the kind who were pretty enough to lure an unsuspecting woman into their clutches, the kind who feasted on them and walked away two dates later.

Better to get eaten by a bear than left by a man.

———

With the cicadas chirping in the surrounding trees, it was hard to pretend I wasn't outside, but I was trying. The sky was getting darker by the minute, and through the canopy of trees, I could see tiny dots of stars.

We were really doing this—staying out here all night long.

Despite my fear of things grungy and buggy, this little foray into the backyard wilderness was growing on me. How could it not with Clay sitting here beside me wearing form-fitting denim and smelling like cedar, smoke, and Irish Spring? If this was camping, sign me up.

The dark sky and intense quiet felt so intimate—just the two of us alone under the stars, a fire crackling and popping at our feet.

I snuck a look at his tight Henley under a half-unbuttoned flannel and reminded myself why it was a good thing that most of the time he sped around campus like a roadrunner with its tail ablaze.

Kept me from thinking things.

Dirty, inappropriate things.

But now I was thinking them. All of them.

Especially now that the intellectual Clark Kent had shown me his mountain man side. Holy Highland Hottie. In a matter of hours, he'd transformed from a friendly English teacher well-versed in classics and track and field to a relaxed, savvy outdoorsman who exuded manliness and sex. This version of Clay was not what I'd signed up for. This version was making me rethink my staunch insistence that he and I could never be more than friends.

Give me a literary quote and the one-two punch of flannel and wilderness skills and apparently I crumbled.

Clay was turning out to be nothing like the man I thought I knew. He didn't act like someone who went around purposely breaking hearts. He was sweet, attentive, considerate. He had taken such good care of me when I got hurt.

If he was good looks alone, I could get past my pesky feelings. But the whole package—Clay's sexy looks and his sincere kindness in trying to help me get past my camping fears—I was hopelessly falling under his spell.

"There's a gap in the firepit." Clay pointed to a space in the circle of stones and pushed up from his camp chair. Going over to a small pile of rocks in a corner of the yard, he returned with a rough stone in his large hands. His forearms flexed when he gripped it. I watched his careful dark-eyed assessment of the other rocks in the firepit while he decided where to place this one. And I stared as he crouched down, quads straining the fabric of his pants.

"Sap," Clay explained, plunking back down into the camp chair. I moved my chair closer to him, seduced by the warmth already emanating from the fire, which cast an orange glow across the sculpted planes of his face. I watched him watch the fire. Then I exhaled a long breath.

"Something about a fire. Hard not to stare, right?"

"Yeah," I mumbled. "It's definitely the fire."

Oblivious to the heat he was creating, Clay popped up and strode over to the cooler. He carried it back and opened it in front of us. The inside was well-stocked and organized. A frying pan tilted against the side, tongs upright next to it. A butcher-wrapped white package. A bowl of pre-sliced peppers and onions covered in plastic wrap. A blue cannister I couldn't identify. Marshmallows, graham crackers, and chocolate.

"Ooh, are we making s'mores?" Even without spending time in the wilderness, I had experience with the melted campfire treat. I started unwrapping a chocolate bar and held up the bag of marshmallows.

At Clay's head tilt, I explained, "I know it's dessert, but I actually know how to do this part of camping. Can I make you a little dessert before dinner?"

I scooted my camp chair closer to his and bumped him with my shoulder. At this new proximity, I could feel enough heat emanating from Clay's body to melt my s'mores ingredients. And I'd happily lick them from his bare skin.

A muscle in his jaw flexed. I could tell that doing things out of order didn't sit right with him, but I waited patiently as he reasoned with himself.

"Fine. One. Just one."

"Deal. Don't want to spoil our appetites." I unwrapped the chocolate and broke off two squares. Clay handed me a long stick with a two-pronged tip that looked expertly chosen for double marshmallow roasting. It was then that I realized how hard he'd worked to make everything go smoothly for my sake. So I'd get through my first wilderness experience in one piece. So I'd love it.

"Clay, thank you so much for taking time to do this with me." My hand went to my chest gratefully. It touched me that the rugged, stoic, super sexy man I crossed paths with daily had such a soft heart. And it astounded me that I'd never given him the chance to show it until now.

When I met his eyes, I caught a glimpse of something I couldn't identify—confusion, gratitude, appreciation? He was looking at me as though I was a stranger, even though we'd known each other for half our lives.

Maybe we were strangers. The version of Clay he'd shown me over the past couple hours was one I didn't know at all. And here I was, trying to figure out what had changed in a matter of hours. Part of me wanted to change it back because the lusty urges I was having toward Clay were unnerving.

But part of me—the part that couldn't believe how wrong I'd been about him and how much better I liked him for it—that part of me wanted him even more.

CHAPTER
ELEVEN

CLAY

"So, explain it to me. Why did you take a wilderness first aid course if you never wanted to be in the actual wilderness?"

"Always be prepared," she quipped.

A week ago, maybe I'd have let her banter me into letting it go, but not now. We were making progress—not just in the "wilderness" but in something I couldn't yet define. Something I wanted to define. I was learning things about her, how she thought, what lay beneath the surface. And I wanted to know more. She owed me a better answer.

"Try again."

Her eyes shot to mine with a look of surprise and maybe a bit of annoyance. "Really?"

"Alexandra, I won't judge. Was it some guy's poor idea for a surprise date? He got you to spend the day with him by promising a hands-on educational experience and then sprung it on you that you'd be relearning CPR? Come on, you can tell me."

She laughed quietly, but her lips didn't form a smile. I wondered if I'd veered too close to the truth. Well, to hell with it. I braced myself for the tales of love affairs and perfect dates.

"Not exactly that." She stabbed the gooey end of her stick at the plate of fresh marshmallows until she'd speared one. Moving it to the firepit, her eyes followed, going glassy as she stared into the flames.

"What, then?" I asked.

I could have let it go. Normally, I'd let it go. What difference did it make? Ally and I were colleagues on a dry run for an extended field trip. Even if a part of me urged this night in my yard to mean something else, my rational side knew it didn't. But maybe I needed her to tell me about the men in her life. Maybe it would make my feelings toward her stand down once and for all.

Maybe bears would dance on my rooftop.

Ally shrugged and continued staring into the fire.

I reached for the frying pan, which now held roasting peppers and onions. I gave them a stir while Ally warmed tortillas on the rocks surrounding the flames. "We make a good team," she observed.

I nudged her under the chin with my knuckle. "Don't try and divert me with niceties. Why'd you take wilderness first aid?" I asked, like a masochist, begging her to tell me about a date with some adventurer.

"It was a promise I'd made to myself." She spat out the words on an exhale like the idea disappointed her.

"What kind of promise?"

"That I'd become self-sufficient and independent. Face my fears. As a woman or a single parent someday or whatever, I need to be prepared for any eventuality. I used to have this romantic idea of the perfect man, the knight on the horse, riding into my future." She laughed. "I read a lot of Regency romance. I guess it rubbed off. But my point is that I get the difference between fantasy and reality. And I choose reality."

"Why can't you have both? You seem like the kind of person who will meet a knight and still remain fiercely independent. Ride your own horse next to his."

She smiled. "If only." The words lacked conviction. I couldn't understand why Ally didn't see herself the way I did.

Tipping back in my camp chair, I decided to fish out the beers I'd stashed at the bottom of the cooler. "Not going to be doing this on the retreat, obviously," I noted, using the handle of the cooler to pop the tops off of two bottles of cold amber beer.

"Obviously," she agreed, taking the open bottle I handed to her and clinking it against mine. "But I appreciate you bending the rules, Scout Master. Glad to see you're not all work and no play."

"Your brother and I used to carry a six-pack each on camping trips back in the day." I shook my head. "So stupid to carry all that weight. But we didn't care. Here, we might as well enjoy the comforts of home."

"But no sleeping inside the house?"

"No sleeping inside the house," I confirmed. "So backing up, you've given up on the knight?"

Her eyes went wide, and she choked on her beer. "I mean, not in theory. But in practice, maybe. Knights haven't exactly shown up for me. I may be better off on my own."

I hadn't noticed the thundering of my heart in my chest until the beating started to subside. Now it just felt like a hyper snare drum. Or a hummingbird flitting inside my chest, trying to escape. Why did the idea of Ally not wanting a relationship amp me up so much?

Because that means she doesn't want one with you.

She shook her head, correcting, "Anyway, I need to know what I'm doing out in the world. I can't be googling what to do for a snake bite if that ever happens. I need to *know*." Clearing her throat, she attempted another sip of her beer, eyes glued to me to ensure I wouldn't say something else to make her choke on it.

My brain continued to swirl with questions she hadn't answered and new ones popping up by the second. "Okay, so you're a control freak, is that what you're telling me? Because lots of people are proficient at adulting without knowing what to do about a snake bite."

On a long blink, she bit her bottom lip. When she opened her eyes, they looked blank. Ally unwound the scarf from her neck, revealing the pale skin of her throat. My hands twitched with the need to feel her skin beneath my fingers. I wanted to wrap one hand around the column of her throat and tip her jaw up so our mouths were aligned.

All my years of dashing around campus had served me well. I'd never been in one place with her long enough to give these physical urges any room to take root. But now . . . shit. Now, there was no reining them in.

I ground my teeth and clenched my fists in an effort to stop myself from reaching for her. This camping practice run had been a terrible idea.

"True," she said. She'd been silent for so long, I'd almost forgotten where we'd left off. "Maybe I am a control freak. I have an earthquake kit in my kitchen cupboard, and we don't even get earthquakes here."

"Are you preparing for the zombie apocalypse too?"

Turning her eyes down, she took the last bite of her s'more and chewed it slowly. I watched her throat move as she swallowed and ached to touch her skin there. I wondered if it would feel as smooth and soft as it looked under my carpentry-roughened hands.

"Not yet. But one never can be too prepared, I suppose," she said gravely, leveling me with her blue-eyed stare. Then her lips quirked to the side and she laughed. That quiet sound that reminded me of tiny glass wind chimes.

I wanted to know more, but I sensed that if I pushed too hard, she might retreat. So I'd tread carefully.

The faint burning smell of seared peppers redirected my thoughts. I stirred the red and green slivers in the pan, noting the blackened backsides and trying to mix them in with the grilled onions so the burned edges seemed less evident.

"Mmm, smells amazing," Ally said, setting up our plates on top of the cooler, which was tall enough to be a perfect table between the camp chairs and the firepit.

As I watched her now, so comfortable out here in the woods just a couple hours after saying she was deathly afraid, it stirred something in me.

"Hey," I said, tucking a finger under her jaw and turning her face to look at me.

"Yeah?"

"I love that you want to be self-sufficient. It's awesome." I met her eyes because this part was important. "But don't forget to let someone in."

I felt her jaw go slack in my hand. Then she swallowed hard. "What do you mean?"

I shrugged. "I think . . . it's amazing to be so independent. To not lose yourself. But there's something magical about being vulnerable enough to trust another person to find you if you get lost. The point is to be vulnerable around the right person. To need that person enough to feel something."

Her sharp intake of breath was the only sound I heard. But I saw the shift in her eyes. They filled with tears that she quickly blinked away until they were gone.

She nodded. "Yeah. Okay."

Yeah. And so *not* okay.

I was already falling hard for her. Too late to stop it. Too late to even try.

———

A half hour later, we'd eaten every morsel of the chicken fajitas I'd cooked up in my sauté pan, rolling it all up in tortillas and adding salsa. Ally's appreciative sighs as she ate were downright addictive. "Everything tastes better when it's cooked over an open fire, doesn't it?" she asked, licking her lips. I sat hypnotized, eyes glued to her mouth as her tongue dabbed at a last dribble of salsa in the corner. "Clay?"

"Um, yeah." It took ten seconds before I realized she was staring at me. "Hey. Let's take a walk."

Springing to my feet, I nearly knocked over my chair as I ambled away from her before she could see the growing bulge in my pants that came from something so simple as watching her lick salsa from her lips.

"Shouldn't we clean up? Won't this attract animals if we leave it?"

"Naw, it'll be fine. Come this way," I called back to her. She was right. It was a terrible idea to leave food out, but I needed to move. As soon as I reached the dozen or so yards of trees that separated the grassy part of my yard from the lakefront, I calmed down. It was darker here and slightly cooler.

"You sure you're okay?" Ally's feet crunched on the fallen pine needles behind me. I waited until she caught up, her face laced with concern.

"I'm good. Just realized I should show you the lake. We missed blue hour, but the darkness is even better."

She walked beside me, weaving around trees and shrubs, until a rogue branch caught on her shirt and tugged her back. "Oops."

I freed her shirt and shuttled her along, having her walk in front of me, guiding her with my hand on the small of her back.

A few paces in, the leaves and branches overhead blotted out the sky temporarily, and it suddenly grew much darker. I led her to a clearing so we could look up at the sky, almost black except for pinpricks of stars freckling the expanse.

"Whoa. I've lived here my whole life, but I've never seen the sky this dark."

"Because we're nowhere near town. Pretty spectacular, right?" I pointed out a few constellations, nothing an amateur with a star map wouldn't know, but Ally seemed suitably impressed.

"Can we just . . . sit here for a while?" she asked, looking on the ground for a good spot. We were standing in a small meadow with soft mounds of green moss that made a perfect carpet beneath us. Ally dropped down without even checking to see if there were bugs or bears in the vicinity.

That's when I knew I'd won her over . . . at least as far as camping went. I'd take that victory. For now.

After Clay and I returned from our stroll under the stars and cleaned up from dinner, we said an awkward good night and settled into our respective tents. Clay was only a few feet to the left of me, but no shuffling or unsettled movements came from his direction. Just silence. But there were other noises . . .

The longer I lay in my tent, the more certain I became that we were not alone in his yard. For one thing, the crickets wouldn't shut up. Their chorus sounded like tiny tambourines played by tiny insect hands.

After straining my ears against their sound for a while, they faded into the background. A kind of forest white noise. Then I heard other things. The whisper of wind tickling the pine needles on the trees. The crunch of a branch brushing against its neighbor in the breeze.

And maybe the footfall of an animal. A small animal like a ground squirrel?

No, definitely something bigger. With bigger feet. And correspondingly bigger teeth. A bear?

I'd spent so much time talking about bears and worrying about bears that my mind was probably playing tricks on me, but I couldn't be sure.

"Clay?" I called out futilely. I listened some more, trying to talk myself down. I was safe in my tent. It was all fine.

Except that I was pretty sure I heard a growl.

"Clay?" I called again, this time louder. And more panicked.

Within moments, he was pulling open the zipper on my tent and peeking his head in. "You okay?"

"Get in here!" I insisted, waving my hands, unzipping my sleeping bag a few inches so I could scoot toward the back of the tent to make room. He obliged, crawling inside on his knees before turning around and carefully removing his shoes to keep my tent clean.

"What? What's wrong?"

I held up a hand to silence him. "Just listen," I whispered. We sat in silence as my eyes darted around, following the hint of a noise here or there. But I heard nothing like the scratching branches and footfalls I'd heard earlier. "There's something out there. At least, there was . . ."

Straining to hear any evidence of an animal, I tipped my head and leaned to the side, not realizing until I heard the soft timbre of Clay's voice that his lips were right next to my ear. "I think you have an active imagination."

I could do nothing to stop the shiver from rolling down my spine from the soft caress of his breath against my skin. "I—I'm pretty sure I heard an animal." Knowing how close I'd leaned toward Clay, I should have pulled back, but I couldn't move.

We sat in the silence for another thirty seconds. The only thing I could hear was my heart thumping in my chest.

"Do you still hear it?" Clay asked.

I shook my head, still listening.

"It was probably a bird or a ground squirrel. Nothing to worry about." He gestured for me to lie back down, and I tried to zip the sleeping bag shut, but a large tuft of nylon was stuck in the zipper. Yanking it in both directions, I tried and failed to get it to budge.

"Ugh, it's stuck. Don't worry, I'll deal with it. I'm good."

Sitting in the tent with Clay's gaze bearing down on me was unnerving. He shook his head. "No, I don't want you to freeze. Do you mind?" He moved right next to me. The space suddenly felt much smaller and a hundred times more intimate.

The roof of the tent only hung about three feet high, so all movement inside had to be done on all fours. Clay sat cross-legged, his knees wedged up against mine, and I scrambled out of the sleeping bag in order to hand him the stuck zipper.

His fingers grazed my hand as he took the lumpy sleeping bag from me. I felt my skin heat where it touched his, and the warmth spread down my arm, quickening my pulse and sending an involuntary shudder through me.

Clay tugged at the zipper but it refused to give way. "Fabric's stuck." He pointed at where a chunk of red nylon was intertwined with the zipper, jamming it in both directions.

"See, it wasn't just me," I said, waiting until he looked away to mop a rivulet of sweat from my forehead. The air in the tent was heating up with his presence like someone had turned a thermostat to a hundred. I contemplated crawling outside and letting him work on it while I sat in the cool, dark yard. Leave it to Clay Meadows to make me want to be alone in the wilderness.

"It's really jammed, but I don't want to tear the fabric." He wrestled the metal tab up and down carefully. "Hang on, I just need to . . ." I watched his forearms flex under his shirt. Easily a hundred fifty degrees in here now. My eyes stayed riveted to his hands. His strong fingers applied pressure to the zipper, but it wouldn't give. A part of me hoped it stayed stuck for hours. The muscles on display in these close quarters were hotter than an August beach vacation.

"Can I help?" I asked, trying to repurpose myself from simply sitting there and gawking.

Clay grunted as he tried once more to strong-arm the zipper into submission. It was giving me ideas. Filthy, delicious ideas about him strong-arming me into submission.

"Here. I think I need to slide it down before I can get it back up." My mind was busy having sex with his words when I realized he was holding the sleeping bag out to me.

"Oh. Right. Okay." Grasping the fabric, I watched Clay drag the zipper down a couple millimeters and I quickly pulled the fabric free.

"Yes! Just like that." His voice strained as he tugged harder at the zipper, our hands touching as he repositioned his to get a better grip. Moving so he was sitting directly in front of me, Clay knelt down and wrapped his fingers around my hand to position it, so he had better leverage on the zipper.

Surprised by the instant spark of electricity, my eyes shot to his. His equally startled look told me I wasn't alone in feeling something.

But there was no time for examining feelings because Clay was putting all his muscle on the zipper and I was pulling equally hard on the stuck piece of fabric. Slowly, the zipper began freeing itself and I tugged even harder. So hard, in fact, that just as Clay finally yanked the zipper all the way down, my leverage on the fabric toppled me over, where I landed indelicately on my side, face bumping on the dark blue denim stretched across Clay's thigh.

"Oh shit," I spat, scrambling to right myself as Clay dove forward to help me back into a sitting position. Now I was upright, one hand on Clay's firm thigh, which I very much did not want to stop touching.

But I had to.

Tearing my hand away like his thigh was ablaze, I tried to make some space between us, but in the tiny confines of the tent, I only succeeded at smashing my head against the tent wall, which immediately created enough static electricity to stand my hair on end.

Silently, Clay reached up and tamed the crazy strands, smoothing them down. Then his hand returned to where it had been a moment before, and I realized that both of Clay's hands lay atop my shoulders. He didn't seem to be in any rush to remove them either.

When I dared to meet Clay's eyes, I saw them laced with the hazy recognition that we could close the gap between us with so little effort. And that maybe we should.

I watched the Adam's apple bob in Clay's throat as he swallowed hard and searched my face, his eyes moving from mine down to my lips. Unconsciously, my tongue swept along my bottom lip to moisten it. He leaned a tiny bit closer as I sat frozen, taking in the campfire smell of him and the tiny yellow flecks in his eyes that I'd never noticed before.

Because I'd never been this close to him before.

I'd always been slightly intimidated by his chiseled good looks, but after spending the past few hours with him cooking and looking at the stars, I'd never see him that way again. Not that he wasn't still intimidatingly good-looking. But he was so much more.

His eyes searched mine, asking for permission. Agreement that I wanted him to kiss me. And I did, but . . .

"A date! I have a date," I blurted right before backing away as far as I could. I felt the canvas of the tent pull again at my hair, but it didn't matter. Actually, it was good. If I looked ridiculous, Clay would lose that gleam in his eye.

He pulled back, startled.

"Oh. Okay." His brow creased and he rubbed his hands on his pants. "You mean right now?"

Befuddled by my own admission and the yarn I was about to spin, I initially nodded. "Yes." Then I realized. "I mean, no. Just . . . soon. I have a date. With a boring-but-stable architect with no pets. Doesn't like animals, actually. Or reading. He lives in Knoxville." I recited these details for no sensible reason, except for the fact that I'd memorized them, all the while detesting the idea of a man who disliked animals and reading.

I would not go on the date, despite my beer-induced softening the other night. Architect Louie sounded as wrong for me as wrong got. But he was the pretext I needed to extinguish the budding romantic moment.

"Okay, well . . . good?" Of course I'd confused Clay with my flowing fountain of information, but I was an unstoppable train, freed from my braking system on a downhill track.

"It's good. So very good," I confirmed, swaying around in celebration of my impending date with the boring guy.

Scooting back, Clay crossed his arms and watched me. His initial look of confusion morphed into one of amusement, which made me realize how ridiculous I looked. My movements pulled to a stop.

"Anyhow, just thought you should know."

He nodded slowly, keeping his distance and his guarded stare. "And now I do."

"Right, so . . ." What was I doing? I was following the script that seemed to make sense when I thought I needed a list of reasons not to kiss Clay Meadows, but now I couldn't remember a single one. "I think I can get this zipped up now. Thank you so much for helping with it."

Clay had already backed up and flipped around so he was sitting in the tent opening, lacing up his shoes. "Of course. Bound to be a kid or two with a stuck zipper. More good training for the retreat."

"For sure." I had my back pressed against the far wall of the tent, the almost-kiss long forgotten.

Except . . .

Hours later, once I heard only silence again in the tent next to mine, I found myself straining to hear any sign that he was still awake. Wondering if he was thinking about me.

Because sure as hell, I couldn't stop thinking about him. More than once I debated calling him back over, but each time, I talked myself down.

Over and over again for several hours until I finally drifted off to sleep.

CHAPTER
THIRTEEN

ALLY

I awoke to the sound of birds. Hundreds of birds, all chirping in harmony on branches of the surrounding trees. My eyes felt glued shut, seduced by the glory of a good night's sleep. Clay was right—there was nothing like sleeping on the ground with the smells of the forest and the chill of the night air to make a down sleeping bag feel like a cloud.

Hands down, it was the best night of sleep I'd ever had. Slowly, I eased my eyes open, surprised to find light streaming through the gauzy walls of the tent. Not that I thought the thin fabric would block out the sun like regular walls, but this was different. I felt the draw of nature beckoning me outside. The day had dawned and I needed to see it.

Unzipping my sleeping bag, I freed myself from the warm cocoon and pulled a pair of sweatpants on over my pajama bottoms. A hoodie over my top.

When I spied my hiking boots in the bottom corner of my tent, I felt grateful Clay had advised keeping them inside. I felt confident no critters had unzipped my tent and hidden themselves in my shoes, but I turned them upside down and shook them for good measure.

I unzipped my tent and shoved my feet into the hiking boots before standing up and inhaling the biggest, most cleansing breath I'd ever experienced in my life. This right here—this air—was the reason people came to the mountains.

I looked around Clay's yard with a new appreciation for the outdoors. This small patch of grass under the stars had transformed itself into a wilderness wonderland. No, Clay had done that, with his walk to the lake and his knowledge of the star maps and his handiness with a campfire.

Which had the effect of giving me a new appreciation for *him.*

Before last night, before we'd almost kissed, Clay was just Clay—a guy I'd known forever and long ago decided was not for me. Now he was Clay, the rugged outdoorsman who rocked a flannel shirt over corded muscles better than any guy I'd ever known. He was the guy with the sharp jawline and smoky hazel eyes who cared enough to make sure I felt comfortable in the woods before I had to show my stuff on a school trip. He was . . .

I needed to stop. It was all just the mountain air getting to my head. The air was thinner up here, wasn't it? Less oxygen. That did a number on a person's brain.

It certainly wasn't because I had actual feelings for Clay. All these years of being colleagues and sort-of friends, I certainly wasn't smitten with Clay Meadows. I was just . . . completely smitten with Clay Meadows.

Well, shit.

There it was.

If I wasn't already standing here fully overcome by just *how* smitten I was, the view before me pushed me right over the top—Clay in a pair of navy-blue hip-hugging joggers and a plaid flannel jacket standing next to the flames of a roaring campfire. Poking at it with a stick, he made the logs pop and crackle while he stared into a metal cup of some sort of steaming beverage.

With the bright yellow rays of early morning sun dancing across his cheekbones, Clay looked more at home than I'd ever seen him on campus. Instead of the greyhound I always saw dashing from place to place and running laps around the track, Clay exhibited a stillness that looked so beautiful it hurt.

I approached him slowly, not wanting to disturb his peacefulness, but the light crunch of pine needles beneath my feet gave me away. Clay turned and smiled, and with the way the sun hit his face, he glowed in the soft amber light.

"Thanks," I said, still a bit overwhelmed by how well the wilderness treated him. Looking down at my baggy sweats and patting the sloppy waterfall of hair, I had no doubt I looked a mess.

"How'd you sleep?" he asked.

"Like a rock. Oh my God, Clay, I had no idea how hypnotic it is to sleep on the ground. What is that about?"

A low chuckle warmed me from head to toe. "Do I detect a wilderness convert?" he asked, his smile morphing into a smirk.

"Hold your horses, buddy. I just said I slept well. Now, what is that delicious-smelling brew?"

He gestured to a French press sitting on one of the stones surrounding the campfire. "Bandit Lake's finest."

"Is the French press an officially sanctioned piece of camping equipment?" I teased as he picked up a second cup and poured coffee for me. Our hands brushed when he handed me the cup, and the jolt of electricity against my skin startled me, confirming that what I felt last night in the tent was no fluke.

I yanked my hand back so quickly that the coffee sloshed over the rim of the cup. Clay's radiant morning glow slowly faded into a look of concern. "You okay?"

Shaking myself out of my spiral of confusion, I blinked away the images of Clay as the fairy-tale prince he'd all but sworn he would never be. So the heat creeping across my skin needed to stop and the romantic in me needed to calm herself. "Um, yeah. Great."

"You sure?" He looked unconvinced.

"Yeah. I, um, just realized I don't need a fairy-tale prince." My eyes went wide at the unintentional admission. "I mean . . . I need to get back. Tell me what I can do to pack up the camping equipment. I want to help."

Clay looked down at his hand where it had brushed mine. His jaw dropped open, then he shook his head. "No worries. I've got this. If you have somewhere you need to be, it's fine."

Pushing the still-full coffee cup against Clay's chest, I stammered, "Okay . . . I do. This was great. Thank you, but it's late and I should go."

Then I pulled the cup back and took a long, satisfying swig of the coffee. Because . . . coffee. "French press. I'm a convert."

I returned the cup to Clay's outstretched hand and jogged out of his yard before I did something stupid. Like reach over to kiss a greyhound who'd only break my heart.

CHAPTER
FOURTEEN

CLAY

Normally, I loved Sundays. Not being much of a churchgoer, I had ample time in the mornings to hike or go out for a run when fewer people were out on the roads.

But yesterday, despite running a cleansing ten-miler, I had loved Sunday a bit less. I wanted it to be Monday. I wanted to go back to school. I told myself I was eager for the typical Monday morning gossip and chitchat in the teachers' lounge, but I just wanted to see Ally and make sure we were good.

I'd almost kissed her, for fuck's sake, and I couldn't decide if I'd ruined a perfectly good work relationship or opened a potentially dangerous door, because I didn't know what lay on the other side.

Certainly, hearing about her date and seeing the lengths she went to ensure we weren't alone together sent a message. It felt like an emotional gut punch, but it told my brain what it needed to hear. We were friends. Nothing more.

That night, I'd stood outside Ally's tent for a long time, listening for any sign she was awake. I'd intended to apologize right then and there, but the last thing I wanted to do was wake her to do it. Eventually, I cleaned up the campsite, making sure there were no food scraps around to attract animals, and crawled into my own tent. It felt really goddamn cold.

The next morning, I'd felt a glimmer of hope when she jerked her hand away. The crackle of electricity when our fingers brushed hit me like a meteor. If she felt even a fraction of the surge of heat in my veins, it was something worth knowing.

Even if I wasn't a fairy-tale prince, if she felt the same way about me as I felt about her, maybe I could be someone halfway worthy. Maybe it was worth trying again.

But after the way she darted from my house, I felt certain I'd come to work and hear she would no longer be my co-chaperone. If she wanted to badly enough, she'd make an excuse to Pindich for why she couldn't go on the retreat.

If she did, so be it. That would make my life all that much easier. I could go back to darting around campus like the greyhound she thought I was and spending minimal time around her. My heart would eventually give up on the possibility of anything more with her, just as it had done in the past.

After she left, I'd plunked myself down into one of the camp chairs, sipped at my coffee, and allowed myself to entertain the wild thought that maybe the intense attraction I felt just being near to Ally might not be one-sided. And what if that were the case?

Well . . . it would change everything.

———

On Monday morning, just for good measure, I ran a few miles before school, even though I barely had time. My hair was still damp when I arrived, so I combed it into place with my fingers. I'd grabbed a cherry muffin from home and made a quick pot of coffee instead of stopping at Donner Bakery like I usually did. The coffee needed reheating by now, and the muffin was too dry to eat.

Walking down the hallway of the main building, I headed for the teachers' lounge. Had to do something about the lukewarm coffee. Before I reached the door, Principal Pindich intercepted me.

"Clay, how are you?" He smiled a little too brightly. He only did that when he wanted something.

"I'm okay. You?"

"Good, good. Listen, I know plans are underway for the carnival and I wanted you to know I've got your back. Just like I imagine you have mine."

"Meaning?"

"You and I go way back—you may not know this, but I worked on your grandmother's estate plan back at the law firm, so I consider you a friend. Your vote in there counts, is all I'm saying."

He clapped me on the shoulder without my making sense of anything he'd just said. I watched him disappear into his office and made my way to the lounge. A peal of laughter rang out from the room, followed by a breathless admission. "Half the women in Green Valley would line up at the kissing booth for him—you don't need to ask twice."

As I got to the doorway, the conversation stopped, and several pairs of eyes turned to me. "Hey, guys. What's up?"

After some throat clearing and mumbling, Witty filled me in. "Spring carnival. Students want to have a kissing booth."

The spring carnival had been a source of debate for months, with half of us agreeing that the students should be free to plan it as they wanted—within reason—and the other half wanting to give them strict guidelines. I was of a mind to let the students' imaginations run wild and tame them only when things crossed lines of decorum or safety. This was their event, after all, and most years there were few variations on the theme of game booths, a mechanical bull, and a dance-off.

I rolled my eyes. "Of course they do. Lemme guess—the quarterback and head cheerleader are the ones fetching top dollar?" It's how it had been in the past. Every senior class came in brimming with "new" ideas, and every few years, we ended up with a dunk tank and a kissing booth manned by the homecoming queen or some version thereof. They generated the most income for the school and proved to be harmless fun, so I never objected.

"No, you are."

Now it was my turn to be silent. A dozen pairs of eyes watched my reaction, which so far was befuddlement. Were we talking about the same thing?

"Come again?" I asked, my voice cracking on the second word. A sheen of sweat gathered on the back of my neck, and I itched to take off the chambray button-up shirt I had on over my T-shirt.

"The student council wanted to shake things up this year, so they proposed having teachers in the kissing booth instead of students. Same with the dunk tank and all the other games."

"Um, why?" The whole point of the carnival was that it was an event run by the high schoolers for the high schoolers. Teachers were only there for supervision, if that.

I looked from face to face, finally landing on Ally. I initially hadn't noticed she was here, and just catching a glimpse of her wide blue eyes calmed me and rattled me at the same time.

The amusement on her face told me I'd missed an important part of the discussion. As if that wasn't becoming dangerously clear.

"This year, we have a bigger mandate," Nick said. "The carnival is supposed to bring in double what it did last year, which means we need to expand our reach and get more people to come."

I still wasn't understanding. Running a hand through my hair, I entered the room and shoved my coffee into the microwave. Maybe if I finished the cup, my brain fog would clear.

While I watched the mug spin on the carousel inside, I tried again for an explanation. "Where are we getting these people? The school is only so large."

"Exactly. The kids figured that having adults running the carnival games would attract other adults," Witty explained, hands out like he was offering me alms. "So, you in the kissing booth, Principal Pin Dick in the dunk tank . . ."

"Well, that's reason enough right there," I said. "Did Pin Dick agree?"

"Not exactly," Witty admitted. "But he won't have a choice. It was a big hit having him in the dunk tank at the Harvest Festival. He was the one who said we needed to make more money. He can't exactly refuse now that the kids have come up with a way."

"So I'm gathering you all think this is a good idea, teachers in the kissing booth?" I asked the group as the microwave beeped.

There was some general nodding and agreeing.

I shook my head. "Pretty sure that's not ethical. We can't be kissing students, even if it is for a good cause."

"Of course not," Nick said. "There would be a separate line for adults. The students would only be able to kiss the homecoming king or whoever. This just adds another income stream. So . . . you'll do it?" he asked tentatively. People were still looking at me like an odd specimen, some kind of science experiment egg they were waiting to see hatch in captivity.

Oddly, it didn't bother me. I was always being offered up as someone's blind date. At least this way, the school would make money from it.

I shrugged. "Sure. Doesn't bother me." I snuck a look at Ally to see what she thought of the idea, but she was smiling down at her phone, tapping with her thumbs. I wondered if she was texting the date she mentioned when we were in the tent the other night.

Either way, I needed to get over it.

The only saving grace to the whole plan was the idea of seeing Principal Pindich in the dunk tank. I'd throw a dozen balls at the target myself. He'd always been a thorn in my side, trying to cut the track-and-field program every year and making me fundraise on my own to keep it. He pulled the same crap with the cheer squad and the fine arts program. Most of us secretly believed the programs weren't in danger of being cut, but Principal Pindich knew that threatening was a way to get us to raise money for the school.

Just one of the many reasons no one could stand the weasel of a man. He resorted to sneaky tactics instead of straight up asking for what he wanted. Seeing him swimming in the dunk tank would only be partial revenge for all the suffering he'd put the faculty through, but it was a good start.

The bell rang before too much more discussion could be had about the carnival, and the air filled with the sounds of chairs scraping against the floor and the resigned groans from my colleagues about whatever the first class of the day would unleash upon us.

With my coffee now appropriately heated, I gathered my books and moved back down the main hallway. Moments later, Ally caught up with me, matching my long stride with her short one, which meant she was walking awfully fast. I slowed my pace slightly and tipped my head in her direction. "Hey there."

"How was the rest of your weekend?"

"Good. It was good."

We walked past students slamming their locker doors and rushing to classes on another floor. I felt certain that Ally didn't teach her first block class in the building where I was headed, but she stayed glued to my side.

"Glad to hear it."

"Thanks." We strode along in silence after that. When we got halfway down the next hallway, Ally stopped. Even though we hadn't been mid-conversation, I stopped too. It felt like the lack of motion was conversation itself.

"I meant, thanks for Saturday night. I feel like I didn't sufficiently express how much I appreciated everything you did to make me comfortable in the wilderness."

I nodded. "You did."

"Sorry?"

"You thanked me yesterday. Don't worry."

Her brow furrowed. "I sort of ran off. I've been feeling badly about it ever since."

"It's okay. Don't worry about it."

"Good." She extended her hand. "Friends?"

I gestured to my full hands with a sheepish grin and a half-hearted shrug, playing it off as the reason why I couldn't shake hers. But in reality, I didn't want to risk touching her and feeling things when she was drawing a clear line for us as colleagues and nothing more. "Yes. Friends. Definitely."

Then I allowed myself to look at her fully, rather than in the stolen glances I'd cast her way in the teachers' lounge. Yeah, no. The way I reacted to her had nothing to do with fucking friendship. There was a reason I moved quickly through campus, and this was it. Stopping to gaze at Alexandra Dalbotten was hazardous to my mental well-being. It made it hard to be happy looking anywhere else.

She had her hair piled in its usual bun. Tendrils fell loose as they always did. Her eyes, wide and blue, seemed primed to swallow me up. Like Jonah and the whale. If I thought I had a chance with her, I'd go into battle without a second thought.

CHAPTER
FIFTEEN

ALLY

"Those two have some moves!" Kendra, the school guidance counselor, raised her glass of pisco sour toward where Nick and Clara were tearing it up on the dance floor at Genie's.

"They sure do," I agreed. John Witty raised his margarita toward us in a toast from where he stood near the bar with a group of teachers, Clay included. We'd all agreed last minute to convene at Genie's to blow off steam before we each had to grade a pile of midterms or projects that would be coming in this week.

Word had circulated quietly throughout the day, with each of us hoping the information wouldn't reach Pindich, who'd have no hesitation about showing up at a teachers-only outing. After thirty minutes, he still wasn't here, which I took as a good sign.

A few other couples were out on the floor, but most of the teachers stood huddled in groups, snacking on bar food and sipping drinks. So intent on not staring at Clay, who looked mighty fine in a plaid flannel, I didn't notice Witty until he sidled up close and nodded subtly at Clay. "Lid for every pot, and you two make a nice set." Before I could deny his assertion or even blush my way to agreeing, Witty was two-stepping away with a goofy grin on his face.

I hadn't spoken to Clay since I arrived, partly because he was already ensconced in conversation and partly because Kendra had grabbed me when I walked in and hauled me to the opposite end of the bar to order drinks.

"Is the principal kind of a close talker?" Kendra asked, voice hushed, which meant I could barely hear her over the music.

I waved a hand around the room. "He stands close to the ladies. The guys, not so much. Just keep taking a step back and make sure you're not near a wall," I advised. As smarmy as Pindich was, there were still members of the faculty who found him charming. I was glad Kendra was noticing his true colors.

She nodded and moved off to where Witty was holding court, telling a dramatic story by the look of his gesturing, and I watched the group from afar. Well, really, I was watching Clay and still thinking about the kiss that wasn't. More and more, wishing it was.

"Don't mess with his head." My brother's gruff voice wasn't the one I expected because I hadn't told him we'd be here. Then again, it didn't surprise me that he'd tag along with Clay—those two were still close, and Jefferson had no problem scooping up the cast-offs from his disinterested bachelor bestie. His last three girlfriends had been interested in Clay first.

"Mess with who?" I asked, taking a proffered beer from Jefferson and sipping the foam from the lip of the glass.

"Clay." He tilted his head in the direction I'd just been looking.

"What's that supposed to mean?" I asked, instantly irritated at the insinuation that my older brother knew something I didn't know—about Clay. Or about me. "I'm not messing with anyone. I'm chaperoning the senior retreat with Clay. He's trying to get me comfortable with camping so I don't freak out in the mountains. That's it."

Assessing me with a raised eyebrow, Jefferson took a large gulp of beer and I watched his Adam's apple bob in his throat as he swallowed. "Not what it looks like."

I rolled my eyes. "Guess you'd better look again. And quit being so dramatic." I snuck a glance in Clay's direction for evidence of what Jefferson could possibly be seeing. All I witnessed was Clay looking perfectly dazzling as usual, with his hair slicked back in that just-showered, perfectly tousled way I saw in the mornings. Expression serious. Focus intent. Polite. As usual.

My stare remained on him slightly longer than strictly necessary to ascertain all these things. As usual.

Clay's eyes briefly left the group of teachers and drifted to me. His lips twisted into a barely there smile, and his gaze hung on mine for just long enough for me to feel a twinge in my chest before he turned back toward the group.

My face heated, and when I looked back at Jefferson so as to prove the nothingness of our interaction, my brother nodded with a smug grin. "Yeah. It's exactly what it looks like."

"Which is what, *exactly*?" I fanned my face because, damn, had it suddenly gotten much hotter in here?

"A thing. You two are a thing."

"We are most definitely not a thing." No. Absolutely not. We were not a thing. But . . . maybe we could be.

I was saved from further consideration of the "thing" by the cool rush of air when the door to Genie's swung open. Mari, the school band director, walked in with her friend Leo. They scanned the faces in the room before turning our way and coming over to chat. Mari and I had grown up together, so she already knew my brother.

"Jeff, this is Leo." We exchanged pleasantries and Mari sent Leo to the bar for drinks.

"Place is packed tonight. What'd we miss?"

I shot Jefferson a warning look, conveying that he'd best not start blabbing his theories about a *thing* that was not a thing to Mari, who'd definitely have opinions on the subject. For once, my brother did as I requested and kept his mouth shut.

Before I could answer his question, Leo signaled Mari over to join him at the bar, leaving Jefferson to explain himself, and I intended to get answers. "What did you mean by not messing with his head? Is there something I should know?"

Jefferson took another sip of his beer, and stared at the ceiling, considering his words carefully. "No. I mean . . . no. Just stick to chaperoning is all."

For all I knew, Clay had put Jefferson up to this, asking him to make sure I was clear that we were merely co-chaperones. Merely friends. "I plan to."

We were interrupted again when the rest of the group came over to dance. Some of the teachers were two-stepping, and a few others partnered up. I swerved to get out of the way of Witty and his wife, which is how I ended up slamming into Clay's rock-hard chest. With large firm hands, he reached out and steadied me before I lost my balance.

"Care to dance?" he asked, rearranging my flailing limbs into proper position and moving us to the beat. Not quite two-stepping, not quite waltzing. It was somewhere in between and Clay's rhythm suited the music perfectly.

Everywhere his hands touched me felt alive with pulses of heat, and I tried to enjoy the feeling and ignore it at the same time. That was near impossible.

I relaxed into his arms, happy to have the excuse to dance with him while my colleagues were all paired up. I avoided making eye contact with Jefferson, who was off in a corner dancing with a blond woman I didn't know.

One song changed to the next, and Clay shifted his rhythm to match it every time. "Clay Meadows, you can dance," I said, tipping my head back to catch the sheepish smile on his face. "Who knew?"

That's when I noticed Principal Pindich standing near the bar, eyes glued to us. It unnerved me as usual, and I was grateful to have Clay as a buffer.

He noticed where I was looking, then spun me around so I was out of Pindich's line of sight.

"May I cut in?" The saccharine voice to my right belonged to Rosalie, a substitute teacher who'd been filling in a lot due to the recent spate of illnesses. She must have just arrived because this was the first I'd seen—or heard—of her tonight.

"Oh, um . . ." Clay dropped his hands from me and I felt a blade slice through my chest. Pure jealousy at the thought that he'd prefer dancing with the young, flirtatious Rosalie.

"Sure. Yeah," I said, taking a step back. Rosalie wasted no time, pressing herself up against Clay and putting her hands on him. He threw me an apologetic glance, eyebrows raised helplessly. "Probably time for me to head home anyway. I'll see you tomorrow, Clay."

He nodded as Rosalie threw her head back and draped her arms around his neck. Clay swept her across the floor with the same careful grace he'd offered to me. Nothing special about either one of us. Clay Meadows could waltz willing women in his sleep. Jefferson's words came back to me. *Don't mess with his head.*

Funny. It felt more like he was messing with mine.

CHAPTER
SIXTEEN

CLAY

When twenty students showed up in the early morning hours, dressed in sweatpants and a ragtag assortment of outdoor gear, I barely looked up from my extra-large coffee cup, which I would need to pull double duty today. Not only did I need to carry an outsized load for two miles uphill, I needed to rally enough energy to motivate the stragglers to do the same.

Yes, most of the students who signed up for the trip were gung ho about spending two nights in the mountains, but there were always two or three who'd thought it sounded like a good idea when they signed up and came to have second thoughts five minutes into the trip. They'd have to hike two miles uphill like everyone else, with me encouraging them all the way. And at their age, I doubted I could entice them with the offer of their favorite colored Skittles like I used to do when I was a camp counselor.

When the last students straggled in looking every bit worse for whatever partying they'd done the night before, I smiled my most encouraging smile, welcomed my intrepid students onto the bus, and shoved each kid's backpack into the luggage area, which was a sea of gray, some dark blues and greens, and a lot of khaki and tan.

And then a flash of bright red. It caught my eye the same way a cardinal would entrance a bird-watcher, and my eye followed the color until I saw the rest of Ally's puffer coat emerge after she closed the trunk of her car. I watched her heft a dark gray backpack onto one shoulder like she was slinging on a book-bag, even though its size made it—and her—list to the side. And I watched her walk toward me in a pair of black yoga pants tucked into the wooly beige socks she wore with her hiking boots.

It was hard to believe only a week had passed since she'd wandered hesitantly into my yard to practice camping. Now she looked every bit the wilderness pro, and I had no small amount of pride in having opened her eyes to the beauty of the outdoors.

Ally's hair tumbled over her shoulders from under a navy-blue beanie which made her eyes look even brighter than eyes had any right to be. My heart began hammering in my chest in an alarming way at the sight of her.

Ever since I'd let the idea into my head that Ally might feel a fraction of the heat I felt humming in my veins, I'd been able to think of little else. Fortunately, after many years of camping, my packing list was rote and I'd written down all the instructions for the students, because I wasn't having much luck staying focused on camping.

Hell, at this point, I needed to cop to being pretty much out of my mind with obsessive thoughts about Ally, and none related to her skills as a chaperone.

Which was why I grunted at her like a Neanderthal when she got on the bus and took the seat across from me. "Not late," she said, pointing at herself with both thumbs. It was then that I noticed her pristine white mittens.

"Nice work. Keep those hands warm. Though they probably won't stay white for long."

She waved a hand. "They'll be fine. I have a pair of work gloves for the grungy stuff. These are just to keep me warm when it's chilly or whatever."

Her smile disarmed me, along with the sparkle in her eyes. "I'm sorry, are you the same woman who professed to hate the outdoors? Why do you seem excited about this?"

She fixed her stare on me, and I felt a surge of heat crawl over the back of my neck. My throat went dry. I felt uneasy. Then she leaned in, bringing her face closer to mine, so close that I could smell the citrusy scent of her skin. I inhaled gratefully, wanting to capture the essence of it.

She whispered against my ear, "Because if it's anything like the night in your yard, I'm going to have a great time."

Pulling back, she settled in her seat, smiled once more, and turned to look out the window. I yanked my hoodie over my head and turned to do the same, willing my racing heart to calm down. And more importantly, worrying about how to get through a weekend around Ally without getting a hard-on in front of twenty teenagers.

Logic would have dictated having Ally hike behind me where I couldn't fixate from fifty feet away on the globes of her ass beneath her heavy backpack. But no, I'd asked her to hike in front of the group, and now I could hear her laughter like wind through the trees and watch the pale strands of her hair catch the sun as she moved up a set of switchbacks just above where I hiked behind the stragglers of the bunch.

Back and forth, we'd been weaving up this long set of switchbacks since we left the bus behind in the parking lot. "How many more?" I heard one of the students ask Ally for the tenth time.

"Just a couple. Don't worry," she huffed, a Mary Poppins of the trails.

"You said that ten minutes ago and we've gone up three since then." I couldn't catch a glimpse of which student it was, but I had my suspicions. Cammie Longmeyer had been in my class last year and she always asked the same thing when I assigned a reading: "How many pages is that? How many chapters?" Some kids always needed numbers. Some adults too.

"Quit counting and you'll feel a lot better," Ally said, and I smiled to myself. She was great with these kids. No wonder they all clambered to be in her class.

I needed her to lead the group and set a reasonable pace. If it felt comfortable to her, it would be comfortable for the students. They wanted to go at a leisurely pace and talk while they hiked.

I had a tendency to tear up the trails without realizing it. I'd get into a thought cycle and not realize I was vaulting up a mountain until I turned to find no one behind me. Long ago, I learned I did better bringing up the rear of the group and letting someone else set the pace.

That meant that I'd been hiking up a mountain for the past half hour like a bunny chasing a carrot, always there in the distance but too far away for me to take a bite. Safer that way for both of us. Even if Ally had wanted me to kiss her in the tent in my backyard, I couldn't exactly do anything to test my theory until we got the kids into their parents' cars, safe and sound. Forty-eight hours from now.

Might as well have been a month.

———

"The doorway of your tent should face away from the lake," Ally's voice called out amid the sea of snapping tent poles and the ruffle of nylon. "You want to be facing downwind, otherwise an animal will follow its little curious nose right into your tent in the middle of the night."

"Really?"

"What kind of animal?"

The chorus of voices were more curious than panicked, and it amused me that Ally was threatening them with the very thing that frightened her the most.

I looked over to see her standing amid three tents with her hands on her hips. Head tilted to the side, she seemed to be considering how big a lie to tell. When she caught me looking at her, she grinned, caught. "Bear, most likely."

I shook my head at her as she bit her lip and turned back to the students. "Okay, probably not, but just face the right way anyhow. Because I said so." I continued to watch her take command over two of the guys who'd decided that seniors no longer needed to turn in homework and were annoying half the faculty with their antics. They each towered over her by a foot and probably weighed double what she did. Cassius yanked the wool beanie off his dark blond hair and shook it like he'd just left the ocean. Picking up one of the tent poles, he bent it into a U shape and let it snap open in his hands, making a *fwak* sound that sounded like a loud fart.

It was off to the races from there. Nothing beat a giant fart in the woods for these guys.

His buddy Miles liked that trick, so he did the same with the second pole. I'd have been more annoyed by them except that they were doing the exact kind of dumb shit Shane and I used to do growing up.

I started to go over there, ready to put them in line, but I stopped myself. She hadn't asked for my help, even if I wanted her to have it. So I waited. And watched.

Ally stood staring at them, expressionless, arms folded across her chest. They continued flapping their tent poles around and a couple kids next to them caught on and started doing it too. She pointed at those kids and shut them down in half a second. "You want to lose an eye with that thing?"

There was some mumbling and head hanging before those two got back to putting their tent up. As to Cassius and Miles, Ally continued staring at them, saying nothing, while they flexed their poles a few more times, each time looking up at her and expecting her to blow her top.

Then, they finally realized they weren't going to get her goat, and they stopped. "You know what's cooler than making fart sounds?"

Neither one answered, but both of them gave it a fair bit of thought.

"Carrying a few poles and some fabric on your back and turning it into a man cave in under five minutes. You want to give it a go? Were you listening when we explained it before?"

Some nodding and grunting followed. Ally pointed to the poles and the slots on the tent, and the guys coordinated their efforts, sliding the tent poles in and anchoring them, then using the full power of their gym-honed backs and shoulders to pound in the tent stays. Within minutes their tent was up and they swaggered away high-fiving each other.

Ally moved on to the next group of tent builders, and I found myself unable to move on at all. I was fully stuck on her.

———

"Who's hungry?" I yelled, tapping a metal spoon on the side of a pot.

"Yes!"

"Me!"

"Yes, please!"

"Word."

The chorus of responses came from down near the lake where half the group had decided to skip rocks before dinner. The rest of the kids were lazing in camp chairs around the firepit where we had a small fire burning. Ally and I had led the kids through the forest to select good-sized logs and kindling, which they'd stacked just off to the side.

A few yards away, twelve pitched tents sat in a clearing, some listing to the side if the kids had pulled too hard on the strings that held them to the ground with metal pegs. Others had their tent flies flapping with the breeze. And despite my very clear instructions, two of the tents faced Sky Lake instead of away from it.

Always one kid who didn't get the memo. Or two.

I didn't hear Ally come up behind me, but I felt her presence. It had been happening all day, this connection to her that came from sensing her presence, a general awareness of where she was at every moment. It was like my body had tuned in to her frequency and I was following it like a lost animal headed for home.

"Hey," I said without turning around. I had to keep my attention focused on the flames roaring from the firepit. Another lie I told myself.

The truth was that it was getting harder and harder to look at her without allowing my eyes to devour her, and I could not do that in front of a group of students. I'd already given in and admitted to myself that I planned to do something about my consuming attraction just as soon as this trip was finished, but I needed to keep myself in check for the remainder of the weekend. I was a runner, for God's sake—I had self-discipline, even if Ally was testing every last shred.

"Hey yourself." Ally gave my back a poke with something sharp, forcing me to turn and identify it. A stick.

"Tents look pretty good," I observed.

"They do. And you were right. I just directed traffic and the kids did all the work. They even pitched mine for me." She pointed to a light green tent sitting on the outer edge of the others. About as far away as possible from the one I'd set up for myself. Good. The farther away she was when she slipped into her sleeping bag for the night, the less I'd think about her.

CHAPTER
SEVENTEEN

ALLY

We taught the kids how to do a "bear hang," in which we loaded our food into a duffel and hoisted it into a tree, out of the reach of bears. There were bear boxes at the campsite where we could put the food, but Clay was right—the kids loved the idea of hanging it, so we decided they could put some of the rations up in the trees for the night.

"You're sure we're good here too? No bears this weekend?" I asked quietly while tying a rope to a bag of food. We were perched facing each other on a fallen log, retying some of the knots the students had done their best to perfect. Unfortunately, a few of them were too loose, and a few students had packed way too much into their nylon duffels, making them unwieldy to hang.

We'd taught them the basics, but now we needed to get real.

A group of kids stood a few yards away, laughing and tossing their food bags back and forth like water balloons. We'd done pretty well keeping them on track all day and making them follow instructions, so giving them time now to get their excess energy out didn't seem to hurt.

Clay laughed. "You know I can't guarantee where bears are going to go."

A loud collective groan sounded when one of the food bags hit the ground with a thud. "Dude, that bag had all the fruit," a guy from the football team scolded.

"Bruh, you shouldn't have thrown it so hard. It's not fourth down."

They opened the bag and inspected a few bruised apples before tying the bag up again and resuming their game.

"I do know that," I said. "Which is why I don't understand why you keep telling me we'll be fine."

"Because you keep asking. And we will be fine. Even if a bear comes through. As long as you're not hiding cookies in your tent, a bear isn't going to come looking for food."

I stopped working on a particularly stubborn knot. "I would never."

"Good girl." His gruff voice sent a shiver down my spine as I imagined him saying that in all sorts of different circumstances, all of them sexual. My face heated at the thought, and I sincerely hoped Clay's wilderness skills didn't include mind reading.

"So, I should've asked . . . how was your date?" Clay's smile was forced. The rest of his face showed signs of painful discomfort.

I stopped working on the knot and glanced behind me, thinking he must be talking to someone else. I saw only trees and rocks, so I turned back to ask Clay what he meant. Then I realized . . .

"Oh, Louie? The animal-hating architect? Yeah, I decided not to go." The fact was that I'd never intended to go. It had only been one more effort to draw a clear boundary between Clay and me, and I was wanting that boundary less and less.

Was it my imagination that Clay's face calmed? Did he seem relieved?

"Huh. Why not?"

I shrugged. I didn't feel like explaining my reasoning to the hot man who smelled like smoke and cedar bodywash and whose muscles flexed each time he wound up a coil of rope and tossed it over a branch. Mainly because he was the reason.

"He isn't the one I want."

His eyes settled on me with an intensity I hadn't seen since the night we spent in his yard. As much as I'd spent the past week trying to avoid just that intensity, it startled me how much I wanted to see it now. How much I needed to see it.

"Okay, then."

I didn't know what that meant, but there was no time to investigate it because three female students came running over. "Ms. Dalbotten, Mr. Meadows!"

They talked quickly and talked over each other, but the gist of the situation was that their friend Jayne wasn't feeling well. Jayne was an awesome drummer in the high school band, and I knew she had a lot on her plate.

I popped up from the log and hurried over to the tent where Jayne lay on top of her sleeping bag, face flushed and forehead hot with signs of a fever.

"I really want to stay. Please."

Clay looked to me, the presumed expert on wilderness first aid, which was certainly not required here. This was simple cold and flu knowledge, but I quickly ran through some basic assessments to make sure Jayne hadn't spiked a fever from heat exhaustion or an infection.

Walking her away from her concerned friends, I found a quiet corner of the campsite where she could sit on a tarp in the shade. The listless way she slumped to the side and her pink cheeks told me her fever was probably over a hundred, but I still sent Clay to my tent to grab the medical kit I'd brought.

"It's in the outside pocket of my pack, the gray one right outside the light green tent."

Clay jogged off toward the tents, and I focused on Jayne's sad, flushed face. "I know there's probably a rule that says I need to go home, but . . ." Her lower lip trembled, and she swallowed back her emotions. "Is there any way I can stay? I've been looking forward to this all year long."

"You want to be with your friends." I nodded, remembering that feeling in high school of not wanting to miss out.

She shook her head. "I want to be here in the mountains. I need it. School's been so stressful this year and I just feel like . . ." She stopped to catch her breath, and she shook her head again. On a long blink, she swallowed hard, and I began to see that there was something else going on with her.

I reached out and put a hand on her knee. "You okay?"

She blinked a few more times, then nodded her head. Her downtrodden expression said otherwise. "Yeah, pretty much. But, you know, this year hasn't been the best for me."

I knew a little bit about it because her mom had called the school to let us know Jayne's dad had moved out. I'd been keeping an extra eye out for her, but she'd seemed to be in good spirits at school, hadn't changed friend groups, and hadn't let her grades slip, as far as I knew.

But I also knew kids worked hard to make sure the surface impression they gave hid whatever they didn't want seen. Just like the battle Clay had fought silently for so many years. Still waters ran deep, and I felt for Jayne, just like I felt for Clay.

"Yes, I know. Is there anything I can do to help you?"

She tilted her head back and seemed to be studying the branches overhead, but when she looked back at me, her eyes were more glassy than they had been a moment before. I felt for her, trying to hold back emotions that probably had little to do with coming down with a fever.

"I just don't want to leave. Being up here, this is exactly the break I needed. I just want to breathe the clean air up here and clear my mind. I'll stay far away from everyone, I promise."

Still sitting, she leaned back on her hands and lifted her face toward the sky. Despite the tree canopy, the sunlight crept through, dappling her face.

I looked up as well, taking in the majestic trunks and leaves. She was right—there was something centering about being out here. I wanted to find a way to let her stay, but Clay and I would need to bend a few school rules, and I didn't know how he'd feel about that.

"Sit tight a minute, okay? Let me see what we can work out."

She nodded and I left, intercepting Clay on his way back from my tent and guiding him out of Jayne's earshot.

He held up my red first aid kit, which was the size of a jumbo bag of chips. "This is heavy. You carried this in your pack?"

"No such thing as too heavy when it comes to safety." It didn't weigh that much. The bag was more awkwardly large than heavy, and I'd had to forego an extra fleece pullover in order to make it fit.

"All my sound words of advice and she learns nothing."

"Hey, I learned a few things. Especially that if you could carry a six-pack up to a lake, I could carry a few bandages."

I found myself not wanting Clay to see me as the anti-bug scaredy-cat who couldn't hold her own in the woods. Maybe I'd gone slightly overboard packing some extra instant ice packs, rolls of bandages, and enough water purifying tablets to make Tennessee's entire water supply safe for drinking. But if my wilderness first aid skills ended up being needed, I didn't want to come up short.

Clay started to walk over to where Jayne looked slightly less distressed sitting in the shade, but I put a hand on his arm to stop him. I wasn't expecting the zing of awareness when I felt his muscles flex beneath his shirt. His eyes shot to mine and I knew he felt it too.

Removing my hand, I stuffed it in my jacket pocket and tried to ignore the unexpected warmth spreading through my veins.

Maybe I had a fever too. These things could be contagious.

"Is there any chance we could bend the rules and let Jayne stay for the rest of the trip? We can quarantine her from the others but at least let her get something from being out here. She did hike all this way, after all."

His quizzical look turned to distress. Clay wasn't a rule bender. "I don't think the school administration would approve. We're supposed to send her home."

"Yes, but that would mean one of us hiking down with her and the other supervising nineteen kids. Does that sound like something anyone would want?"

"It's not a long hike," he said. Ever logical.

"I think it's important for her to stay. I'll go to bat for her. I'd love the chance to get back at Pin Dick by making decisions without him."

His eyes widened slightly as he caught my drift. "Details, Alexandra."

I shrugged. "I told you. The lunches. He's creepy. And vindictive."

Clay waited as though I might say more but I didn't want to tell him my whole maddening history with our school principal, so I took the opportunity to untie and retie my hiking boot.

"That's all you're going to give me?"

"For now, yes."

"How about explaining why you think it's important for a sick kid to stay on the trip."

Glancing around to make sure no students had snuck up behind us, I confirmed we were still out of their earshot. "Jayne and I were talking a little bit and I got the sense that staying here is about more than just FOMO. It feels important for her to be here. I think she needs it. Like, really needs it. For her mental health, if nothing else."

That got Clay's attention. "She say that specifically?"

"Her parents just split. It's senior year. You know how stressful that gets for these kids. She almost broke down in tears telling me how much she wants to be here. These kids need to be out here breathing this air. It's some good shit."

The smile began creeping across Clay's face like the first rays of dawn that don't want to wake the neighbors. Before I had time to duck and cover, the full force of Clay's smug grin was assaulting me with its damned beauty.

"You're a convert. You love it out here."

"I do. I love it."

"It didn't take anywhere close to a year."

"Needing to be right all the time is not one of your more charming attributes."

He kept on grinning, not giving a crap. "I don't need to be right all the time. But I'm glad I'm right about this."

At that moment, we heard a splash in the lake, and both of us turned in the direction of the noise. "Any chance that was a belly-flopping fish?" I asked hopefully.

Clay shook his head. "Doubtful." When we heard the second splash, we started moving in the direction of the lakeshore.

"You think they're swimming?"

"We'd have heard a scream if they were. That water's fifty-eight degrees."

Before I could ask where Clay came up with his precise temperature estimate, we stepped past the last tree blocking our view of the lake. A few yards in the distance, a half dozen kids stood on the lakeshore, some bent down searching for stones, the others testing their throwing arms and rock-skipping abilities.

The next stone to skitter across the lake skipped twice before dropping into the water with a similar splash as we'd heard earlier. "I thought that was going at least four," Miles said, bending down to hunt for more flat rocks.

"Dude, not with that throwing arm," Cassius mocked, cocking back an arm and letting his rock fly. It skipped three times and plopped into the lake. "That's how you do it."

I leaned toward Clay, hoping he'd agree with me about Jayne.

"Can we say we made a judgement call that the hike down would be more dangerous to her health than staying overnight? Reassess tomorrow?"

"You're the one with the medical expertise."

"I need to answer to the principal for my decision."

"I'd defend you against Pin Dick if it came to that."

A part of me really wanted to see him do that. I was so busy imagining Clay standing up in a court of law giving testimony to Pindich that I almost didn't hear what he said next. "Since we're out in the fresh air, she should be fine if she stays six feet away from the other students. I don't want to make her feel like an outcast, but of course, she shouldn't share a tent with anyone else."

He was looking at me meaningfully, and it took a minute to catch his drift. We hadn't brought extra tents.

"Oh."

"It's fine. She can have my tent and I'll sleep outside on the ground."

"You can't do that. You'll get eaten alive by bugs, for one thing. Plus, it's cold. You're the one who stressed the importance of the tent shelter."

"That was more for the kids."

I shook my head. "No way. You can share with me. We'll just flip around so your head is by my feet to give us a little privacy."

"You really think I want my head next to your feet after you hiked up here in stinky boots?"

"Fine, enjoy getting bitten by mosquitoes. Too bad I didn't bring any hydrocortisone in the first aid kit to help with the itching."

"I apologize. I'm sure your feet smell lovely."

"They do."

"Fine."

We'd share a tent like two normal adults, and I'd go home after the trip and sleep for a week. Because I sure wasn't going to get any sleep for the next two nights, trying to maximize the distance between me and a man who made my heart pound every time he touched me.

So. Not. Fine.

EIGHTEEN

CLAY

We were on our twenty-ninth campfire song and my voice was getting hoarse. Not wanting to overpack, I wasn't about to lug a full-sized guitar up a mountain, but the tiny ukulele I tied to the outside of my pack proved just enough to give us a melody.

Several of the kids took turns strumming it and proved that it's a lot harder to play a ukulele than it appears. Eventually it made its way back to me, and now I was picking out the melody for "Dust in the Wind," which only a few kids knew the words to, judging by the fact that Ally and I were doing most of the singing.

From time to time I'd forget we were sitting amid a circle of students. The wind chime sound of her laugh was nothing compared to her clear, soft singing voice and I kicked myself for not knowing she was a singer. I'd have recruited her long ago to join us for a Friday jam session at the community center.

She seemed to know the words to every song I came up with. Before long, it became a competition between us to see how quickly she could identify the next song I planned to play after hearing only a few notes. The kids got in on it too, cheering her on when she correctly identified the song and started singing. Somehow, they all seemed to be Team Ally, and I didn't mind one bit.

After we'd sung "Oh! Susanna" for the second time, I noticed the kids were starting to lose steam. They'd proven they knew the words to the song an hour ago, but now less than half of them were singing. It was time to send them to their tents and wish them sweet dreams.

"Okay, guys. You can stay up for a while inside your tents, but if it gets crazy loud, I'll make you turn off the flashlights."

A chorus of hiking boots scraping the dirt followed as everyone made their way from the campfire area to the tents. Everyone, that is, except Ally and me.

Normally, after a day of hiking and chaperoning, I'd be so dead tired, I'd be in my tent and half asleep five minutes after dismissing the kids. But tonight, I felt myself lingering by the campfire.

Because sharing a tent with Ally felt so much more intimate than it would with just about any other member of the Green Valley High School faculty. Not just because she was a female. But because she was her.

What had I been thinking, agreeing to her plan to sleep head to feet? Like that would make it any less awkward.

Lost in my thoughts, I didn't realize for a moment that Ally hadn't left the campfire either. When a cascade of sparks rushed into the air, I realized she'd poked the logs with a stick.

"We should make sure this is out—like really out—before we go to sleep," she said, staring at the flames. "I don't want to have to evacuate this bunch because we set the forest on fire."

I got up from the rock where I'd been perched for the past hour and stretched my legs. They felt creaky and hike-weary. Normally, sleeping on the ground after a good hike was my favorite thing in the world. Tonight, I was riddled with anxiety.

I felt my heart hammering in my chest, and I knew it wasn't in delighted anticipation of inhaling the mountain air as I slept. It was in nervous anticipation of inhaling Ally's citrus shampoo in close quarters and pretending it didn't affect me.

Shuffling over to an area where I'd piled up some loose dirt, I scooped a handful and brought it back to the fire. Before I could dump it on the flames, Ally stopped me. "Do you have to put it out? Can I sit a while?"

"Oh. Sure. I figured you were tired."

She shrugged. "A little tired, but it's only ten, so I doubt I'll fall asleep. I'd rather hang out here a bit longer." In the darkness, I couldn't see her face well enough to notice a crease in her brow or other signs that would show she felt a similar trepidation about sharing a tent.

She probably didn't. She was a mature adult who knew that two colleagues could take one for the team and sleep in close quarters without it being a big deal. I needed to get out of my head.

I let the dirt sift through my fingers onto the ground and sat back on my rock across from her. It took every bit of self-control not to edge closer, and I mentally berated myself for not taking better advantage of this same situation a week earlier when we didn't have twenty teenagers roaming around aware of our every move.

It didn't take a crack detective to pick up on the gossip that roamed the halls at school. If students so much as saw a pair of teachers showing anything other than purely professional affection, the rumor mill blazed to life.

Last year, Witty had the poor judgement to stand in the lunchroom line behind Rosalie and use a plastic fork to comb her hair. Instead of swatting him away, Rosalie laughed, and by the end of the day, half the student body was convinced they were having a fling. Episodes like that taught me long ago to keep my hands—and my forks—to myself or risk a public outing of feelings I didn't know I had.

Except now, the feelings were real and I'd spent much of the day avoiding being too close to Ally for fear of exposing myself.

The flames licked at the remains of the logs and lit up her face in pinks and oranges.

"Today was a good day, don't you think?" She leaned forward to warm her hands, holding them open in front of the flames.

"I'm just happy you're not miserable. There's a big difference between camping in my yard and coming up here."

"Yeah, two dozen teenagers. How do you ever get them to quiet down and go to sleep?"

A gentle breeze rustled the leaves on the trees and blew a few strands of Ally's hair loose. She swatted at them to tame them. I ached to scoot closer to her and tuck the strands behind her ear. But I did nothing except watch her in the dim light, hoping the darkness would hide the evidence of my thoughts.

"They're more tired than they realize. They'll have fun making a commotion in the tents for a while, but eventually, they'll drop. Just wait. Something happens after an hour or two and suddenly it's dead silent."

She cupped a hand around her ear and listened. "Yeah, not yet. Not at all."

"Patience, grasshopper."

I should have been telling myself the same thing. Tonight would be fine. I needed to relax and stop worrying about the future.

"So tell me more about Jayne," I said quietly, glancing behind me to make sure we were really alone. "I didn't get a heads-up from the school counselor about depression. Is it a new issue for her?"

"Oh, I don't think it's new. She's been struggling with it for a while, but she manages it with meds."

She didn't look pointedly at me when she said it, and I almost wondered if she'd forgotten what I'd told her after she'd crashed on the track. She *had* hit her head.

"How's it going for you?" she asked with quiet concern, like a friend. Like it wasn't a source of constant anguish for me as I resisted my doctor's advice to up my meds.

"It's going okay, thanks."

I'd looked away, so I didn't notice that she'd moved closer until she bumped my hip with hers. "Hey, no pat answers. I'm asking for real."

Exhaling a lungful of mountain air, I realized how few people cared enough to ask, and that was my fault for not letting people in. "It's been up and down since my grandmother died. Lately, I've . . . struggled a bit more."

"She was your person in this, huh?"

I nodded. "She understood. I guess I haven't looked to find someone else who does. My fault."

"I could be that person, you know. I am your friend and I'm here. So just, you know, talk when you want to talk."

Even if I'd wanted to talk, I couldn't have, due to the sudden lump in my throat. Barely able to swallow over it, I simply nodded.

And even though she'd offered, I wasn't willing to tell her everything. I didn't want her to know the part of me that sometimes struggled with feeling despondent when I was alone at home. I didn't want her to feel sorry for me or judge me for not trying harder to be happy, as though it were a choice. "Do you know much about mental health issues?"

It's not that I thought she was necessarily holding out on me with her own struggles, but I wanted to know how open-minded she might be about the severity of mine if I told her more.

Even in the dim light, I could see her eyes go wide with surprise. "I mean, I don't think you can teach students for ten years and not know about mental health issues. Right?"

"True. I guess I meant more specifically."

"You mean have I worked one-on-one?"

"Yeah."

She patted her lips with a finger, thinking, and I stared at the plump shape of her mouth, not quite a pout but full, pillowy lips. I was such an asshole. I'd asked her an important question, and now I was sitting here ogling her lips.

"I've had a couple of students confide in me. Jayne is one. Last year I had two others. I wanted to make sure I was telling them the right thing and not just spouting moronic philosophy, so I did a lot of research."

"Does Jayne seem like she's handling it? Any red flags?"

She shook her head. "No, she's managing. She knows what she needs to do to keep herself 'out of the pit,' as she calls it."

I knew the pit. I knew that there were days when it didn't matter how objectively fine life looked. There was no climbing out of the pit and no desire to try.

I could tell Ally how far down I'd sunk. I could let her know me better.

"Okay. Good for me to know, though. I'll look out for her a little more than usual."

No, I wouldn't tell her. Not yet. I wasn't ready for her to see me differently.

Ally was watching me, and I realized I had my palms against my cheeks, resting my chin in my hands, elbows tucked against my body protectively. I lowered my hands to my lap and stretched my shoulders, but her gaze stayed fixed on me as though she knew something about me despite my effort to hide it.

Then she leaned back and grabbed a small red duffel bag I hadn't noticed. Her eyebrows bounced as she pulled the string and opened it, producing a package of graham crackers, a chocolate bar, and a half-full bag of marshmallows.

"You didn't hang that in the tree with the rest of the food?"

"Not yet. I had a feeling I'd want a little extra dessert. Join me?"

I nodded. "Sure."

I fished around on the ground for some fresh sticks and speared a marshmallow. The longer we sat out here, the less time we'd be alone together in a tiny tent.

CHAPTER
NINETEEN

ALLY

Eventually, we both ran out of excuses.

I'd eaten three s'mores, which was two s'mores more than I'd ever eaten in one sitting in my life, and I felt a little sick to my stomach. Clay had stopped after two, claiming he didn't want to open a new package of chocolate, but he was probably just as ill as me.

The fire had died down to a few lonely embers, which made the air around us much colder. We'd have to put another log on the fire if we had any chance of continuing to brave the elements, and there was no reason to do that when the whole point was to put the fire out.

So I watched as Clay scooped up the dirt and small rocks he'd piled nearby and dropped them on the embers. For a moment, a rogue flame shot up, somehow enthused by the dirt dousing. "You sure you don't have kindling mixed in with that dirt?" I asked.

"Reminds me of a time Shane and I went camping as kids and did exactly that. Our dad told us to scoop some dirt on the dying fire. To a couple of kids, that meant throwing the closest dirt pile on top and getting inside our tents."

"Uh-oh. Tell me you didn't burn down the Smoky Mountains."

"No, but about an hour after I went to bed, I opened my eyes and saw the fire had kicked back to life and was blazing in the firepit. In the middle of the forest with no one watching it. I started screaming and kicked out of my sleeping bag, unzipped the tent, and ran out barefoot. And there was my dad watching from inside his tent."

"Why didn't he just put the fire out himself?"

"Because then I wouldn't be a stickler for fire safety twenty-five years later."

"Smart dad."

"Yup. Still is."

I made no move to get up, content to sit out here a while longer if it meant getting to know Clay bit by bit in the darkness. As he stood and stretched his arms toward the sky, his shirt rode up, exposing some nicely defined abs and a light trail of hair. I couldn't tear my eyes away, wondering where it led and how it might feel to touch. "I'm gonna feel that pack in the morning," he said.

Leaning toward me, Clay extended a large, strong hand to help me up. Grasping it, I flashed back to the litany of tasks I'd watched Clay's hands perform over the past few hours—hefting logs like they were lightweight sticks, commandeering rope to throw over tall branches, tossing vegetables in a frying pan like a master chef.

With each grip of his hands on the equipment, my brain registered and added up his skills one by one. And each time, I felt something.

At first it was appreciation for all the things he knew how to do and seemed to take for granted. Appreciation for how different wilderness Clay was from the musclebound Clark Kent who darted around campus and let people think he was disinterested in relationships. I'd gone along with it too, assuming that what I saw was all there was to him, even if I knew better than to judge a book by its cover.

And when the cover looked that good, reality felt like even more of a betrayal.

But now, with my palm firmly in his grip, I felt something entirely different. It was electric. My hand felt gripped by flames hotter than the ones we'd just doused with dirt. The heat crawled along my skin and begged me not to let go.

I wanted him to touch me everywhere, and it wasn't until that moment that I really, truly realized how completely fucked I was agreeing to share a tent with this man when nothing would or could happen between us.

And it wouldn't. I knew that.

I also knew I'd lie awake for most of the night trying not to accidentally wrap my body around his.

"I guess we should hit the hay." Clay's pronouncement pulled me from my thoughts.

"Um, yeah. And I should brush my teeth, make sure a bear doesn't come find me and kiss the marshmallow off my mouth."

Clay's jaw went slack at the suggestion. I swallowed hard, then cleared my throat, searching for something else to say. I found nothing.

We walked in silence toward the bear boxes, our path lit only by Clay's head-lamp, which bounced light over the grassy terrain. After stashing the s'mores supplies in the box, along with my toothpaste and toothbrush in the small Ziploc of toiletries I'd brought, Clay secured the box and gave it a fierce rattle. "Seems bear-proof to me."

"Ha. I'm pretty sure a determined bear could rip through the metal if he was hungry enough."

"No doubt. But at least this'll keep a bear busy so he won't come nosing in the tents."

We began walking toward the lone tent opposite from the student tents, where it sounded like a house party was happening. "Do we need to tell them to quiet down?" I asked, fairly certain it would be a futile effort.

"Nah, let 'em go. They're not bothering anyone out here, except maybe the animals. And that'll just keep them far away."

"In that case, they can scream all night."

He laughed, and even though I'd heard the sound before, in the quiet empty space of our campsite, it felt more seductive. Hotter. Like a siren song, luring me to a place where panties were incinerated on contact.

I was losing my mind. This was just a normal night. He was just a teacher. A colleague. Jefferson's dorky friend. The hottest man I'd ever spent time with.

The tent looked forlorn sitting in its small clearing among the trees. And also perfect. A charming home away from home, which made me question yet again why it had taken me so long to conquer my fear of the outdoors.

And here, now, I had a whole new host of fears and none of them had anything to do with camping.

Clay unzipped the front of our tent and gestured for me to climb inside. "After you."

I crawled into the tent, then flipped around so I was sitting down with my feet sticking out. I leaned forward to unlace my boots. While I worked on the double-knotted laces of the first one, Clay crouched down and began unlacing the other.

I felt my face heat as I watched him carefully untangling the knot with his long fingers and tucking his large hand under the heel of the boot to wrench it off my foot. When I'd finished unlacing the other, he grabbed it and easily pulled it off too.

Not wanting him to see my flushed cheeks, I scrambled inside the tent and moved toward the back wall. Clay's large form joined me a moment later, sitting in a similar position as I had while he took off his own boots.

When he scooted back and zipped the tent closed, the tension in the small space ratcheted up a million or so degrees. Pressing my back so hard against the tent wall that I risked tearing the fabric, I still couldn't bring myself to look at Clay. His presence was so strong I felt overwhelmed.

Clay placed his flashlight under a white shirt, giving the light a muted glow. What had I been thinking, saying we should share a tent? I'd slept in these tents at Clay's house, and I knew they were barely big enough for one person, let alone two.

Maybe you want to be in close quarters with him.

Well, sure. Who wouldn't want to be in close quarters with this hunk of Clay? But could I handle the swarm of butterflies in my stomach and the raging libido he unleashed? Doubtful.

"Alexandra." We were only a couple feet apart. Clay wasn't speaking loudly. But the tent had an echo chamber effect, which meant his voice came at me from all sides, the lilt of his Tennessee drawl coating me like a pour of warm pancake syrup. I shuddered unconsciously.

"Yes?" I asked, looking anywhere in the tent but at his face. I busied myself smoothing out my sleeping bag and maneuvering it so my head would be as far away as possible from Clay's while we slept. As if I'd be able to sleep with him so close by.

"Look at me."

Tipping my head up only enough so I could see him through my eyelashes, I told myself I had complete control over my reaction to him. I could look at him without feeling a lurch in my gut, right?

Wrong, wrong, and triple wrong.

His chiseled features had dissolved into a look of concern that creased his forehead and removed all traces of his smile. And somehow he appeared even more beautiful. No one had ever gazed at me like that, even my parents, and I knew empirically that they loved me. This was something different, and my body responded to its magnetic pull. I was powerless to resist him, and as much as it thrilled my senses, it annoyed my brain.

He's just a guy, a colleague, I told myself in what was becoming a truly useless refrain.

Reaching with a steady hand, Clay tipped my chin up with the knuckle of his index finger. Chills raced over my skin. "What's wrong?" he asked.

"Nothing. All good," I said, my voice crackling like the fire we'd just extinguished. And now the damn hottie was lighting a new one. I forced a yawn. "I'm just super tired. Probably should get some sleep."

He let his hand drop to his lap, and I felt suddenly cold. But that was a good thing. Keeping my distance, I shoved my feet into my sleeping bag without taking off my socks, and shimmied into the warm cocoon until I could barely see Clay. I heard him rustling around at the opposite corner of the tent, and I assumed he was loading himself into his own sleeping bag.

More rustling. And a few jerky movements. He wasn't settling down, and after another minute, I became curious enough to peek over the edge of my purple sleeping bag, only to find Clay sitting cross-legged, rummaging through several small nylon sacks he'd taken from his backpack.

Cue tiny orgasm from organizational porn. The man had everything sorted in small bundles, and I couldn't help but stare as he opened one and removed a long-sleeved tee. He then reached for the neck of his fleece and pulled it off, along with the shirt beneath it. My jaw went slack at the sight of his naked torso, all carved into muscular bas-relief like a granite sculpture. His abs flexed as he folded—folded!—his fleece and packed it into the small sack.

When he pulled on the long-sleeved shirt, I let out an exhale of thanks for taking mercy on me. Apparently, it was a loud exhale. Clay looked up, so I quickly buried myself again under the top of the bag.

"Alexandra," he said.

"Yes?" My voice was muffled by three inches of down and nylon.

"Is this going to make you uncomfortable?"

"This?" I sounded like a squeaky bird.

"Sharing a tent. I really don't mind sleeping on the ground. You can have the tent to yourself." He gestured around as though he was highlighting the spaciousness of a villa instead of a tent spanning four square feet.

His words hit me like a shovel to the back of the head. I was being ridiculous. It was just a few butterflies, and I was the strong, capable sort of person who could talk them down. Mind over matter.

"No, no. You don't need to do that. Head to feet, we're all good."

But we weren't all good because he didn't slide his feet into the sleeping bag for another ten minutes, during which time I snuck more looks at his flexing biceps while he organized more small sacks of camping items. He changed out of the socks he'd been wearing all day and put on a fresh pair, reminding me I'd shoved my dusty, socked feet into my bag and now I'd have the pleasure of sleeping that way.

Unfurling a pair of sweatpants that he'd rolled into a tidy bundle, Clay glanced in my direction. I hunkered down in my bag, wondering if he was about to take his pants off in the tent. Instead, he opened the tent, tossed a thin camping towel onto the ground outside, and stepped out. I could only see him from mid-thigh downward, but when he dropped his hiking pants, I caught a shadowy view of some very muscular runner's legs before he stepped into the dark blue sweatpants and crawled back into the tent.

My heart clenched the moment he zipped the tent closed and I realized how small the space felt. I began to rethink my insistence that this would be fine. Was it me, or was there suddenly less air in here?

Finally—finally—he slipped his feet into the sleeping bag and stretched them out toward my head. His own head was about as far away from me as it could be without sticking out of the tent.

Clay fished the flashlight out from the corner and flicked it off. The darkness provided its own kind of relief because I could no longer worry about catching sight of Clay. But then I had a different problem—hyperawareness of his every shift and movement, which I could feel because our sleeping bags had no distance between them.

It was so quiet for such a long time that I assumed Clay had fallen asleep instantly.

I was making a mental note to ask him in the morning how he managed that, when he shifted in his sleeping bag and started talking.

"Hey."

"Hey."

"You comfortable?"

Was I . . . what? In a list of words to describe my state of being, "comfortable" would round out the very bottom.

I'd been lying there for fifteen minutes, stiff as a wooden plank, trying to breathe quietly and stay on my side of the tent. My muscles were so tense and tight that I'd make an excellent soldier, ready to spring into action at a moment's notice. Not to mention that there was a rock or a pinecone underneath the tent, and no matter how I positioned myself, it kept jabbing me in the back.

I couldn't help it. I started to laugh. "Um, not really. I was afraid to move because I thought I might wake you."

His laugh joined mine. "Oh, thank God. Me too. I've been waiting for you to fall asleep so I can exhale."

"Impressed that you can hold your breath for fifteen minutes."

"I am a runner, you know."

I heard some shuffling in the dark, and a moment later, the flashlight popped back on, muted by the same white shirt. It gave the tent a warm glow under the low green ceiling.

"What are we gonna do?" His voice was a low grumble. Sleepy and deep. Almost intimate.

"I don't know. Tell each other ghost stories?"

Still inside the sleeping bag, I sat up, finally relieved of the pesky rock. I rubbed my back. "I was so busy telling all the kids to check the ground for rocks, I somehow neglected to do it myself."

"There's a rock under you?"

"More like a shard."

He sat up. Now we were facing each other, only a foot of space between us. Then he started scooting toward me. "Here, switch places with me."

"No, I'm not making you sleep on a rock."

He was already moving toward me like an inchworm, but in the cramped tent, there was no way for him to get past me without contact. Before I knew it, he'd picked up the bottom half of me, still in the bag, and propped my legs on his lap. Then he wrapped an arm around my shoulders and swung us both around until he was sitting in my former half of the tent, and I was in his.

But he didn't let my legs go.

Acutely aware of his legs beneath mine, I stopped breathing momentarily.

When I glanced up, his gaze was bearing down on me. In the dim light, I was close enough to see gold flecks dance in the hazel of his irises. His muscled arm wrapped me up in heat. I let out a shaky exhale and felt him do the same.

Unconsciously, I leaned forward, drawn in by him. I wanted to memorize the details of his face in case I never got this close again. He tipped his head down slightly. Now we were mere inches apart, and it would take only the slightest movement for one of us to close the gap.

Clay's lips looked soft, and I fixed my gaze on the corner of his mouth that crooked to the side the way I always liked, as though he was fighting a smile.

I felt his exhale as though it were my own. When he rolled to the side, I wanted to roll with him. Instead, I lay frozen in the dark, afraid of moving a muscle lest I inadvertently climb on top of him.

Finally, Clay settled down and seemed to find a comfortable sleeping position because he stopped moving and I could hear his even breathing.

I started to shiver. It made no sense because my sleeping bag was plenty warm, but I knew it had nothing to do with being cold. The proximity to Clay was making me tremble with anticipation that something was about to happen. We could ignite ten campfires with the sparks shooting between us.

Then Clay turned abruptly, and my eyes locked on his. I watched them heat, irises turning a deeper color, pupils dilating.

"What's happening right now?" he asked.

"I guess I'm a little nervous."

"Why are you nervous? It's just me."

"Exactly. It's you." I didn't know what I was saying. And then again, I knew exactly what I was saying. It was Clay, the man I'd fantasized about for half my life, even as I told myself nothing could ever happen between us. I'd used him as the cautionary tale, convinced myself I was better off staying far away from the greyhound who'd never stop moving.

But that wasn't the guy I'd seen over the past couple weeks of spending time together. And the man I was getting to know now had my insides melting. He had me wanting things I'd convinced myself never to believe I could have.

I wanted those things. And I wanted him.

I couldn't say all of that to him, not when we were chaperoning a group of students, not when telling him how I felt made me feel intensely vulnerable, not when I couldn't be sure my feelings would be reciprocated. Easier to chicken out. "I guess I just . . . I don't know."

His head fell forward, almost in defeat. "Ally . . ." The growl of his voice in the small space sent a cascade of chills down my neck. "Why do I make you nervous?"

Bunching up a wad of sleeping bag in my fists, I exhaled a long breath and closed my eyes. I could feel my heart hammering in my chest. His proximity made me nervous. The heavy air between us. The simplicity of moving a few inches closer and feeling the warmth of his body.

The inescapable pull of him. The electricity I felt sizzling in my chest, daring me to lean closer, take a whiff of him, touch his skin.

And yet . . . I still had a chance to reel it back. Or at least diffuse the situation. Despite spending half my life trying to convince myself I didn't flat-out want Clay Meadows to kiss me, I could admit the truth now—at least to myself. But I didn't have to admit it to Clay.

Had I learned nothing from my mother—and my father? Had no wisdom lingered after my failed relationships to convince me that I was better off on my own?

I wished I could believe it. I wished the romantic in me still didn't wish to be proven wrong. I'd always imagined someone like Clay—or Clay himself—making a case for the fantasy. Proving I could have the fantasy I secretly still dreamed about.

"I think I've changed my mind about the fantasy."

He flinched almost imperceptibly. Eyes heating. Losing their color to a molten darkness.

My heart thundered in my chest like an entire orchestra woodwind section. I moved closer to him, near enough that I felt the heat of him, saw the pulsing of his heart in his throat, felt the sharp inhale of breath.

"Ally . . ."

A warning I ignored.

"Yes?"

His hands flexed and he looked around the tent before his eyes returned to me. Boldly, I leaned in a little more. Our faces inches apart. My nerves raking my skin with goose bumps.

I heard him draw a shaky breath. "I can't have you this close to me and not kiss you."

I swallowed hard. "So kiss me."

He didn't. He stared, eyes searching mine for something—a sign I didn't mean it? A reason to back away? There were plenty.

"Goddammit." A growl mixed with a curse. The snap of tension.

He yanked me toward him. The nylon shell of my sleeping bag swept along the floor of the tent as he reduced the space between us to zero.

The feel of his lips against my jaw was sensory overload. His breath was hot against my skin, one hand slipping along the side of my face and into my hair.

He kissed my jaw, my cheek . . . finally my lips. His mouth was soft, tentatively tasting, exploring without being insistent.

This was the first time I'd experienced Clay moving like he wasn't in a hurry. The first brush of our lips turned into a languid, slow burn that made me moan for more.

I licked Clay's bottom lip and his mouth opened, fusing with mine. Our tongues found each other and tangled mercilessly, impatiently.

Clay tasted delicious, a faint hint of campfire, chocolate, mint from his toothpaste. And as my hands roamed up the hard planes of his chest and wrapped over his shoulders, I felt my heart contract in my chest. Blood rushed hot through my veins.

This was the side of Clay I'd wondered about all these years and never had the temerity to believe I could have. Not that I really had him. This was pure lust and opportunity. Of course I knew that.

But it didn't mean I wouldn't enjoy every minute of it.

Until Clay abruptly pulled away, looking a little surprised. Almost like he'd forgotten I was there with him.

"I'm sorry. I . . . shouldn't have done that."

"You didn't. We did. I'm here too." I wanted to be clear on that because that kiss was very consensual.

He looked at me, and I watched his eyes trace the contours of my face, warming my cheeks as his gaze rippled across them, making my lips ache to be touched when his stare finally landed on them. Hot, wanting. "So you don't feel cornered?"

I'd been so certain he and I were on the exact same page, his words downright baffled me. "Cornered? No. Not at all."

"You're sure?"

"Clay, stop being so polite."

"Ally . . ." His voice was low, gruff, aggravated mostly with himself. He shook his head slowly. "If you knew the things I crave when it comes to you, you'd never accuse me of being polite."

"Try me." It was a challenge, and his eyes grew darker, molten.

The next kiss was more intense, slower, dragged out as Clay's tongue tasted every part of my mouth. His teeth came down on my bottom lip, and I let out a quiet moan. He soothed the skin with his tongue.

His forehead tipped against mine and we both steadied our breath. My cheeks felt flushed, and I left my eyes closed briefly to soak in the lingering imprint of Clay's lips. When I blinked my eyes open, I saw softness in Clay's eyes coupled with firm resignation in his jaw.

"We can't do this. Not here."

"I know."

It was crossing every line of proper chaperoning, and my thoughts immediately turned to our responsibilities. I backed away from Clay until I was pressed up against the nylon of the tent. It felt damp from the chilly evening air, but I needed to cool myself down.

"But . . . we're only here til Sunday." The gruff insinuation of what might happen after Sunday sent a zing of awareness through my body.

"Sunday."

Clay nodded and reached for the hiking boots he'd stashed in the corner of the tent. Roughly shoving his feet in, he unzipped the tent and pushed both feet outside. The brisk air hit me, bringing me back to my senses.

"I'm going to check on Jayne, make sure the Tylenol is working to keep her fever down."

"Good idea."

He zipped the tent closed, and I exhaled the remaining air from my lungs. My fingers went to my lips, tracing them and recalling the feel of Clay's mouth over mine.

When Clay returned a while later, I'd rearranged our sleeping bags head to foot and was slithered down in mine, my back to the wall of the tent. Plenty of room between us. No chance of accidentally touching him.

"All okay?" I asked.

"She's good. Try to get some sleep," he said, shucking off his boots once more and zipping the tent shut.

"Will do. G'night, Clay."

"Sleep tight, Ally." Clay shoved his feet into his sleeping bag and zipped himself in. Then he settled in and stopped moving. After a while, his breathing evened out and I imagined he'd fallen asleep. I spent another good hour reveling in the proximity of him, even if I knew nothing could happen between us on this trip. Just the feel of him kept me awake, delighting in how it felt to kiss him. Until I dissolved into dreams of the same thing.

TWENTY

CLAY

When I woke up in the morning, Ally had migrated toward the middle of the tent. I found her sleeping half on the foot of my sleeping bag and tried not to wake her as I extracted my feet and quietly unzipped the tent. I heard only silence in the direction of the students' tents and I was tempted to wake Ally so she could experience one of my favorite parts of camping—the cool morning mist on your face and the first deep breath of still mountain air.

But watching her sleep peacefully, her blond wavy hair splayed everywhere, with the peaceful, syrupy smile of someone who was drunk with a good night's sleep, I couldn't bear to tear her out of it. Instead, I allowed myself to gaze at her for a couple minutes, marveling at how good it had felt to kiss her. Finally. The way I'd dreamed about for half my life.

Then I sorted through my bag, quietly pulled out a fresh set of clothes, and left the tent to get dressed before I got any new ideas about kissing her again.

I walked down to the creek and carried a few liters of water back to boil for hot chocolate once the kids woke up. Then I gathered more wood for a campfire.

In the past, it always seemed like there were loads of morning chores to do and never enough time to do them, but this morning, I ran out of ideas once I'd set up our cooking equipment and walked the perimeter of the campsite to make sure there was no evidence of animals disturbing anything during the night.

With the kids still asleep, I had time to leisurely set up breakfast and enjoy the slow morning pace. It was what I loved most about camping—the sunrise hour felt clean and unhurried with the twists and turns of the day still to be determined.

I loved the sense of possibility. After one kiss, I loved it even more.

It might end up biting me in the ass, but I didn't care.

When I caught sight of Ally, I walked over to the large flat rock where she stood at the lookout above the valley. I put my hands on her shoulders briefly before dropping them by my sides.

"G'morning." My voice sounded like sandpaper working over dry wood.

She turned around with a shy smile that cracked open when she saw me. It was almost enough to ignite the desire I felt to throw her over my shoulder and find a hidden spot in the woods where I could see where that one kiss would lead.

Almost. But, no. Not here. Not now.

"Hi," she said softly. "How'd you sleep?"

"Great." It wasn't a lie. I always slept better on the ground, but waking up in a tent next to Ally Dalbotten was a whole other sensation. One I planned on replaying all day while I stole glances at the woman who'd be just out of reach for the next two days. "You?"

"Pretty well, once I got settled. You were out cold, greyhound. The mountains speak to you, I can tell." She pressed her lips closed as though debating whether to admit something. Nodding her head, she whispered like it was a dirty secret, "They speak to me too."

"I'm glad." Now it was my turn to smile. "The wilderness looks good on you, Alexandra Dalbotten." I allowed my gaze to rest on her longer than I normally did, finally taking all of her in—her easy smile, the golden halo of waves that fell around her face, her wide blue eyes that made it hard to view the sky the same way again.

A part of me felt nervous about letting myself think of her as someone I could be with. She still didn't understand the parts of me I hadn't let her see, and I wanted to show her, despite the potential consequences.

Just stay in the present. Stop worrying about the future.

It was a radical thought. It felt so easy to be with her that all my fears and what-ifs about the future washed away, leaving me squarely in the present. For the first time, I understood what my therapist meant when she encouraged me to live in the present.

Before now, her words had sounded like . . . well, words. They seemed like platitudes that people in her field are obligated to say to people who sign up for therapy.

Live in the now.

It didn't seem sustainable. After all, we need to rely on knowledge of the past and anticipation of the future to help us make wise decisions. But God, it felt good to forget all of that during each stolen moment with Ally.

Once the kids started rustling about, we went our separate ways, Ally heading over to retrieve the food from where we'd hung it and me divvying up pots and pans to boil water and start cooking breakfast.

From there, we took the kids on a day hike, with me in the lead and Ally bringing up the rear. The park ranger would be at the campsite all day to check on Jayne, who said she was feeling slightly better after a good night's sleep. She was still running a fever, and I felt grateful to have the extra help on the trip.

From time to time, when I was at the top of a rise, I caught bits of Ally's conversations with the hikers who brought up the rear. "I like the back of the pack. No pressure to hike fast," she said. It made me smile after the pace she'd kept leading us up the mountain. But that was her way, always making other people feel better by empathizing.

Every so often I'd glance back and catch a glimpse of her, hair tied back uselessly, strands breaking free of the hairband at every opportunity. She'd swat the strands away like irritating gnats and smile while never breaking stride or stopping her story.

Finally, I stopped the group at a wide lookout point. It was the entire reason for the hike, an earned view of the mountains to the north, a wide expanse of sky, and a deep crevasse below. The park service had installed some railing along the edge, and every student felt the need to push the boundaries by leaning out over it and looking down, where a vast chasm extended so far beneath us, the bottom was invisible.

A waterfall slipped between boulders about halfway down the cliff, crashing down on the rocks and sending a spray upward to where we stood.

The trail continued farther, winding through the trees and eventually dropping down into the valley, but this was our stopping point for today.

There was space for the students to spread out, finding nooks on rocks or fallen logs where they could sit and write in their journals. There was a collective groan when I pulled the stack of black-and-white composition books from my pack and started handing them out. "Oh, come on, this is an English class retreat. You didn't think I'd bring you to the woods and not have you reflect on Henry David Thoreau, did you?"

More groans preceded some grudging acknowledgement that my assignment did, in fact make sense. As the students took their books and roamed around looking for writing spots, I stole a glance in Ally's direction. She stood focused on the view.

"You want to do some journaling? I brought extra books," I said, coming beside her, but leaving about ten feet between us. She turned and smiled.

"Nah, I'm good. Taking mental notes."

"Works for me." I lingered longer than I needed now that she'd answered my question. Her gaze drifted back to the view, and I turned to go.

"Thank you for this," she said quietly. I had to take a few steps closer to hear her well, and I wanted to hear this.

"This?" I pointed at the view. "I'd love to take credit, but I didn't create any of it."

She nodded, still staring out over the steep drop and the waterfall beneath us. "Not what I meant. I appreciate you giving me a new appreciation for the wilderness and getting me over some of my fears."

Her chest expanded as she inhaled a cleansing breath, the kind you use to fortify your nerves. I waited, letting her gather her thoughts, which she did by pacing in a circle and finally settling her gaze back on the view over the valley. "Contributing to my self-sufficient life."

A rustle behind us made both of us flinch. We turned as a ground squirrel ran in front of us with a small acorn or tree nut in its mouth, and we watched it until it scurried under a bush and disappeared from sight.

"I'm glad you feel more confident, but didn't we talk about this? Don't give up on the fantasy of the knight if that's what you want, Ally."

A quiet hum of voices came from the direction of the students. They were finishing up their journaling and ready for an activity. But I really wanted to hear her answer.

"Yeah. I do want it . . . I just don't know if it's out there for me. That's why I'm grateful to be able to take care of myself if I'm ever left behind in the woods."

She extended her hands to our surroundings as though these were the very sort of woods where she might be left alone.

"Who would leave you behind in the woods?"

"I don't know. People."

"Not the sort of people you should be hiking with, if that's what they're about."

Her lips quirked to the side in amusement but the seriousness in her eyes told a different story. "I mean, sure, I'd like to have someone in my life who *wants* to do the dishes and fix the leaky sink without me asking. But I don't *need* anyone to do those things for me. I don't need to worry about being left behind, in the woods, naked and afraid, possibly injured. I'll be skilled enough to fend for myself."

She was serious. In making her feel more confident, was I also pushing her away? If I was honest with myself, I didn't want her to be so empowered that she didn't need me. I just didn't know how to tell her.

"I would never leave you behind in the woods."

"That's nice of you, Clay, but—"

"No, you're not understanding. That future you're imagining where you're alone and left to your own skills and devices to solve every problem, I'm just saying, you're not alone. You have tons of friends, family—people are here for you. *I'm* here for you."

What I wanted to say was that I would always be there for her. I'd be that knight she fantasized about riding up on a stallion and catering to her every whim. And I'd relish the job. But what if it wasn't mine to have?

What if I opened myself up to the possibility of being with Ally and it didn't work out? Would my mental health spiral out of control? Could I handle it? Could I take that risk?

Until I knew the answer, I couldn't say the words.

But it felt liberating to be thinking them.

TWENTY-ONE

CLAY

We couldn't have asked for better weather on our second day. The high clouds slid back and forth in front of the sun, so no one was baking in the heat, and the white puffy shapes made for beautiful reflections in the lake.

I watched Ally poke the ground on the far side of a log before stepping over it, explaining the logic to three students who were hiking with her. Quick study. It made me proud as a teacher, sure, but my smile when I watched her all day long was for other reasons. Reasons I hoped to repeat tonight, which couldn't come fast enough for my damn taste.

"Do we really have to do the trust exercise?" Cassius grumbled after lunch when we assembled the students around the campfire area, where enough felled trees and large rocks gave everyone a place to sit.

If it were left to me, I'd cut out all of the activities the school district listed for me. Bonding was hardly a concern this late in the school year, and most of the exercises were designed for new students to get to know each other. Made sense if the retreat fell at the beginning of a school year, but in the spring, most of it felt like nonsense.

"I hear you, Cash, but this stuff is mandated by the district, so we have to do it," I replied.

"I don't want some dude catching me like a fainting princess or some shit." Cassius looked at the other guys in an attempt at solidarity. There were some general mumbles of agreement.

"Language, Cash," Ally reprimanded for the fifteenth time on this trip.

"Sorry."

"I can make him do it," Ally whispered to me. It was the closest she'd been all day, given that we were spread far apart during the hike. The small stolen glances would have to do for now.

"Hey, Cash, come here. You too, Miles." Ally beckoned them with her index finger, pointing to a spot in front of her.

They looked at each other, shrugged, and sauntered over while the other students watched. The breeze made its way through the overhead branches and rippled the leaves on the white oak trees.

Ally inhaled a fortifying breath and turned back to the two rabble-rousers in our group. "Cash, if you were on the football field during an important play, you wouldn't drop the ball, right?"

"'Course not." He crossed his arms, seeming unsure where she was headed with this, but I already knew. She was brilliant with these kids, knew just how to handle their insecurities and attitudes.

Turning to Miles, she asked, "And if you were making a key tackle, you wouldn't feel weird about touching a guy, correct?"

Both of their expressions shifted at the same time as they figured out her angle. "Fine," Cash muttered.

"We'll do the trust thing," Miles agreed.

Ally had them go first, clearly knowing that if she put them in key positions as "leaders," they'd eat it up. Inside of an hour, we had every kid falling backward into the arms of a fellow student. Trust achieved. Sharing a tent with Ally an hour nearer. Level unlocked.

All in all, it was one of my more successful senior retreats. Other than Jayne's flu, we'd had no mishaps and I could tell the students were eating up the lessons learned in the wilderness. But man, if ever a person wanted to slow down the pace of time to a syrupy crawl, this was it—standing ten yards away from the woman I'd been dreaming about for half my life was making my body burn with need.

"How's it going?" Ally delivered three students to where I was getting ready to build tonight's campfire. "We have some willing fire builders."

Our eyes only connected for seconds before one of the girls took over the conversation. "I saw an area at the end of our hike with big chunks of fire-wood. If we use those, we won't have to collect as many logs."

"I told her it might take longer to get the bigger pieces to ignite, but you're the fire whisperer," Ally said, moving off before she'd finished her sentence and causing a dull ache to lodge in my chest. "So you should take it from here."

"So can we? Use the bigger logs?" the girl asked.

I tore my gaze away from Ally's retreating form as I drew my attention back to the students. "Sure, let's give it a go. I have a trick with kindling that will help."

When I looked up again, Ally was over by the tents in the distance. I let my gaze linger on her for an extra moment before exhaling my surrender and bending down to collect more kindling.

Every time we got close enough to each other for me to graze her hand with my palm, there would be some new issue that needed our attention. It would have been comical if it wasn't killing me slowly.

A couple hours later, after cooking dinner over a healthy-sized campfire, I looked around and saw that all the students were occupied making s'mores, so I sidled up to where Ally was stacking the clean camp dishes.

"I just want a moment alone with you. Is it me, or does it seem like the sun isn't setting until midnight tonight?" I asked quietly, eyes on the students to make absolutely sure they weren't looking. No one was paying any attention to us.

She laughed. That gorgeous uninhibited laugh that I could listen to for days. "We're just talking. We're allowed to talk without anyone thinking it's weird." All the same, her eyes scanned the students too.

With barely any motion, I reached for her hand, entangling our fingers. Just that small bit of contact would get me through the next few hours.

At the same time, we noticed Miles had lit a stick on fire and was holding it up like a torch. We both sprang to our feet. "Hey, not okay," I said, Ally on my heels.

We spent the next twenty minutes lecturing everyone about fire safety. The feel of her hand in mine lost to our chaperoning duties. But every time I snuck a look in her direction, she seemed to sense it, glancing back my way if for only a moment.

"Okay, kids, time to wrap it up," I said at ten on the dot. They'd spent an hour longer than I'd planned competing in a group sing down of songs that had to have the word *black* in the title. Then it switched to *fire*. They'd have gone on and on if I hadn't forced them to go to the tents. And even that took an extra hour by the time everyone got their teeth brushed, and I still heard them squealing over pranks and talking over each other.

And just when I thought I could finally have a moment alone with Ally, she dashed over to check on Jayne. "My turn with her tonight. See you soon, roomie." Then, she looked back at me and winked.

Who knew a wink was something I'd feel in my soul?

CHAPTER
TWENTY-TWO

ALLY

By the time the kids were all in their tents on that second night, I fully understood the beauty of sleeping outside. I was so exhausted that I'd have happily slept on a pile of rocks.

"It's only nine," I told Clay when I backed into our tent so my feet stayed outside while I unlaced my hiking boots and took them off. "Nine, and I'm ready for bed. I feel like it's one in the morning."

Lying on top of his blue sleeping bag with his ankles crossed, he chuckled. "Hiking wear you out?"

"No, the kids, the hiking, the constant fear of bugs and wilderness . . . that's what wore me out. But I'm excited that I can go to sleep at nine."

"I'm excited for you. How's Jayne doing?" Tonight, I spent some one-on-one time with her while Clay entertained the kids by the campfire. She'd brought a small drumming pad and drumsticks in her pack, and she demonstrated how she practices at home without making much noise.

"Feeling much better. I think she'll be back to her old self just in time for pickup tomorrow." I stuck my feet into my sleeping bag and wiggled my toes in my socks. "I guess this is the point of camping—to get so worn out that sleeping on the ground feels amazing."

Our head-to-feet arrangement didn't feel nearly so awkward tonight, and as we both hunkered deep into our respective sleeping bags, there was enough moonlight for us to see each other in a silvery glow. "I wish you could see how beautiful you look," Clay said, raising himself onto his elbows to look more squarely at me, and making my view of him that much better.

"Something pretty about moonlight. It's working for you too, greyhound," I admitted.

Lying back down, he reached for my hand, which I had draped outside my sleeping bag. Intertwining our fingers felt like a victory. Somehow so much more intimate in the quiet of the tent, now that we were alone. My skin buzzed at all the places his fingers touched mine, as his thumb softly rubbed circles over the back of my hand.

Lying here with him, I felt a sense of calm contentment that I'd never experienced before with a man. I didn't hear my usual warning voices telling me that guys like Clay were only bound to break my heart. This man—the Clay I'd gotten to know over the past couple of weeks—seemed like the kind who had my back. That's what he'd been telling me, and I was starting to believe it. "This is nice." My voice sounded as sleepy and contented as I felt.

Clay sat all the way up and brought my hand to his lips, kissing each knuckle. The feel of his breath over my skin sent a ripple of warmth through me and I sighed quietly.

"C'mere," he said, pulling me up to sitting. "One kiss. Just to tide me over, yeah?"

I nodded, my movements slowed by the desire to stretch this moment to infinity. Clay slowly pulled me closer until our clasped hands were sandwiched between us. When his lips swept across mine, I breathed him in and my eyes drifted shut.

His mouth covered mine more fully and our lips melded. Discovering, tasting, hinting at more. Then Clay pulled away and brushed his nose against mine before leaning back to look at me. I drank in the strong line of his jaw, the warmth in his hazel eyes, the stubble on his face that I ached to have in my hands.

Hands still joined, we each lay back down on our sleeping bags and I heard a deep sigh rumble from Clay's chest. It mirrored how I felt. And how I felt surprised me.

In all the years I'd observed Clay from afar, I'd done so with the idea of him being off-limits. My brother's best friend. A guy who couldn't commit. The very sort who my mother warned me against. And yet, this wasn't the Clay I'd gotten to know.

Maybe I didn't need the fantasy I'd always imagined. Maybe I could allow myself to enjoy something—even just a kiss—without worrying about commitment or labels or the fact that Clay didn't do relationships. And about that . . .

"Clay, I just need to ask . . . what's your deal? Why do you not do relationships? Is it just that it's annoying to be fixed up all the time? Or do you like to keep your options open? Or are you a loner or a commitment-phobe or a—"

"No. It's none of those things," he interrupted, squeezing my hand.

"Then what?"

"Alexandra, it's pretty simple. The only woman I've wanted is you."

Maybe in my wildest romantic fantasy sequences, someone like Clay would say something like that to me. But not in real life. "Wh-what?"

"You heard me."

And I had no idea what to do with that information. "Since when? Since our camping trip in your yard?"

"Since forever."

I raised my head to get a better view of Clay and found him staring up at the tent. The moonlight cast shadows on his face, but I could still see the furrow in his brow. "Clay . . . *what?*"

"It's been years, Ally. I wanted to stop thinking about you. I tried to stop. But I . . . can't." His voice cracked on the last word, and I heard it strain. It sounded feral, a tight guitar string on the verge of snapping. "And I don't want to try anymore."

"I thought . . ." I couldn't articulate what I thought without spilling a lifetime of insecurities, and right now, I didn't want Clay to know that side of me.

"I know. I've never been clear with my intentions toward you."

"Your intentions . . ." He was speaking like one of the heroes from my historical romance novels, and instead of suitably swooning, I was repeating his words and looking at him with round, blank eyes.

"Yes. My intentions."

"Which are . . . ?"

"Everything. All of it."

"We've worked together all these years. How come you never even . . . asked me out?" It seemed like the very most basic concept.

He continued staring upward and let out a long exhale. "It's kind of a long story."

I barked out an incredulous laugh. "We're in a tent with nothing else to do. Seems like a good time for that."

He was nodding, but when I could see that he wasn't ready to look at me, I dropped my head back down and stared up as well. When he began speaking, his voice was so steady and soft, I almost mistook it for a faint gust of wind.

"I told you I'd been diagnosed with depression. What I didn't tell you was that it came on the heels of a bad breakup. I'd been dating a woman who'd moved here from Colorado. This was years ago."

I thought back and tried to figure out a timeline. I'd all but lost track of Clay when I was in college, and until we'd started teaching together, I didn't know what he had done.

"We dated for a year and a half," he went on. "I fell hard and fast. It was my first serious, long-term relationship, and it happened right as I was starting to feel heavy signs of clinical depression, but I didn't know how to recognize that's what it was at the time. I needed her for my endorphin rush. She was the only thing keeping me happy, so I decided I wanted to marry her."

Jealousy had no place here, but I couldn't help the ugly twinge in my chest. It shouldn't have pierced my heart to hear him describe his feelings for someone else right after he'd just finished telling me that he's wanted me for all these years. But it did.

"It sounds a little ridiculous saying it now, but I didn't understand what was happening with my mental health. I just knew she became the lifeline that made me feel better, and I thought she was the key to being happy."

"It doesn't sound ridiculous," I said, feeling my heart squeeze at the kind of pain he must have felt.

"Anyway, long story short . . . she was separated from her husband when we met and she kind of abruptly decided to move back to Colorado and try again with him. I didn't see it coming. And I . . . spiraled. Like, it was bad. Your brother knows. He's the only one."

"How bad?" I wanted to understand, needed to know.

"I called Jeff, told him I was sitting with a bottle of pills. He came right away. We tossed them in the toilet, made some calls to psychiatrists. It took work, but he got me straightened out. I owe him . . . everything. And as to why I don't do relationships, I guess I was always afraid of it happening again—all of it."

I sat up and scooted across the floor of the tent in my sleeping bag until I could wrap my arms around Clay. He sat limply for a moment, letting me hug him, before finally encircling me with his arms.

We sat like that for a long time, not talking. It felt good to return all the warmth Clay had shown toward me, even if I wasn't sure it was enough.

"How do you feel now? Do you feel afraid with me?" I asked, finally. Clay loosened his grip and backed away enough to look at me. His eyes were dark, deep thoughtful pools that swallowed me in their intensity.

"No. With you, I feel really good."

I leaned forward and kissed Clay's cheek, trailing my lips down to his and placing a soft kiss there. I moved back to my spot, head next to Clay's feet, and closed my eyes.

"That's why . . . ," I said, slowly realizing, "my brother told me not to mess with your head."

"He did? When?"

"The other night at Genie's. I had no idea what he was talking about, and it was Jefferson—he sometimes makes a big deal out of things that aren't big."

"This one's big."

"Yeah. But it's not insurmountable."

"No, not insurmountable. At least I hope not." He squeezed my hand.

I sat up and brought it to my heart. If he could trust me with this, I wouldn't betray him. Even if we weren't right for each other, I wouldn't let him fall. "Okay, then," I told him. "Let's start with that. Let's start with hope."

CHAPTER
TWENTY-THREE

ALLY

I slept like a felled tree and woke up to cries of "No way!" and "You messed up, dude!"

The sun was already shining brightly through the gauzy nylon of the tent, but that only meant it was after six in the morning. Other than that, I had no idea what time it was. Telling time by the sun's position would have to fall into next year's camping tutorial.

Looking next to me, I saw that Clay was already up and out of the tent—no surprise that he'd heard the call of the wilderness. He probably had already prepared breakfast for everyone. But the continued shouts of various students in the distance had me curious, and if they were awake, I really needed to put my boots on and join them.

A few minutes later, with my hair piled into a typhoon of a ponytail and a flannel shirt buttoned up beneath my puffer coat, I strode over in the direction of the voices. Under the tall pines, I found Cassius and Miles standing with Clay and the park ranger among the trees where we'd practiced hanging food the day before yesterday.

Since the bear hang had only been an exercise, we'd taken all the food down and stowed it in the bear boxes. All but one bag, apparently.

And it looked like a bear had found it overnight.

The nylon sack itself was in shreds, easily torn in two with a bear's claw. The food that had been inside—a loaf of bread, a bag of trail mix, and several packages of hot chocolate mix—was now mostly an assortment of torn wrappers on the ground.

"Ms. Dalbotten!" Cassius yelled when he saw me and dashed over. "Check it out."

I walked carefully in the direction of all the chaos, where a couple more students who'd heard the yelling now joined. Chatter erupted anew as Miles and Cassius filled them in on the bear visit last night.

I caught Clay's eye and cocked my head. "No bears, huh?"

"I just promised you wouldn't be visited personally. I didn't say black bears don't exist out here."

The ranger chimed in with all kinds of statistics about bear sightings in the surrounding area, all information I was glad I didn't know about before the trip. "But no one's been attacked, in part thanks to the bear boxes. This here, though"—he pointed up at the paltry-looking rope dangling from a branch right next to the trunk of the tree—"that's just bear bait, hanging so close to the trunk. A bear has no problem climbing up there to get it."

"Clearly," I said, surveying the damage again. Clay was still eyeing me quietly, probably waiting for me to freak out. I surprised us both by calmly nodding and concluding, "Guess we got lucky. Good lesson for the kids on how *not* to do a bear hang, right?"

"Exactly," the ranger agreed. "Not so good for the black bear because sourdough isn't exactly part of its diet, but I'm not chasing down a bear to say so."

The near bear sighting had all the students so fired up, they helped make breakfast and cleaned the campsite without needing much instruction from us. Within a few hours, we'd packed up and hiked down the trail to where the bus took us all back to campus.

The weather had cooperated all weekend long, but by late Sunday afternoon, the clouds rolled in as if to say, *We did our best to hold off as long as we could, but now we're coming.* The first drops of rain splattered on the blacktop in the parking lot as the kids hugged each other goodbye and we loaded them into their respective parents' cars.

And then . . . it was just Clay and I in the parking lot standing next to Clay's blue truck.

He took my hand and led me around to the passenger side, popping the automatic lock. Then he opened the door, swept me up into his arms, and deposited me on the seat, just like he'd done that day I'd splatted on the track.

Clay and I drove back to his house in silence, but the rush of blood in my ears with each beat of my heart would have drowned out a conversation anyway. Clay kept my hand grasped in his own, every so often raising it to his lips. I nearly swooned every time he did it, my heart so full of feelings for him.

When we pulled into his driveway, I had an idea. "Clay, do you still have the tents pulled out from when we camped in your yard?"

"Yeah, they're in my shed. Why?"

"Can we sleep in them tonight?"

He started to laugh, swinging open his door and coming around to my side of the truck. "Are you serious?"

I shrugged. "I like the close quarters." He took my hand and helped me down from the truck, ever gentlemanly.

"Don't you worry, Alexandra. I'm keeping you close for the rest of the night." He kissed my temple and left a lingering kiss on my cheek. "I love your new appreciation for camping, but we're sleeping in the house. On sheets. In a bed."

I grinned. "I like the sound of all of that too."

The last time I'd been here, we'd barely spent any time inside the house, other than as a passthrough to the yard. Tonight, Clay gave me a tour of the downstairs, pointing out the living room and den and guest bathroom, all of which were decorated with modern furnishings and masculine grays and blues. Pulling us into the kitchen, Clay rummaged through the refrigerator.

"Chicken burrito? Will that work?" He held up two packaged burritos with the guilty smile of a kid who's about to eat a box of sugary cereal.

I nodded, and Clay popped them into the microwave.

Leaning against the marble counter, I watched him set the timer, liking the domesticity of the moment. After misunderstanding him from afar for all these years, I loved seeing him with new eyes, performing simple tasks.

Turning back toward me, he smiled and lifted me onto the kitchen counter. Stepping between my legs, he was the perfect height to kiss me. He leaned in, cupping my cheeks in his hands, and his lips found mine. Soft, tender, unhurried.

I wrapped my arms around his neck and surrendered to a kiss that felt like it lasted for hours. Only the ding of the microwave gave me a sense of time.

Clay poured some salsa into a dish, and we ate side by side on barstools at the counter. He held his burrito in one hand and let the other rest on the back of my neck, where he gently rubbed out the muscles that were sore from carrying my pack.

When we'd finished eating, he walked me upstairs, never taking his hands off of me, never leaving more than a few inches of space between us. It was like an invisible barrier had snapped, and now we were two magnets unendingly pulled toward each other.

Wordlessly, he opened a cupboard in the hallway and handed me a fluffy white towel. "Three days in the wilderness. You earned yourself a hot shower." He pointed me in the direction of a guest bathroom with a white-tiled shower, and came back a moment later with a pair of sweatpants and a tee. After a minute, I heard the water turn on in another bathroom.

I loved that he knew me well enough to understand that I'd endured bugs and dirt without complaint, but now I wanted a shower more than anything else. I loved that he'd given me a change of clothes without my having to ask. I loved so many things about him, and that made me a little nervous because of all my mother's warnings.

And then I reminded myself that I was not my mother. And not all of her warnings applied to me.

The hot water felt amazing, but I showered quickly, noticing a soap dish shaped like a duck and a neat display of river rocks in a bowl on the blue-tiled counter. Checking my reflection in the mirror, I wound my wet hair into a bun and put on Clay's oversized clothes.

When I padded down the hall toward his room, I could hear the soft notes of blues playing, and I could smell the heady scent that was all Clay.

I hovered in the doorway and took a moment to gaze at Clay in his bare-chested splendor, as he stood shuffling through music on his phone in the dim evening light through the window. Hair wet and slicked back. Abs still damp above a navy pair of boxer briefs that hugged sculpted thighs. The blues track changed to a quiet instrumental and Clay seemed satisfied.

"Hey there, greyhound," I said as Clay looked over at me lingering just outside the room.

"Hi, gorgeous." In two strides, he reached me, extending his hand and pulling me toward him. Walking backward, he led me to his bed, covered in a large white comforter with big square pillows rimmed in blue stitching. In a quick motion, he swept me up and placed me in the center of the bed.

Almost like he knew where my mind had wandered, Clay took both of my hands in his and held them between us while his mouth claimed mine in a searing kiss.

Our bodies folded into each other, his hard muscles finding my soft places. Everything fit, and Clay released my hands, freeing them to roam over his sculpted pecs and along his strong shoulders.

My heart fluttered in my chest like a panicky hummingbird. My breathing came out in uneven exhales, even as I tried to steady it.

How could I feel so much and crave this man so much when he'd barely touched me. The mere proximity of him had me feeling more alive than I'd ever felt. Every nerve flared on high alert. Every tremble across my skin raced through my body, ending in a hot bundle of nerves at my core.

"Ally . . ." He closed his eyes on a long blink that made me wonder if I was trying his patience. When his lids lifted, there was a fiery determination in his eyes that hadn't been there moments earlier. "Always. I've always wanted you like this."

I swallowed hard, a nervous tiny voice telling me there was still time to back out.

I didn't want to back out.

I nodded.

Clay leaned closer, and for a moment, time hung there in the space between us, gobbled up by the infinite possibilities of what could happen next. "There's something magical about the pause, isn't there?" His quiet voice danced across my lips. "The holding of breath, the knowing, and anticipating, and waiting just another moment before . . ." He lingered there, and I felt his breath against my lips, a quiet caress that was almost enough to throw every nerve ending into overdrive. Almost.

The proximity of him was making me dizzy. All sexy stubble and angular cheekbones. Pine scent mixed with soap. The faintest hint of mint from his toothpaste. My eyes drifted shut and I leaned closer. Millimeters separated us, and all of my other senses came alive when I stopped fighting them.

Clay's hand cupped my chin, sending chills down my spine and making me lean into his touch as he slid his hand along my skin and into my hair. He grasped the back of my head and turned my face slightly, leaning back to look at me. Like he was giving us one last chance to change our minds.

I nodded, eyes locked on his.

I saw the moment his resolve shredded. A tiny crack in his controlled façade. A softening of his jaw and a darkness in his eyes that hardened with decision. Then he angled my face to the side, his hand twisting into my hair as he drew me closer.

It was a different brush of his lips, a hint of something deeper that leveled my senses with such force that I gasped. But there was no time to feel self-conscious about the sound because he wasn't stopping, kissing me like I was a salve to his aching body, not just hinting but insisting. I kissed him back with equal fervor, overwhelmed by a hunger I couldn't explain because it was so unfamiliar.

I just wanted him. I wanted his hands touching me in more places, his lips on me everywhere.

When his tongue swept inside my mouth, I moaned a little and grasped his shoulders again for purchase, digging my fingers into the sculpted muscles. They were every bit as rock hard and broad as they looked, and feeling them beneath my hands, I felt a little faint.

Then there was no end of me or beginning of him. We were locked into a steamy, languid kiss that went on and on.

When Clay pulled back again to look at me, I saw his eyes had heated to a deep molten color that made no mistake about what he wanted.

"Yes," I breathed. Yes to everything. I wanted him more than I'd ever craved anything or anyone in my life.

Rolling me onto my back, Clay moved over me, holding himself up on his forearms on either side of my head. The tender way he looked at me made me feel cherished. The feral gleam in his eyes left no doubt about what he wanted to do with me.

Then the weight of his body bore down on me, his hard length pressing exactly where I needed him. I moved beneath him, needing friction, but he lifted away, teasing me with tinier kisses and withholding what I wanted until I moaned in protest.

Pecs that looked carved from marble, abs that rippled, and a deep V that led exactly where I wanted my hands to go.

I took one more opportunity to let my eyes roam his chest and double-check that he was real. That I was here with him.

"Holy shit," I mumbled appreciatively. His lips tipped up into a smile, and he bent to nip at my neck.

One hand trailed along my shoulder and drifted across my collarbone. Chills erupted over my skin as he bent to kiss the dip at my throat. Trailing kisses lower, he tugged at the collar of my shirt with his teeth before his hand drifted beneath it, gently stroking the skin along my waist.

I was all ready for him to rid me of the shirt when he stopped, his gaze roaming over my face, my chest, his eyes locking on mine. The look of utter reverence startled me.

"What?" I gasped, half expecting him to tell me this was a terrible idea. It was, but I didn't care.

"I don't trust myself. If I have a tiny bit of you, I won't be able to let you go."

"Then don't." I was too amped up to stop this now, and he needed to stop wrestling with his fear about seeing me back at work or whatever was concerning him about this fling.

His eyes heated and he nodded. "Deal."

His hands lifted off the giant tee, baring me to him. I heard him suck in a breath as his eyes traveled over my curves. Then his lips returned to mine with more fervor. He nipped at my bottom lip and soothed it with his tongue. I heard myself whimper, and I'd never been a whimperer.

We'd had two nights of holding ourselves back, and the result was this— hunger, haste, curiosity, abandon.

It was like we'd flipped a switch. There was no more hesitation, no thinking. Clay kissed my breasts, taking one in his mouth and sucking hard. His hands trailed lower, tickling the skin of my abdomen as he went.

Clay slid down the sweatpants, ridding me of them, and moved down my body, laying kisses in a trail across my hip.

His hands trailed up the inside of my thigh and my eyes drifted shut as his hands parted my legs. He nipped at the sensitive skin at the apex of my thighs and soothed it with his tongue. These were moves I'd only read about, imagining someone would want me enough to have me like this but never being able to form a solid picture in my mind of who that someone would be.

Now it felt clear that Clay was the only possible someone in that picture, and this was the only fantasy I wanted.

His tongue lapped straight up my center and I gasped, my hands tangling in his hair. His hands teased my inner thighs while his mouth took me to a place I'd never been.

I felt my orgasm build—hell, it had been building since the day Clay administered first aid to me on campus—and Clay's deft tongue had no mercy. He sucked hard on the sensitive bundle of nerves and my senses exploded in fireworks, earthquakes, rolling thunder. The natural world had nothing on this man and he took me to places I'd never imagined existed. Places I never wanted to leave.

"God, Clay . . . ," I moaned.

As he moved back up my body, I felt light-headed and slightly crazed. My lips fell to his neck, which hit me with the manly scent of pine.

Reaching inside his boxer briefs, I wrapped my hand around his hard cock and felt all logic and rationality leave my brain. As I stroked the length of him, I heard him suck in a breath. "Ally," he growled. "Fuck."

His curse fueled me. "I want you inside me," I breathed against his neck.

"Ah . . ." Then he froze and pulled back to look at me. "I . . . wasn't exactly planning this. I don't think I have any condoms."

I was baffled. This was Clay, notorious bachelor. Didn't he carry a roll of them in his wallet at all times?

"You—you don't?"

A quiet laugh escaped his lips. "No, Alexandra. I don't keep condoms here because I don't bring women back to my house."

"Oh. Well, I'm on the pill," I said, unhelpfully, because if anyone called for a condom, it was a notorious bachelor.

"Okay, well, I haven't been with anyone for over a year," he said, as though it made any sense at all.

"You haven't?" I didn't mean to sound so disbelieving. But come on. This was Clay Meadows.

"No. I haven't. Why does that surprise you so much?"

"Just . . . you're you."

"And?"

I had no interest in explaining when I had Clay Meadows, still clad in those damn boxer briefs, hard and here and so damn sexy. Ridding him of the last stitch of clothing, I felt emboldened. I gestured for him to roll onto his back and I straddled his legs.

Clay's hands slipped up my torso and he palmed both breasts as I ground against him, already feeling another orgasm starting to build.

I rolled my hand over the tip of his cock before edging it inside. Slowly. An inch at a time. Until he filled me.

When we started to move, it had none of the clumsy first-time feel to it I'd come to think of as normal. We were a symphony conducted by a maestro. Seamless, blissful harmony.

"Fuck, Ally," he bit out as I rode him. Watching his half-lidded eyes as he began to let go fueled me. I loved having this effect on him.

And then we were both falling, useless at anything, perfect at everything. Coming apart and melting into each other.

This was not the man I thought I knew. He was so much better, and that would make it so much harder to get over him when I eventually had to, but I didn't care. Right now, I'd give myself over and live out every fantasy with him. I could let myself have a little fun.

Or a lot. Hours of it, to be exact.

TWENTY-FOUR

ALLY

Three days after the retreat, the seniors were still buzzing about how much fun they'd had. And I was still buzzing from the night afterward that I'd spent with Clay. Given that it had been a Sunday, and we didn't sleep much, it was making for a very exhausting week. A week of stolen glances and lingering kisses when Clay picked me up and dropped me off each day, which he'd insisted on doing.

This morning, it was early, even earlier than the teachers arrived for sunrise classes. No students were anywhere. The sun was barely up. But I'd already been awake for hours, thinking about Clay.

"You want to . . . go on a date with me? Tonight?" I sputtered, trying to wrap my brain around what he'd just asked.

Clay's laugh sounded hollow. "No, Alexandra. I don't want to go on a date with you. I want to go on a year of dates with you. And I want to listen to your weirdo thoughts and stare at your face when you tell me stories about the students you saved. All of them. But mostly, I want to fast-forward to the end of the dates to where I get you alone and I can peel the meddlesome layers of clothing away and see all of you. Devour all of you. And I don't just mean with my eyes."

"Oh."

"Oh?"

"I just mean . . . you're known to date women only once or twice. Is this how you let me down easy, by taking me on a date?"

He looked more amused than disappointed, hand ruffling his hair, mouth quirking up into the unintentional smile I loved.

"Is that what you want, to be let down easy?"

"No." Did I answer too quickly?

"Okay, holding you to that."

"I just . . ." Unsure how to finish the sentence, I stopped with my mouth hanging open and stared at the way Clay's hazel eyes warmed when he watched me squirm. He was definitely amused.

"What?" he asked, gently tucking a few wild tendrils of hair behind my ears. "What are you worried about?"

I couldn't calm the butterflies in my stomach long enough to come to a conclusion on that. I just knew he made me nervous and excited and overwhelmed with feeling, and I didn't know what to do with all of that.

"So you want to go on a date with me. A first date. The first of one hundred?" I couldn't get the idea through my head. I'd prepared myself for an ending. And now . . . I was on new ground.

"You don't get it. It was never about dating lots of women. It was only ever about distracting myself because I didn't think I could be with you."

Well, that did it. I grabbed his face in my hands and pressed my lips to his. It didn't matter how many hours we'd spent doing this already. I was just getting started. He responded in kind, lifting me so I could wrap my legs around his waist.

Clay turned us and pressed me up against the door of his truck as I ground into him, finding the exact spot I needed to get the friction I craved. He kissed my cheek, running a row of tiny kisses along my jaw and nipping at it before pulling back to look at me.

"Do you get it now? The way I am with you is different than anything I've ever felt before. I don't know what to do with it. And I tried to stop feeling it. I tried so hard to stop thinking about you. Wanting you. But I can't fucking do it.

"Going on a date sounds far too polite for all the things I want to do with you. I want . . ." His eyes were wild and dark as he shoved a hand through his hair in an aggravated, frustrated gesture. "I want to fuck you until you can't sit down and make you come until you don't remember your name. Is that clear enough for you?"

I nodded. "It's clear. Let's go on a date."

———

Clay wined and dined me at the Italian restaurant in Knoxville where they really did "know what to do with pasta," before insisting we go dancing at Genie's. "Are you sure?" I asked. More than once.

Going on a date at Genie's was like announcing your relationship to the entire town, but apparently that was what Clay felt like doing.

"I'm damn proud to be with you and I don't care who knows it," he'd said when I suggested going someplace a little less popular.

Clay led me around the dance floor to an upbeat country song. "I haven't been able to get the image out of my head of you leaving this place five minutes after I had you in my arms," he said. "Tonight, when you leave, you're leaving with me."

My heart beat faster at his possessive tone. His large hand on my back made my insides warm and my heart flood. "So this is kind of a do-over date?"

He nodded. "If I'd have been able, I'd have danced every dance with you that night."

"Pindich would have probably fired you. He was glaring at you the whole time we danced."

"Yeah, he came up to me after you left and said some weird stuff about knowing why I was deeded the Bandit Lake house. Said he knew my grandmother back when he practiced law, made it like they were the best of friends. I asked what year he passed the bar, and that shut him up. I never understand what angle he's working."

"That's why I try to avoid him."

Clay brought me down for a dip and swept me back up and into his arms. His lips brushed over mine and I heard a few people around us hoot and holler. Something about being with Green Valley's most eligible bachelor was giving people a lot to look at.

"People are gonna talk," I teased. "Your reputation's on the line."

"Let 'em talk."

"Oh, they're gonna." The stern voice next to me could only belong to my brother. "Is this your way of telling me you two are an item?"

We slowed our dancing and I took in my brother, who looked downright entertained by the sight of us. "Do you just lurk at Genie's all the time?" I asked.

Jefferson shook his head and pointed at Clay. "This guy invited me to join him here. I thought we were having a drink. So I repeat: is this your way of telling me something?"

Clay's rueful smile said that it was absolutely his way of showing my brother what he had no ability to put into words. "I'm crazy about your sister, and I wanted you to see it and understand it. If I just said something over the phone or whatever, you'd come over and belt me, so I wanted you to see up close and personal that it's real."

Clay smiled confidently, but his nerves showed in the way he swallowed hard.

Jefferson mock-glared for a second before breaking into a grin. "Joke's on you, stress-nozzle. I saw the way you were looking at each other a week ago and could've told you your story myself. But now that you dragged me down here, you'd better buy me a drink."

That was the end of the dancing for a while, as my brother crashed our date. But after he finished his beer, Clay sent him moving along and led me back to the dance floor. He wrapped me in his arms and we swayed to a slow song, and I couldn't remember being happier.

Things were going well. Better than well. Maybe my mom had been wrong about romance, wrong about men. And wrong about me.

———

Secrets didn't stay secret for long in Green Valley, to say nothing of secrets at the high school. Within two days of our date, everyone knew.

On Tuesday, every chair in the teachers' lounge was taken when I arrived. Witty was eating something green that had the stench of day-old broccoli without looking nearly as healthy. As usual, I didn't ask.

As usual, the same mugs festered in the sink and the same individuals had made coffee with the Keurig machines, without removing the used pods.

As usual, no one sat on the green couch against the wall, even though it meant two teachers were teetering on one chair together, half-cheeking it and nearly toppling over each time one of them reached for a bite of lunch.

And as usual, Principal Pindich made a beeline toward where I stood by the coffee machine. "Pour me a cup, would you?" he asked, reaching over my head to retrieve a mug and missing my face by mere millimeters in the process. He gave me the creeps, but I took a step back and tried not to choke on the musky smell of his body spray.

As I filled Pindich's cup with coffee, I could hear Clay's voice in my head telling me not to drink "that swill."

I had no problem pouring it for our dear principal.

He leaned in again, uttering a whispered "Thanks," but before he backed away, Clay "accidentally" tripped and splashed cold brew all over Pindich. Shaking off the cold coffee and muttering something about a dry-cleaning bill, Pindich moved away to search for paper towels.

Thank you, I mouthed to Clay. My heart squeezed at his protective gesture.

As he moved past me, his chest grazed my shoulder, and he placed his hand on the small of my back. A tiny gesture, but it set off a firestorm in my veins.

Guiding me away from the coffee maker, Clay tipped his head toward the hallway. I felt Pindich's eyes on us as we left. The curiosity in them had turned into a glare.

Wordlessly, Clay moved us outside to the teachers' parking lot and drove us off campus for lunch. "I swear to God, Ally, if Pin Dick does anything even the least bit skeevy to you, I want to know about it. So help me, he'll barely live long enough to regret it."

One hand on the steering wheel, Clay drove, his fury evident in the crease in his brow and the set of his jaw. We pulled up to Daisy's.

Clay hopped out and came around to my side. He didn't extend his hand to help me out of the car like he usually did. Instead, he leaned in, bracketing my head with his forearms on the frame of the truck, and kissed me like it was his final dying request. Lips. Teeth. The scrape of his stubble. I felt it straight down to my core.

When he backed up an inch, I let out a shaky breath before inhaling the pine-and-soap scent of him. My eyes fluttered open.

"Hi." The sexy rasp of his voice was a balm to my senses.

"Hi."

His lips were on mine again and dizziness took over. It was an authoritative, claiming kiss, and as much as Pindich irritated me, I had to credit him with bringing out this protective side of Clay. I loved it.

The sound of approaching voices immediately put space between us, and Clay wrapped his hand around mine and pulled me out of the truck. Before we went into Daisy's, he grabbed my hand and brought it to his lips. "You free tonight?"

I nodded. *Tonight and every night,* I wanted to say. But I didn't.

I wasn't ready for Clay to know how smitten I was with him. I wasn't even sure if I could admit it to myself. Except that, yeah, I had to admit I had it bad for him.

And also . . . so good.

CHAPTER
TWENTY-FIVE

CLAY

A light bluegrass soundtrack snuck through the speakers I'd installed in my living room and the music followed us onto the deck that overlooked my yard.

I'd made an effort to come up with an activity for us this afternoon, so it wouldn't seem like all I wanted to do was kiss Ally and carry her to my bed. But when she showed up in a plaid flannel shirt, painted-on jeans, and hiking boots, all bets were off.

"C'mere," I said, leading her into the house. "We need to get you out of those clothes."

She looked down. "What do you mean? I thought this was the perfect outfit for a hike."

"It is. But I won't be able to think straight watching your tight little ass in those jeans if I don't have you first."

I didn't bother taking her upstairs to my bedroom, not when I had a perfectly good couch right here. "Ah, okay. Understood. Have your way with me, greyhound."

I loved how easy things were with her. We functioned like a singular being, and it both delighted and scared the shit out of me. The better things felt, the harder I fell for her. The harder I fell, the more I worried about what would happen if things ended.

I knew it was the wrong thing to be thinking about, but the worry never left the back of my mind.

Well, that's not entirely true. She did have the ability to make me forget everything, if only for a few hours. And those were the best hours of my day.

As my eyes roamed the milky skin of her naked body splayed on the couch beneath me, I stayed in the present. "You are so goddamn gorgeous, I'm about to lose my mind," I growled.

And then I slid inside her. Heaven found. Mind lost.

———

After I'd ravished her body, I reluctantly let Ally get dressed, but only because of how much I enjoyed seeing her in those jeans. Then I guided her outside to a trail behind my house, where I'd promised her a fun date.

"I'm not feeling the fun yet," she panted as we crested a hill.

"No?" I laughed, stopping so we could catch our breaths and enjoy the view. Bandit Lake lay below us and to our right was a lush green meadow. Our destination.

"It is pretty though."

"That it is," I said, enjoying my view of her. When she turned and caught me staring, she blushed. I loved that I could make her do that simply by telling her the truth.

The sun was high overhead, so I guided us to a shady spot in the meadow, where a winding trail cut through the greenery and led to a mossy flat area.

"Okay, here's where we take your survival skills up a notch," I said, kicking over a rotting log and revealing a colony of half the varieties of bugs that lived in the state of Tennessee.

Ally took a step back but observed the bugs, which crawled every which way, now that I'd moved their shelter. I rolled the log back with my foot, but a few escapees roamed on the moss around it.

"Um, what do you have in mind?" she asked, raising an eyebrow skeptically.

"I know how much you want to be self-sufficient, and I figured you might like to have some wilderness survival skills to go along with the first aid."

I didn't know what I was expecting. A laugh? An eye-roll? But the look on Ally's face was pure gratitude. "You want to help me be more self-sufficient?"

She brought a hand to her chest and cocked her head. Her eyes may have even been moist, but I couldn't really tell behind the sunglasses.

"I—"

She wrapped her arms so tightly around me I almost lost my breath. Then again, I felt breathless around her most of the time anyway.

Moving the log again, I set the bugs free and watched them splay out across the ground. I searched for the one I wanted and saw it on the desiccated log. "Here, this is a good one." Picking it up, I held the small brown insect out for Ally to inspect. Still standing a few feet away, Ally leaned slightly toward it but mostly observed it from afar.

"Why is that a good one?" she asked.

"Bark beetle. They're plentiful around here, and they have a lot of protein. So if you ever run out of food, these are a good option. What you want to do is bite the heads off and spit them out, then eat the crunchy body."

"I absolutely do *not* want to do that."

I handed her the bark beetle, which she accepted in her palm, observing it. I watched her watch the bug. Then I saw her make a decision. Closing her eyes, she brought the beetle to her mouth and hesitated, screwing up her face in disgust.

"Wait!" Her eyes popped open when I took the beetle out of her hand. "I didn't bring you here to eat bugs."

The look on her face was priceless. Part relieved, part murderous. "I almost ate that bug."

"I wouldn't have let you."

"You can't stop me. Here, hand it over." Was she serious? She nodded at me and held out her hand. I put the beetle back in her palm and watched her steel herself. "This is really safe to eat?" she asked.

"A hundred percent."

"Okay . . ." She brought the beetle to her lips, and I prepared myself to fall hopelessly in love with this woman who had been scared of the wilderness a few weeks ago and was now willing to eat a bug.

Ally opened her mouth, but instead of taking a bite, she placed the beetle back on its log and smiled. "Maybe next time."

Looking for a place to sit, she inspected the ground for evidence of bugs, critters, and rogue leaves.

"Hang on." I grabbed her hand to prevent her from lowering herself to the ground. Then I took out a blanket from my backpack and spread it out. "Here. Much better."

"Oh. So much better," she agreed.

Settling down next to her, I unzipped the inner pocket of my pack, where I'd stashed a bottle of wine, plastic glasses, and the makings of a charcuterie board.

"I'm absolutely taking your wilderness survival training seriously," I assured her, "and I plan to give you a full lesson while we sit here. But no eating bark beetles when wine and cheese is an option. Bugs are purely for an emergency situation."

We unpacked the food and poured the wine, and then I gave Ally a lesson on wilderness survival, using a pad of paper to jot down notes for her and draw makeshift representations of some bugs that make good protein sources in a pinch.

"And whatever you do," I cautioned, "no eating mushrooms on or off the trail. That's where you get into trouble."

"I think I knew that one."

We spent most of the day in the meadow talking about hikes we could take and short backpacking trips that would test her wilderness skills. I respected her desire to take care of herself, but the more time I spent with Ally, the more I wanted to take care of her.

"You know, being self-sufficient doesn't mean you have to go at it alone."

I was lying on my back with Ally's head resting on my stomach. She tilted her face to the side to look at me. "What do you mean?"

"Just that you can be strong and vulnerable at the same time."

She swallowed and blinked up at me. I watched her process this information. Finally, she nodded. "That's a good way of putting it. I guess I was taught that being vulnerable would lead to heartbreak."

"It won't with me," I said, intending to live up to that promise.

She smiled. "Gonna hold you to that, greyhound." She gave me a poke in the ribs, which left me no option but to tickle her until she cried uncle. Which led to me wrapping her in my arms and pulling her onto my lap.

"This is good. I like this," she said.

"I like it too." I loved it. And I fucking loved her. Which was why I briefly allowed myself to think about telling her everything about how despondent I felt sometimes and how messed up I felt on medication. Here I was, waxing poetic about Ally allowing herself to be vulnerable, but I needed to do the same. I could trust her—this I knew with certainty. Maybe I had to trust myself, trust that I would be enough for her, exactly like this. Exactly as I am.

Then, maybe . . . maybe it could work?

I was so lost in thought that I didn't realize Ally was asking about my other weekend plans until she waved a hand in front of my face. "Earth to greyhound?"

"I have a family dinner on Sunday," I replied, half distracted by the idea of seeing my parents, who required a whole different set of survival skills to be around. "Actually, would you like to come with me? It'll make the dinner much more pleasant, though you might be done with me afterward."

"I very much doubt that."

"Yeah, maybe they'll behave. There's always a chance."

It was crazy to invite her to a family dinner. My parents were half the reason I'd never felt comfortable with my depression diagnosis or the meds that kept me functional. Nothing good could come from her seeing the whole family dynamic in action.

And yet, a part of me wanted her to know that side of me. A large part. I'd never believed Alexandra Dalbotten and I had a future together, but every day I spent with her was making me want to believe.

"Will you come to dinner?" I asked.

She agreed readily, and for the first time, I found myself starting to believe.

TWENTY-SIX

ALLY

When Clay's brother, Shane, and his fiancée, Julia, walked into their parents' house, it was like Prince William and Kate had just arrived. Apparently, that made us Harry and Meghan.

"Look at what you brought us!" Judy exclaimed, cradling a loaf of sourdough bread like it was a newborn baby. Never mind that both Shane and Julia worked at Donner Bakery as bakers and hadn't exactly driven far to come up with their donation to the dinner spread.

Not that I begrudged them bringing sourdough. Donner Bakery's bread was the best in town and people often came from other areas just to get it. My point, though, was that Clay's parents were gushing over it like it was the next best thing to . . . sliced bread. And Clay and I had spent a half hour assembling a charcuterie platter, garnishing it with dried fruit and flowers.

In addition, after this morning's run, Clay had gone to a flower shop and selected the yellow and white blooms that were his mom's favorites. Then he'd stopped by an art gallery and chosen a blown glass vase he thought his mother might like.

"Oh, Clay, did you find these on one of your runs? You're always off on those long runs," Judy said, smiling through what sounded like a criticism.

"Too soon for wildflowers," Clay reminded her. "I went to a shop."

"They're sweet. I'll put them in the vase." She spun off to the kitchen to add water to the vase, returning a few minutes later with the charcuterie platter and a vase full of white roses, which she placed in the middle of the dining table. Clay and Julia were busy talking, and Shane looked away when I tried to catch his eye. Was it strange that his mom had foregone Clay's flowers for these other ones?

I decided not to make something of nothing and reached for a cracker and a slice of Gouda. Clay's mom watched me chew, and I made sure to keep my mouth closed in case she was studying my manners.

"How's work?" Clay's father, Clayton, asked the room.

Shane and Julia, who I knew from around town, effused about how busy Donner Bakery had been helping the Lodge cater a large wedding. Clayton nodded and turned to Clay, who put his arm around me.

"Still love teaching," Clay said. "And this is the fun part of the year when the senior projects come in and we have the carnival, grad night, all the big send-off events for the seniors."

"You teach at the school too?" Clayton asked me.

"I do. I have a lot of the same students, so it's a fun time for me too, putting finishing touches on senior pages before the yearbook goes to press."

Clay's parents nodded and said a few pleasantries about teaching being a noble pursuit. His parents were kind, polite. I probably would have thought nothing of their manner or anything else except for the way they positively doted on Shane.

"And tell us about the symphony, Shane. Will you be there regularly? Should we buy season tickets?" Judy squealed.

"Nah, just a couple times a month when they're playing composers with large French horn parts. The rest of the time, I'm happy playing at the jam sessions with Clay."

"Did Clay tell you Shane used to play for the New York Philharmonic?" Judy asked me.

"Yes, that's amazing." Clay had also told me that his brother hated it and promptly quit the job and moved back to Green Valley to bake bread. That somehow didn't make it into his mother's story. "I just think it's awesome that we have local jam sessions with such talented folks," I said, willing Clay to brag about being a great guitar and ukulele player.

To hear his mom talk of it, Shane practically hung the moon by himself using only his left hand, while his right worked the bell of the French horn.

Wanting to make a good impression on Clay's parents, I considered keeping my opinions to myself. But I was getting more and more riled up each time Clay started talking about his students and one of his parents interrupted and went off on a tangent. Finally, I couldn't take it anymore.

"You should see how much the students look up to Clay. I've had at least a dozen put Shakespeare quotes on their senior pages because he inspired them to read the Bard," I said.

His mother stopped fussing over the flowers and looked at me with a blank expression. "It's nice that you two have similar interests."

"It's more than just an interest. Your son is great at his job. He's molding these kids and they're all the better for it."

She nodded, but said nothing. It made my blood boil seeing his parents be so dismissive of the man I was falling for.

Clay's dad was an older version of Clay, firm jaw, full head of graying hair, and hazel eyes that had the power to evoke a reaction. But he lacked all of Clay's warmth. While Clay's mouth turned up at the corner in that way I loved, his dad's did the opposite, making him look vaguely disappointed, even when he was telling his wife how much he liked her baked Brie appetizer.

"Did you know Clay is running a faster mile time now than he did in high school?" I couldn't help bragging. Clay's hand wrapped around mine and he squeezed, but his face showed no emotion.

"Yes, the running's been a thing since then, that's for sure." Judy blinked at Clay, assessing. I couldn't figure out why his running seemed to bother her rather than make her proud. When I turned to Clay, a question in my eyes, he shook his head and held up a hand to stop me from going farther down that conversational path.

"Are we ready to eat?" Shane asked with more cheer than necessary, pointing us to seats around the table. I tried to make eye contact with Julia—surely I couldn't be the only one who thought this was strange, but Clay's hand wrapped around mine under the table and gave it a squeeze.

"I'll explain later," he said quietly.

We ate dinner around an antique oval dining-room table with high-backed chairs and itchy, uncomfortable cushions. I couldn't imagine Clay growing up here. Everything I knew about him now, including his love for the outdoors and the exuberance with which he taught his students, felt lost in this formal environment.

Dinner went by quickly, with all of us oohing and aahing over Judy's cooking and the bread Julia and Shane brought. Clay was quieter than I'd seen him, and while we were finishing up the meal, I caught Clayton staring at his son with his head cocked to the side, like he was trying to figure out a puzzle.

"You handling everything okay?" he asked so quietly, I wasn't sure anyone else heard him since I was directly next to him. But Clay answered immediately.

"All good."

His dad nodded.

"People count on you. No problem's anything a good attitude can't solve, right, Clayton?" Judy piped up.

It bugged me that she called him Clayton, even though, obviously, it was his name. It didn't fit him. It fit his dad—a little bit stuffy, a little rigid, a little emotionally unavailable. Not that it was my place to come into her home and tell her what to call her son.

Judy rounded the table putting down dessert plates. Her constant motion reminded me of how I used to think of Clay, but lately, he'd slowed down. For me.

"Have you seen Clay's house?" Judy asked me.

"Oh, I have. It's in such a pristine spot there on the lake. He's so lucky to be there."

"Not exactly luck," Clayton grumbled from the head of the table. Clay had told me how he'd inherited the house from his grandmother who felt a kinship with him because they shared some traits. It was starting to make sense now—they'd both suffered from depression, and his grandmother had been his true north when he dealt with the worst of it. Meantime, his parents resented that she'd left the house to him.

"Dad, stop," Shane said, his annoyance seeming like this conversation happened often.

"I'm just saying luck had nothing to do with it. Hard to argue with fact."

"Okay, enough. Can we not discuss this again?" Judy patted her lips and pushed her chair back from the table. "I'll bring out the dessert. Julia, will you help me plate the pie?"

"Of course." Julia looked at me and mouthed, *Sorry,* before following her future mother-in-law from the room.

———

"What the hell was that about?" I whispered the moment the screen door to the back porch slammed behind us. Now that we were outside in the backyard, I felt the air returning to my lungs, but I was no less riled up.

"Don't worry about it. It's just them."

"Meaning you're fine with your own parents treating you like second best when you're awesome in every possible way?"

I had more to say, more anger for these people, more confusion, but it was stifled for now by Clay's large hands cupping the sides of my face and his lips landing hard on mine.

He didn't hesitate for a second out of fear we might be seen by his parents or anyone else. His kiss told me how much he'd been holding back while we were inside the house. Every impassioned answer to his parents' prickly questions, every bit of determination to live a life on his own terms poured out in this kiss. Hungry, insistent, plundering.

His hands gripped my hair like he was afraid he'd lose me if he let go. Lifting my face and angling my lips more squarely against his, he groaned as I pressed against him. He walked me backward with the certainty of someone who knew the terrain and had a plan. I trusted that he wasn't guiding me into a ditch and didn't drop my lips from his.

The light changed, growing shadowy, and I opened my eyes to see we'd entered a stand of trees at the perimeter of the yard.

"Thank you," he said before dipping down to kiss me again. I knew he wasn't taking me 'round back for a quickie before coffee. He just needed to get out of that house as badly as I did. "Thank you for being you," he said in between kisses.

"I will always be me. You don't have to thank me for that."

"Thank you for caring enough to get upset with my parents." His hands didn't leave my face, and he tipped his forehead against mine. "That's just my parents. They don't totally . . . get me."

"What is there to get? You're amazing. They're lucky to have you as a son. What's with all the weirdness?"

He shook his head. "They just don't understand my depression. Never have. They kind of think mental health isn't a real health issue."

I was floored. "Not a real health issue? How can they think that?"

He shrugged, leaning against a tree. He spun me around so my back was to his front and he wrapped his arms around me. Now when he spoke, his voice was soft near my ear. "When I first told them about the bad episodes I was having, they told me to cheer up, try to look at the bright side of things. My mom would remind me how much worse some people have it."

"Like Shane," I said, realizing.

I felt him nod against my neck. "I mean, it's how they see it. He had a real, visible challenge that he was born with, and he's overcome it in amazing ways. My depression hit me later in life and it's not something you can see. Maybe that's why they'd rather think it's not there."

I turned in his arms to face him. "Do not let them convince you of that. It's real and I'm glad you're dealing with it."

On a long blink, he nodded, but the anguish on his face told me there were complicated layers he still hadn't shared. Did he want to share them with me?

"Ally," he whispered, tipping his forehead against mine. "I don't know what I'm doing."

I felt that sinking feeling again in my gut. Reining in my expectations, I reminded myself of everything I knew about Clay. He moved quickly through life, never got pinned down, didn't have relationships. "It's okay, Clay. I'm not expecting anything. You don't have to worry."

"That's not the thing I'm worried about," he ground out, shaking his head.

"What, then?"

He took a step back and his eyes washed over me like a painter studying a subject and deciding where to put the first daub of paint on a canvas. Assessing, undecided, appreciative. He shook his head.

"Clay, you can talk to me."

He stared at the ground for so long I began to worry the earth was receding beneath our feet, so I looked down as well. I saw Clay's feet move, but then I felt them standing toe to toe with mine. His hands cupped my face and he kissed me again, harder this time. All the unanswered questions satisfied with this kiss. It was wet, deep, so swoony. I had the sense of falling, tilting off my axis and into an abyss, a black hole where nothing exists except this kiss.

And that's where I wanted to stay. But I also wanted to understand what was troubling Clay, which is why I was the one who pulled away this time.

"Talk to me," I insisted, taking a step back so he couldn't scramble my brain with another kiss. "Why do you look like you're in pain each time you kiss me?"

He made no effort to look less agonized. "Because I'm scared that each kiss you give me might be the last. Because I've wanted you since I showed up at my friend's house years ago and understood what it meant to fall for someone at first sight. Because I might want you, but I need you more."

"I need you too."

He shook his head. "Stick with me." It was a plea, but I nodded like it was a basic fact. I was falling in love with him, so I saw no other choice.

Clay threaded his fingers between mine, and I leaned my head on his shoulder as we walked. I'd stick with him, even if I worried that he didn't feel the same way about me as I did about him. Even if he'd end up leaving.

We went back into the house to say our goodbyes. Clay's mom embraced me warmly and asked me to come again soon. It was such a strange contrast to the way she'd treated her own son so coolly all night long.

"I love your son." The words slipped out, but I meant them. I wished I'd told him first. Wished I'd been able to formulate the simple three-word phrase when I'd stood in the yard moments earlier, but this final bit of indifference from his parents pushed me to say what I knew I felt.

Clay squeezed my hand, but I didn't look at him, keeping my eyes focused instead on his mom.

"Well, that's nice to hear," Clayton said, clapping his son on the back. "I hope he's smart enough to feel the same."

"He is," Clay said, dipping his face next to mine and kissing me on the temple. Plucking one of the stems from his mother's vase, Clay gazed at the bloom before presenting it to me. His arm circled around my waist. "He loves her too."

My heart cracked open when he said the words. Not because I needed to hear them, but because I could see how much Clay needed to say them. He needed to believe in us, and for the first time, I felt like he did.

CHAPTER
TWENTY-SEVEN

ALLY

"This looks great," I told Carrie Layton as I stood over her shoulder, reviewing her page design for the sports section of the yearbook. She'd overlayed sheer images of students playing their sports on top of the requisite team photos. A baseball player's bat making contact with the ball. A soccer player shooting a goal. A gymnast mid-somersault off the beam. The action shots in the background brought the team photos to life.

She'd devoted the next page spread to more action shots, each one with speech bubbles scattered around the photo with imagined crowd cheers and commentary: *Great shot! Homer!*

"I was trying to give it a little action, make it feel like the sports were happening," Carrie said, assessing the page to see if she'd accomplished that.

"That's how it feels. It's a good choice aesthetically, as well. People will stop and look at these pages because they're interesting," I said.

"That's what I'm hoping. Normally, people kind of skim past the sports pages because they're just team photos, but these athletes work really hard. They deserve better."

"They do."

The bell had already rung, and with a glance at the clock on the wall, Carrie pushed her chair back and began organizing the art supplies in the bins on the desk. "I could do this all day. It's my favorite class," she said.

"Aw, I love having you in this class. You have a great eye."

Carrie slung her backpack over one shoulder and smiled. "Thanks." She hesitated for a second, then reached out and hugged me hard, hands balled into fists. Backing away just as quickly, she looked at the floor. "Sorry."

"Don't be sorry," I said. "You're allowed to express emotions. We're artists in here. That's what art is for."

Raising her gaze, she bit her lip and nodded. "I think so too." Backing away as though she didn't trust herself not to hug me again, she smiled once more. "I'll be back during my free block tomorrow. Is that cool?" she asked.

"Yes. Great. See you then."

I turned back to the art tables to straighten them up, expecting to hear the snick of the door latching behind her. Instead, I heard the approach of footsteps behind me.

Clay.

I turned expectantly, a smile already sneaking across my face at the thought of seeing him. Instead, I was greeted with Pindich's smarmy smirk. Closing my eyes to block out the sight of him, I turned back to the tables.

"Hi there," I said, hoping he'd stumbled into the wrong classroom.

"Ms. Dalbotten." More of a statement than a greeting.

I went back to straightening up. I'd asked the students to leave computer printouts of the pages they'd been working on so I could look at them all together for consistency. Computers were awesome, but I still liked to see things on paper. For that reason, I was shuffling through assorted pages when Pindich came up behind me.

"Messy business," he commented.

"Art gets messy," I said, trying to hide my physical reaction when he came near me. It was hard not to shudder when he got closer than about five feet away. Almost like a force field radiated from him. A force field of sleaze.

He came closer than he needed to, peering over my shoulder at the pages I was straightening. I moved to the side so he could look without being in my physical space. I was so tired of him lurking closer than he should under the pretext that he just didn't understand personal boundaries. He understood them, and he violated them on the daily.

"This is the yearbook?"

"Yes." We were in the yearbook classroom. If it walked and talked like a duck . . . But I held my tongue and swallowed down all the snarky comments in favor of being cheerful and upbeat. "I love it when students make the year-book their own instead of following the cut-and-paste template." I fanned out the pages, hoping he'd say something appreciative about the work they'd done and we could move on.

"Template's there for a reason," he grumbled.

"We're not deviating in any ways that will end up being problematic."

He harrumphed. "We'll see, won't we?"

Was this why he'd ambled into my classroom, to warn me about taking liber-ties with the yearbook design? I was about to ask him when he perched on the edge of a desk facing me and crossed his arms over his chest. His legs stretched out almost far enough so for his feet to touch me, but he left about an inch of space between us. It had the effect of pinning me in place lest I move a fraction of an inch and make contact.

I shifted and put my hands behind me, which allowed me to hop up on another desk and create a little more distance.

"Yes, we shall see. I'm sure you'll be happy with the result. Are you concerned? Do you want to see more of the pages?" I asked.

I would just shower him with sweetness until he agreed that our yearbook was the best-looking version we'd produced in years.

"No, no. That won't be necessary. I trust you," Pindich said.

"Great. Thank you."

He crossed his feet at the ankles and stared me down. I wondered if his gaze was supposed to be intimidating because the dour expression on his face was anything but frightening.

"So I'm here in an unofficial capacity," he began, watching me to gauge my reaction.

"Meaning what?" Was this where he'd put the moves on me? Tell me my job hinged on going on a date with him? People knew Clay and I were dating, so it would be silly for him to choose now, of all times, to hint at it.

If I hadn't been making this list of possibilities in my mind, I may have been better prepared for the words that actually came out of Pindich's mouth. But as it were, he left me flabbergasted when he said, "I assume your new boyfriend has kept you in the dark about the real reason he's suddenly taken a girlfriend. And since you're a smart woman, I assume that long before that, you questioned why Green Valley's most notorious bachelor would be attracted to someone who, let's just say, falls outside his normal type."

So. Many. Words.

So many warring thoughts. My mind buzzed at the sense of doom in his words. And the implications that there was something I didn't know.

In all the time we'd spent together, I'd gotten to know Clay in a way that ran contrary to his reputation. He'd told me why he stayed away from relationships and explained to me why I was different.

And yet . . . was there something I didn't know? Of course, I questioned why he suddenly made a move after all these years. He'd never quite answered that question—why now? Was it just the coincidence of being thrown together on the retreat? I did fancy myself to be a smart woman.

I also felt defensive. About myself as someone worthy of Clay. About Clay as someone who was much more than his shallow reputation allowed people to see. But mostly, I felt defensive of our new relationship that didn't deserve scrutiny from anyone else, especially not our school principal. It was none of his damned business.

"This is none of your damned business," I said before I had a chance to edit my words.

Pindich's surprise spread across his face like lukewarm cream cheese on a bagel. "Maybe, maybe not. But I like you, Ally, and I want the best for you. Selfishly, you being happy makes for a copacetic workplace."

Oh, he was so full of crap. He knew he wasn't making me happy right now with this tease of a scandalous story, yet he persisted with a smile on his face.

"I'm fine. You don't have to worry about me at work," I said. I didn't want him to tell me more. The little he'd said already had me flushed and upset, but letting him see that would give him all the power. I needed to get out of here. Then I'd find Clay and he'd put an end to Pindich's rumor, whatever it was. "I really should go."

I scooted along the desk until I was far enough away from him to get up and make my way toward the door. But my bookbag and purse were stashed in a cubby at the back of the classroom, so I didn't make it out the door before he leveled another verbal blow.

"Clay made a bet that he could get the Green Valley Spinster to fall for him." He waited for my reaction and I did my best not to betray the heat rising in my veins, but my cheeks went rogue. "Didn't know people called you that? Yeah. In case you thought he was interested in you for more noble reasons."

I should have walked out of the room. I should not have let Principal Pindich see that he'd rattled me. But what we should do and what our brains and bodies direct us to do in a moment of crisis are rarely the same thing.

So I stopped before pushing the classroom door open and turned to face him. "Sorry, what?"

His face twitched. He was trying to suppress the world's largest shit-eating grin.

"I think your hearing is fine, Ms. Dalbotten." It annoyed me that he kept calling me Ms. Dalbotten, as though offering me some degree of respect. But I knew that was far from his intention. Normally, he called all faculty by their first names, even when he was referring to one of us in front of a student. Heck, the students called us by our first names half the time, even though they weren't supposed to.

"It's hard to know when you encouraged the district to go with the cheaper healthcare plan, Principal Pin Dick."

He made the same face he always did when I drew out the syllables of his last name. It looked like he was smelling rotting cabbage and extruding it from his rear end at the same time. "Pi-en-deech," he said with a strange accent. "It's German. I shouldn't have to remind you that accuracy is vital when you're around today's youth."

"I never studied German. I'm unfamiliar with the pronunciation of certain words," I said.

"It's a matter of respect, making an effort. Which is why I call you by your proper name, with your chosen pronouns. Respect."

No, this was his way of faking respect, as though he was providing information from one esteemed colleague to another. But Pindich always had an ulterior motive. In fact, I wondered if his insistence that I go on the retreat was somehow part of a larger plan. Not that he could have known Clay and I would fall for each other—on the contrary, he probably assumed I was the safest possible choice to throw in Clay's romantic path because he'd never go for someone like me.

"I don't know who he made the bet with, but I heard about it that night when the staff went to Genie's. Thanks for the invitation, by the way. I just don't want to see you get your feelings hurt when this all blows up." He watched me for a reaction, and I did my best to school my features and give him nothing. "Which it will."

He hadn't budged from his position against the desk, as though he had all day to sit here until I gave him the reaction he wanted. I refused.

The one benefit of having been a wallflower for most of my life was that I didn't allow myself to get bullied by jerks like Pindich because I had nothing to lose by standing my ground. Could they take away my social status? Not if I didn't have any. Could they mess with my self-esteem? Not if I'd already been humbled. Could they make me doubt my intelligence? Nope, not ever.

Jerks like Pindich rarely understood this, so they kept on nudging, trying to get me to care about what they had to say.

I would not react. Instead, I calmly stared back at him, knowing he'd find nothing in my expression. "Who told you this?"

It certainly wasn't the most important piece of information, but I did want to know the answer. In fact, it was the only thing I really wanted to know. He could have been making all of this up to mess with me. Get back at me—again —for turning down his advances over all these years.

And no, I wasn't bulletproof.

A tiny part of me found it all too easy to believe what I felt certain most people knew to be true—Clay, with his pick of every woman in Green Valley, most certainly wouldn't choose me.

Right?

"I was there that night, remember? Let's leave it at that," he said. If he'd had a mustache, no doubt he'd be twirling it.

I couldn't shuffle through my various questions and insecurities in Pindich's presence, and his beady-eyed stare was making me more uncomfortable by the minute. The best thing I could do was show little reaction to what he was telling me and go talk to Clay.

"Thanks for your concern, but you don't have to worry about me." I turned for the door, opened it, and stepped into the hallway before I heard Pindich's final retort.

"Careful . . . ," he warned. "I'd be careful if I were you."

Giving him a final definitive glare, I responded, "I'm always careful."

Then I let the door slam behind me.

TWENTY-EIGHT

CLAY

I'd rounded my third lap on the track when I saw her.

At first, the warmth spread in my heart as usual whenever I caught a glimpse of Ally. Even from a distance, I could see the blond escapees from her ponytail, which always made me think of little children misbehaving. The way she shoved them back into place and ignored them when they sprung free again brought a smile to my face even though I was burning through a six-minute pace.

I slowed a little when I came around the next bend, so I could intercept her as she came closer. On the off chance she hadn't come out here to find me, I wasn't about to let her get away.

As she drew nearer, I noticed an intensity to her stride, mirrored in the consternation on her face. I came to a halt just as she ducked around the bleachers and emerged at the side of the track.

"Hey, you okay?" I asked before she stopped in front of me and crossed her arms. "What's wrong?"

I guided her to where we could take a seat, high up in the bleachers, which gave us perspective over the field. Maybe that would give her perspective on whatever was bothering her. It sometimes worked for me.

"I just had a conversation with Pin Dick," she said, spitting out his name like a curse and emphasizing the end of his name with a hard *k*.

A bolt of panic stabbed at my chest. Even though I knew there could be a host of irritating reasons he'd come talk to her, she seemed upset and I feared the worst.

"Did he do something to you? Say something?" Maybe he'd suggested another one of his "lunch dates."

She turned to me and I saw fire in her eyes. That was heartening. Better than an accusatory glare. "He told me you made a bet that you could get the Green Valley Spinster to fall for you." She pointed to herself with both thumbs. I'd have laughed at the nickname—because it couldn't be more ridiculous—except that she looked so upset. "Please tell me this is just Pin Dick being his usual douchey self. Tell me that's not why you suddenly took an interest in me."

My heart flooded with an unexpected tangle of emotions, but for once, I had no trouble finding words to express my thoughts. "Suddenly?" I shook my head.

I should have been honest with her from the beginning, but my paranoia had kicked in. I'd worried about drawing her in when I knew I didn't deserve to have her.

"Did you hear this rumor?" she asked and shook her head. "You know what, this is stupid. I don't care what Pin Dick said." She huffed a laugh and shrugged. "Unless it's true, obviously. Then I stand by what I told you weeks ago, that I'm giving up on my knight fantasy in favor of harsh reality."

With her hands on her hips, she took on a fighting stance and I thought about everything she'd told me about wanting to be self-sufficient. I didn't think she really believed something so ridiculous as what Pin Dick had said, but her comment about the knight told me she didn't *not* believe it.

And there it was, the sickening pit in my stomach that I knew so well. It wasn't sadness. It was fear mixed with self-loathing mixed with hopelessness. I knew it wasn't rational. Depression wasn't rational. But I felt it—all too familiar.

This was how it began after my ex left, and I'd forgotten how far down it took me.

Rationally, I knew this situation was night-and-day different, but again, rational thoughts rarely factored in when I felt the pull of depression. It was just a feeling. A dark feeling closing in.

But I gave it one solid effort to turn the tide. Maybe I could move the serotonin to where I needed it through sheer force of will and a good attitude.

"Alexandra, I would marry you today if it would convince you that everything Pin Dick just told you is garbage. Today."

"Oh, no, I wasn't trying to trap you into—"

"Ally, if you only knew . . ."

It wasn't the afternoon sunlight that made her squint at me. She had no idea what I meant. Of course she didn't. I'd done too good a job of keeping my feelings hidden.

"Knew what?"

"How long I've fucking loved you. It wasn't some crush all these years. I loved you," I choked out, hating myself for having waited so long to tell her.

Her eyes went round in disbelief. "Clay . . . what?"

I knew I needed to do better than uttering confusing proclamations without anything to back them up. If one of my students turned in an English paper with only a topic sentence and no supporting details, I'd hand over an F without even reading the thing.

"Years. You've captivated me since the day I walked into the kitchen with your brother and saw you baking a cake when you were fifteen. You had flour on your hands and a stripe of it along one cheek, and you didn't notice it. I had to ball my hands into fists to keep from reaching over and wiping it away. Then it was all I dreamed about for months—touching your skin. It was an obsession and I had to tamp it down."

"How did I not know this at all? You were at our house all the time and you basically ignored my existence."

I wiped a bead of sweat from my cheek with my forearm. "It doesn't matter now. All the missed opportunities I had don't matter."

She wrapped her hand around my arm and nodded. "Exactly. We're where we're supposed to be now. So forget about what Pin Dick said. I shouldn't have even mentioned it, but he just gets me so riled up."

And therein lies the problem. "But you believed him."

"No, I didn't," she protested.

The icy feeling of panic was spreading in my chest. I could see where my logic would take us, but I didn't have another option but to pursue it. "Can you tell me there wasn't a small part of you that wondered if he was telling the truth? Wondered about me and my intentions toward you?" I asked.

The dawning on her face told me my answer. "Clay . . . that's not fair."

"Maybe not, but I saw it. I saw how ready you were to believe the worst and lock yourself back down. Self-sufficiency above all else?"

"Come on, Clay. That's not what I'm doing. I'm not running away."

"Not today, but you can't guarantee me that you won't in the future."

She came at me and grasped my arms with both hands. "Clay, listen to what you're saying. Of course, I can't guarantee that. You can't guarantee that you won't get hit by a bus tomorrow. No one can guarantee anything. So we try. We do the best we can and we try."

I looked up at the sky as though some skywriter would have written instructions for what to do when you feel your heart breaking. I wanted to trust her. I wanted to believe that I could be vulnerable and it wouldn't blow up in my face. But all I knew was the fear—fear of ending up back where I'd been with that pill bottle in my hand.

When I looked at Ally, she was shaking her head. "You're going to sabotage this, aren't you? Because of something Pin Dick probably made up. He's getting exactly what he wants—do you realize that? And for what?"

I couldn't come up with an answer. The feeling of defeat roared in my head and drowned out all rational thought. Even on meds, the depressive thoughts still had a stronghold.

"I don't want to give up, but maybe I need to take a beat and get my head in order. Make sure I'm on the right dosage of meds. You deserve someone who's ready to be vulnerable."

She nodded. "I do. I do deserve that. And you're the one who made me believe it. You're the one who convinced me I could hold out for the knight. And now I want to convince you to hold out for me."

"I want to . . . but right now, I can't."

"Try harder."

I felt like a child being reprimanded by a teacher for adding two plus two on my fingers and somehow getting five. Right now, five seemed like the only answer. My brain couldn't get on the same page as hers.

It was unwilling, too afraid of falling more in love than I already was, too afraid to make myself that vulnerable. It felt like too big a risk.

"I want to trust you. I want to be all in. I just don't know how to get there," I admitted.

"You do it by asking for what you want, regardless of the baggage your family has laid on you or your misguided perceptions of yourself, and making something of whatever you've got."

I wanted to take her words at face value and believe she was correct. It sounded simple enough. But maybe I was too far gone to be rescued by words. I'd spent most of my life feeling broken and maybe even love couldn't fix me.

"You were ready to give me my fairy tale, Clay. Why can't you let me do that for you?"

I shrugged. "Because it terrifies me."

"I know. I know it does. But I'm telling you that you can trust me. So come find me when you believe it."

She began stepping down the bleachers, but not before I saw her eyes brim with tears that she wiped with her fingers. And then I just saw her back as she walked away.

CHAPTER
TWENTY-NINE

ALLY

I thought I'd hear from Clay within a day. But as a day turned into three days, I started to lose hope.

At first, the voice inside my head told me that my mother was right—Clay was no different than any other man. Destined to leave.

I'd heard the same refrain—and played it again in my own head—for so many years, it was like a blasted anthem. Only now, I didn't recognize the tune. For the first time, I didn't believe my mother's proclamation.

Her words seemed defeatist—a defense from someone who'd been burned and who'd given up instead of keeping the faith in her own pursuit of romance. I had no idea what had made my mother give up, what had made her cling to a ridiculous bear story and instill her so-called wisdom in me, but it didn't matter now.

Clay had convinced me I was worthy of a happily ever after, long before he'd proven he was the very guy I wanted to give it to me. Long before he'd let his own fears clamp down on him. I still had faith that he'd come around, but when he did, I needed to have my shit sorted.

And I knew what I needed to do to make that happen—I needed to talk to my mom.

Tracking her down on the commune wasn't easy because they had chores they did to keep the place going, and I knew from experience that my mother could be anywhere from the kitchen to the garden at any given hour. She spent long hours tending to vegetables and cooking meals—that was the way she contributed.

I'd never visited her in California but I had an image of what life must be like there—lots of free-spirited women working together to farm and cook. Women who sang folk songs or played mahjong in the evenings.

My mom answered her cell phone after three rings, her face filling the screen of the video chat. "Is this my sweet girl?"

Her cherubic face looked tanned and healthy, with a few more lines than I remembered but the same heart-shaped face as me. Her hair was a touch more gray, hanging in a long braid over her shoulder.

"Hi, Mom. Are you in the garden?" I could see something blurry and green behind her and a fragment of blue sky.

"Yes. I've been working here all morning." She flipped the phone around to show me rows of red chilis hanging on tall plants and bushes bursting with tiny tomatoes. Turning the camera back, she smiled. "How are you doing? Everything okay?"

"Actually, not really. I wanted to talk to you about the whole self-sufficiency thing. I know you think men are only bound to leave and you want me to be independent and on my own . . ."

I waited for her to tell me I'd gotten it wrong, that I'd overcorrected. I wanted her to tell me I should still aim for all the fantasies I'd always had about meeting someone great—like Clay—and believing in a future with a man.

"Yes?" she prompted.

"You don't really think all men are destined to leave, right? I know that was your experience, but it doesn't have to be mine."

She was silent and still for so long that I thought our connection had frozen. "Sweetie, I don't know what you want to hear. I'm just trying to save you from the heartache I experienced. Isn't that what a parent does?"

Her eyes looked so clear that I almost mistook their clarity for sound judgement. And I realized I vehemently disagreed. After meeting Clay's parents, I disagreed even more. Parents were simply humans who brought their own baggage along and had an important choice when it came to raising children: they could push their ideas onto them, or they could give them the tools they needed to form their own.

I didn't know why it took seeing my mother standing in a field in California for me to finally understand that she and I were not the same person. What was right for her didn't need to be right for me.

I was not my mother. And I still believed in love.

"Ally? Everything okay? I should get back to the gardening before it gets too hot." My mom shook me out of my reverie with a tone of impatience more than concern.

"Yes, Mom. Everything's okay. I just wanted to tell you I met someone and I really, really care about him. And . . . I'm happy."

I couldn't tell if maybe she got some pollen in her eye because she started blinking and eventually shaded her eyes from the sun so I couldn't see them. But she nodded. "Okay, well, if you're happy, then I'm happy for you."

And that was it. She didn't add a warning or tsk-tsk me for failing to be a lone wolf. She was happy for me. Which made me happy for myself.

CHAPTER
THIRTY

CLAY

The timing was good at least. If I was going to ruin my life and spiral down into despair, at least I had Senior Project Week to do it in.

While the seniors worked on their final projects, teachers had the week off. In theory, we were available to supervise students and give them feedback on their work, but all of my students had taken the opportunity to work off campus at a Shakespeare festival that would be premiering *As You Like It* in a few weeks.

Some of them had found jobs painting sets or sewing costumes, and a few were learning theater production from the lead producer and would be working through the summer during performances.

All of that made for the perfect setup for wallowing, which was what I'd been doing all week. Eating bags of chips and greasy take-out burgers. Running miles and miles. Drinking too much coffee and not sleeping for days. Now it was Saturday, but it felt like any other day.

The junk food made me feel nauseated and hungover even though I didn't touch a drop of alcohol, but the coffee made me hollow and jittery. I was punishing myself, and the worse I felt, the better I felt, strangely.

I really wanted to avoid having to think, but I'd done some of that as well, evidenced by the full journal I'd written over the past few days. Some of it was illegible due to late-night writing in the dark, but the upshot of my soul-searching was that Ally was correct and I was the idiot who'd listened to her but didn't hear her.

Of all the people in the world, Ally deserved the knight on the white horse. Not sure how or why she imagined I might be that knight, but she was smart enough that I shouldn't doubt her.

Now I just had to figure out how to take a chance.

"Go away," I said to no one. Well, not no one. I said it to whoever was out there pounding on my front door, but it didn't matter who it was because I didn't intend to see that person. Might as well have been Walt Whitman himself, telling me to get into the woods and inhale some fresh air. Didn't matter. I wasn't going to listen to him or anyone else.

I'd been on my couch for the past twenty-four hours at least, minus a couple bathroom breaks and a few staggering trips to the kitchen to refill my coffee cup. Even that was a failure. If I'd been smart, I'd have brought the pot over to the couch so I wouldn't have had to get out from under the gray blanket.

Yes, the same gray blanket I'd wrapped around Ally that first night we'd spent in my yard. It still smelled like her, and I wasn't ready to give that up yet, even though I'd all but given her up. Even though I'd sabotaged us.

The banging continued. I did my best to ignore it. If I didn't acknowledge the person outside, eventually they'd get bored and take off.

Well, a normal person might do that. Unfortunately, Jefferson Dalbotten was not a normal person.

So not normal that he figured crawling in through my kitchen window made perfect sense. I'd left it cracked in order to get some circulation going—even I knew the place was feeling musty after just a day of me staying inside here moping—and apparently Jefferson took that as an invitation to push the sash up all the way and make himself at home. I ignored the rustling in my kitchen the same way I'd ignored the knocking.

Eventually, the man strode into my living room, after having made himself a fresh cup of coffee and having poured one for me as well. Then he walked right past me and opened my front door, where my brother, Shane, stood leaning one shoulder against the frame.

"Jesus, both of you?"

It wasn't going to be a problem. One, two—twenty—it didn't matter how many bros, real or otherwise, showed up at my doors and windows. I didn't feel like talking to any of them, and it was dark enough in my house that if I sat still long enough, they might forget I was here.

Good thing I had that attitude because my parents walked in after Shane. That was new. I eyed him to see why he'd organized a fam bam and he returned my look with a stony stare.

"I think it's time you had a little more support," Jefferson said.

"Yeah? That's for you to decide?"

My mom knelt down next to me. "Well, I'm glad he did. Honey, how could you not tell us how bad things got?"

I rolled my eyes. "Can we not do this?" I looked accusingly at Jefferson, then at Shane. They looked back at me as though I was the problem. I'd never considered it because keeping things to myself just felt like I was saving everyone else the trouble of dealing with my issues.

My dad, ever stoic, nodded. "We're not here to do anything. We're just here to let you know we've got your back. All the time. Anytime." His voice cracked on the last word.

I had no idea what Jefferson had told them—I presumed he'd told them all of it —but it had the effect of visibly shifting something in my parents.

"That's all we came to say," my dad said, moving toward the door. My mother bent down and hugged me. A wave of flowery perfume washed over me, and it struck me for the first time as vaguely comforting. Something I didn't mind feeling.

After the door closed behind my parents, Shane's weight landed on the arm of the couch, judging from the way it shifted. At least he knew enough not to sit down right next to me. I'd either vomit coffee on him or slug him. "That was pretty good, for them," he said.

Arm over my forehead, I nodded in agreement.

"Getting back to the question of why we're both here," Jefferson started, "my sister called me. I went to see her, made sure she was okay. Then I called Shane."

At the mention of Ally, my heart sank. "Is she? Okay?" The sandpaper in my voice made me stand and stagger to the kitchen for a glass of water.

"She's upset, understandably. But she gets what's going on with you. She's smart that way," Jefferson said. "By the way, congrats on finally making a move on my sister. Took you long enough."

I returned to the room to find him half grinning, half grimacing. "How long have you known?" I asked as I got back under my blanket.

"How long have I known you had a thing for her? I dunno, fifteen years? How long have I known about the two of you . . . Well, I saw you that night at Genie's, remember? It was pretty obvious."

"I like to think I have a poker face."

"Yeah, you fucking don't," Shane said.

I refused to move out from under the blanket except to take another sip of my water. Somehow the two cups of coffee hadn't made me feel more awake. Just more morose.

Yeah, pretty sure it was more than two cups. Then, late at night, an attempt to sleep, feeling terrible about myself, more fitful sleep, more coffee. I'd lost count, but somewhere along the way, day had turned to night and that had predictably turned to day again. Not that I could tell much with the shades drawn.

No sooner had I put the glass on the table did Jefferson move it aside, just out of my reach. "Here. Drink this instead." He yanked a bottle of orange juice from his pocket and handed it to me.

"You're a magician now, Jeff?" I grumbled.

"No, I'm your friend, and you're an asshole."

I threw an arm over my eyes, blocking him out. "Correct. Now that we all agree, can you please leave and let me wallow in peace? I know I fucked up. I just needed to figure out what to do about it, and I haven't sorted myself out yet." I was exhausted.

I heard Shane grab handfuls of fast-food wrappers and crumple them into a ball. The smell of grease and sauce made me sick to my stomach.

"Stop that," I ordered. The room went silent. For a moment, I wondered if Shane was still here. Then I heard the sound of him pulling the blinds open a crack. When I chanced a peek through heavy-lidded eyes, the room was light enough for me to see Shane, but not much else.

Shane plunked his solid frame into a chair opposite the couch, crossed one foot over his knee, and sipped his coffee while he assessed me. "You look like a therapist. I don't need a therapist," I said.

"Debatable. And you need me."

Jerking my hand up with the open juice bottle in it, I spilled a good amount of juice over the side. Great, now I'd have to clean the carpet. "That was your fault."

"For making you drink coffee until you were jittery?"

"For coming here. For existing, basically."

I glared at him because he was annoying the shit out of me, looking well-rested and pleased with himself. And why did he need to look so damned perky? "Why are you so damned perky?" I demanded.

"Went for a long run this morning. Something you oughtta do."

"Yeah, yeah."

"Seriously, you'll feel better and then we can talk."

I slumped back on the couch, dipping into a shadow that I hoped would camouflage me completely. Maybe Shane would think I disappeared and go find another errand to do. Or another soul to save. I was beyond salvation.

It didn't occur to me to wonder why Shane was the only one in the room talking to me until Jefferson showed up again with my running shoes in his hand. At least I think they were mine. I couldn't take the two of them moving around so much. The fatigue was real, and they were making it worse.

"Here. Put these on and let's go do some speed drills," Jefferson said.

Exhaling an aggravated sigh, I pulled the blanket fully over my head. That only magnified the scent of Ally's shampoo and made me feel sadder, so I threw the blanket on the ground. I squinted at the two men tag-teaming me in my living room and assessed whether there was any chance they'd go away if I didn't do what they wanted.

The odds were down near zero, since each of them was easily as stubborn as me, and I didn't have the stamina to out-stubborn them.

"Fine. I'll run. But we're not talking."

Jefferson held out his hands like a minister. "Fine. Wear your headphones, I don't care. Just get moving."

I didn't bother changing out of my grungy gray sweatpants and the Green Valley High tee with the brown bear on the front even though I'd probably get hot. Hunching over my shoes, I laced them up and tried to find any excuse for why I needed to be alone in my misery. But Shane didn't give me enough time to come up with anything before he was slapping a baseball cap on my head and shoving me out the door.

All the running I'd been doing had taken a toll on my muscles. I was sore and achy with new blisters on several toes. As promised, Jefferson didn't try to make me talk. I plodded along a couple paces behind him, working the soreness out of my legs, which felt like leaden tree trunks. All of me felt like it had taken root in stale dirt and grown old. That was the effect of self-sabotage.

But as my feet hit the ground, I felt differently than I'd felt the past few days, running alone. The fact was, I wasn't alone. Not like I had been in my twenties. My life was different now—with different, better people in it—and I had to allow for the possibility that I was different too.

I took care of my mental health. I took my meds. And in just a few weeks' time, I had opened my heart to the possibility of loving the only woman I'd ever wanted, and she wasn't scared off.

Until I got in my own way.

Jefferson kept a brisk pace and I forced myself to keep up, though I still trailed him by a couple yards. Every so often he'd glance back and make sure I was still there, but with music playing on his AirPods, he didn't seem to have much interest in me. Which was perfect.

After fifteen minutes, my legs started to feel semi-normal and I picked up my pace a little, almost coming up next to Jefferson before he edged ahead, going faster. Fine. I could play this game.

I lengthened my stride the way I taught my team to do when they wanted to inch up on an opponent without using too much energy. Then, once they drew up parallel, they could pour on some speed and blow right by. It was a morale killer and was often the difference between first and second place in a race.

Without realizing it was happening, the fog began to dissipate from my brain. As I took in a lungful of air and blew it out, I felt like it made room in my body for a deeper breath. It felt good. I inhaled and started feeling human again.

My pace slowed to a jog because I didn't have anything else to prove. Taking more deep breaths felt more important than speed. Jefferson caught up to me and I slowed even more until both of us were trotting at a cooldown pace. It wasn't until then that I looked up and realized he'd taken me on a loop down the road and back along the path near the lake. We were already back at my house.

The scent of bacon hit me as we walked down my driveway, and despite the lingering nausea from lack of sleep, the idea of food didn't repel me. Shane had made a fresh pot of coffee while we were gone and started some eggs and bacon in a skillet. Hash browns cooked on a flat-top grill on the adjacent burner.

Wordlessly, Shane handed me a glass of water. I took it into the bathroom and swallowed down my antidepressant before returning to the kitchen.

Ally was right. My psychiatrist was right. I needed the meds. I needed to think and feel for myself. I was the one who battled it every minute of every day. Not them. If I needed medication to be okay, then I could accept it.

Shane flipped the fried eggs with a spatula in his left hand, separated them, and slid them onto three plates. Pressing down on the hash browns to make them sizzle against the pan, my brother was a great cook. He knew how to get the right amount of crispiness on the potatoes. Those went on the plates next. Last was the bacon, a thick slab, which we all preferred well cooked.

Jefferson raided my refrigerator for ketchup and hot sauce as well as the cream for our coffee.

Then the three of us took our plates back to the living room. With the first sip of coffee, I nodded at them. A run, a cup of coffee, my antidepressant meds—that was the recipe for every good day I'd ever had. At least until I started spending time with Ally.

No one said a word. The only sound was teeth working through the thick bacon and crunching through slices of sourdough toast. About halfway through the meal, I'd caved and let Shane open the blinds about halfway so a horizontal strip of light brightened up the room.

I scooped a final bite of eggs onto the remaining corner of toast and popped it into my mouth, realizing when I looked up that both Shane and Jefferson were staring at me.

"What?" I asked through the mouthful.

Jefferson tipped his head at Shane, giving him the go-ahead to speak. Then he picked up his coffee mug and leaned back in the leather chair, settling in for something that looked like I might hate it.

"You gonna be okay?" Shane asked.

I forced a half smile onto my face and nodded, maybe with too much enthusiasm to be believable. "Sure. Of course. When am I not okay?"

Yeah, I'd overdone it. Both of them squinted at me and grimaced like I was hard to look at.

"Right now," Jefferson said, pointing at me. It felt antagonistic. I was tempted to thank them both for cooking and running and then ask them to leave.

"Listen, it was nice of you to come, but—"

"I should have said something to them earlier," Shane blurted out, standing up and pacing around the room. He shoved a hand in his hair. I couldn't figure out why he was so agitated when I was the one who'd been ambushed.

"Explain." I still wanted to kick them out, but I'd at least listen to whatever he had to say. Shane was an insightful guy. It was bound to be interesting.

"Mom and Dad."

"Still not following."

"I knew how they were with you, but I was too wrapped up in my own self-loathing at the time to be much help to anyone else. And frankly, I didn't know everything."

My fault for not telling him, but he was my younger brother, and it wasn't his job to look out for me. He was the one with symbrachydactyly. Not me. He was the one who had no choice but to have his disability thrust into the spotlight every time he shook hands with someone new.

I was the one who had it easy because my issue was something I could hide from the world. *I* was the one who looked out for *him*.

"It's managed," I said.

"I'm not talking about the depression," he corrected. "I'm talking about how they minimized its existence. They didn't understand it."

We'd never talked about it. I dealt with my shit on my own. It wasn't his problem to solve.

"I get it, feeling like a stranger in your own body sucks." He held up his hand, something he rarely drew attention to—that's how evolved and fine he'd become with his disability. "I can't imagine what it must feel like to be fighting against your brain."

There were so many things I'd thought about saying to my parents and my brother over the years, desperate explanations of how I felt. But I never said anything. That wasn't their fault. I needed to own it.

And I could do better. I could talk to them now. Let them in. Stop resenting them for not understanding when I didn't understand it myself.

"Thank you." I looked at Shane for a sign of what else he needed to hear from me, worried I'd let him down as an older brother.

He nodded and came over and put an arm around me. He knew when it was best to stop talking and give me space.

Shane and Jefferson cleared the plates and sauce bottles off the table, and I picked up the coffee cups. We carried everything to the kitchen and dumped it in the sink. Dishes could be dealt with later.

Shane glanced up at the clock on my wall, drawing my attention to the time. I was right—it was early in the morning, but it was later than I thought. Half past nine.

"You are still going to the carnival tomorrow, right?" Shane asked.

Right. That.

"I should talk to Ally first. I don't want to just show up there without clearing the air."

Jefferson pulled something out of his pocket and handed it to me. A single pink ticket. "Yeah, or you could just show up there and figure it out."

No. I wasn't ready for that. I needed to think some more, make sure I could really do what Ally had urged me to do before I pushed her away. And hell, maybe she wouldn't even want me now.

No, that was wrong. She said I could trust her and I did. I just needed to prove it.

THIRTY-ONE

ALLY

Lucy didn't need a CPR refresher, even though she swore up and down that physician's assistants needed regular training just like everyone else. I didn't doubt that, but I assumed she'd have been able to fit in a quick course at the hospital, rather than signing up for a Saturday session at the community center with half the babysitters and teachers of Green Valley.

But Lucy was the kind of friend who'd pretend she needed a CPR refresher and spend half a day pumping on the chests of plastic dummies if it would keep me company on a day when I needed re-certification. And more than that, when I needed to figure my life out next to a willing friend.

"Are you sure you don't just want to stay in? I can make us breakfast," I offered.

Lucy looked around my small rustic kitchen, peeked at all the take-out containers in my fridge, and shook her head. "We need to get you out of the house before you become one with the furniture."

"I've been out. I go out every day to work," I protested. It was a half-truth. I'd been to work, but I'd pretty much come and gone without lingering or chatting with my colleagues. Most of them probably just thought I was busy working on signage for the carnival and didn't give it a second thought. Only Witty had reached out to make sure I was okay, either because he'd caught wind of potential drama or because he missed having me as his dutiful audience in the teachers' lounge. Likely both.

Meanwhile, Lucy called my bluff on breakfast. "If you can show me where you have an egg or some fresh cheese, I'll let you make me breakfast. Otherwise, we're getting out of here."

I mentally tabulated the contents of my fridge, then admitted, "Fine. You win."

I'd signed up for the class months ago as part of my recipe for self-sufficiency, and this morning, I'd called Lucy to back out.

Fifteen minutes later, she showed up at my house with a vanilla latte. The creamy delicious drink made me think of Clay, which she knew it would, and before I'd finished half of it, I'd told her everything. Somehow, in the process, Lucy had managed to get me out of my yellow plaid pajamas and into a pair of equally comfortable sweatpants.

"These are more fit for public display," she said, pushing me out the door before I had time to protest. I was too bleary after a week of poor sleep to argue.

As we drove to the center of town, Lucy began a monologue she'd obviously prepared before coming. "I just want to say I'm proud of you."

She paused and waited for me to ask why. So it wasn't so much a monologue as a planned discussion. Either way, I groaned at the thought.

"Don't you want to know why?" she teased, her voice lilting over the words.

"You're going to tell me either way, right?"

I didn't have to look at Lucy to know she was smiling, happy she'd caught me in her conversational net. "I'm proud of you for standing up for yourself and asking for the kind of relationship you want. The fairy tale."

Throwing a hand over my eyes, I cringed. "I'm an idiot. Telling that to Clay was idiotic, and look where it got me. Here, with him running for the hills just like my mama warned me he would."

Lucy tsk-tsked, waving a finger while keeping her other hand on the steering wheel. "No, he freaked out because of his own baggage, and you did right, telling him to deal with it." And now I regretted having filled Lucy in on every detail of our breakup.

"But I'm talking about you," she continued. "You did good. You asked for what you wanted and you should always continue to do that. Whether it's with him or somebody else."

"But I want it to be with him," I whined, finally saying the truth out loud.

"I know, honey, I know. And if that stubborn greyhound removes his head from his ass, it will be. I sincerely hope he does."

After that, Lucy stopped talking and let me nurse my latte. Nothing else needed to be said.

———

When we arrived at the community center, I snapped back to reality. Too many people. Too many potential conversations. Too much in general.

And wouldn't you know, the first person Lucy and I ran into was Rosalie. "Hi, you two. Fancy meeting you here, Lucy Gibson. Are you the one teaching the class?"

"Hey, Rosalie." My greeting lacked enthusiasm, but Lucy picked up the slack immediately.

"Aw, good for you for getting certified, but I'm just here for fun."

Rosalie popped her hip out to the side, giving Lucy the once-over with furrowed brows. "Fun? Well, that's sure good to hear. I was worried this class would be a bore."

Lucy didn't have time to respond because the instructor stood at the front of the room in hot-pink scrubs clapping her hands rapidly. Her high ponytail bobbed as she bounced on her toes and greeted us with a smile that instantly gave me a headache. It was just too . . . perky. "Okay, everyone, find a partner and we'll get started in a minute."

The room was empty save for a handful of blue exercise mats in the center and a bunch of folding chairs that had been set to the side to make room for the thirty or so people who were now abuzz with chatter as we partnered up.

"I'm going back to bed," I threatened, turning toward the exit and running smack into John Witty.

"Oh, no you don't." Witty's hair was slicked back like he'd just gotten out of the shower, and it pained me how many people in Green Valley were up and oh so perky at the frightening hour of . . . ten in the morning. Okay, maybe slothful, wallowing Ally needed an intervention.

"Why are you here?" I half whined.

Witty grinned. "Ran into Lucy earlier and she mentioned y'all were taking this class. Since you've been draying around school all week, and Clay's taken five personal days for the first time in forever, I decided all teachers ought to know CPR, including this guy." He pointed to himself with both thumbs.

I couldn't help it. I smiled at my goofball colleague who'd rather lie about wanting to learn how to do two hundred chest compressions than make me ask for help.

I reached out and hugged him and gratefully accepted his return embrace. "Don't be a lonely pot when there's a lid out there that suits you," he whispered.

Before I could answer, our teacher started barking instructions over the din in the room, pointing to the loosely clothed dummies on the blue mats and telling us to gather around them. Witty couldn't help himself—he checked inside our dummy's pants. "It's a dude."

"It's no such thing," Lucy admonished. Witty shrugged.

"Still not sure why you're here," I grunted at Witty, glancing around the room to see if any other high school teachers had shown up, specifically one who taught the senior English seminar. I'd mentioned a couple weeks ago that I was signed up for the course and Clay said he might come along. I couldn't decide whether I was relieved or disappointed not to see him here.

Relieved. No, disappointed. No, just exhausted.

"I'm here for moral support. To encourage you to follow your heart while simultaneously being good to yourself."

And maybe Lucy was right. I had stood up for myself and my romantic aspirations, even if they wouldn't end up coming to fruition with Clay. I was a dreamer, a romantic. I wanted the fairy tale, and dammit, I was going to keep believing in it.

"How do I do that?"

"You do more things that fuel your own happiness," Witty said, producing a white bakery bag seemingly out of thin air and opening it. The scent of a freshly baked almond croissant hit my nose and reminded me that I'd barely eaten in a week.

He took one from the bag and handed it to me, then offered the bag to Lucy.

I took a big bite of the almond pastry and let it dissolve on my tongue. Normally, eating one of Donner Bakery's specialties was something that fueled my happiness. But today it tasted less than good, just like everything felt.

"I'm not sure what those things even are."

Witty chimed in, "You go to work. Engage with your students. Make the carnival the best Green Valley High has ever seen. And you wait for your dumbass boyfriend to come to his senses. Ask me how I know he will." Witty bounced his eyebrows and waited for me to ask him about this newest piece of gossip.

"Not interested, Witty. Not today," Lucy told him. "This is about Ally being Ally. Not self-sufficient Ally or girlfriend Ally. Just Ally—whoever she wants to be."

No one had put it that way before, but upon hearing Lucy say it, I knew she was right. I wanted to be that person, whoever she was, without being guided by her mom's fears or her own self-doubt. "I want to go to Donner Bakery and eat my weight in cake. Then I want to paint signs for the carnival," I said. "So let's revive these dummies and get going."

"Deal," Lucy said. "The cake is my treat."

CHAPTER
THIRTY-TWO

ALLY

Green Valley High had put on great carnivals in the past, but this year's was the best yet, even if my heart wasn't fully in it. I wondered who would be working the kissing booth next to me, since I didn't have faith it would be Clay.

Despite my brother's insinuation that Clay would come around, the entire week had gone by, and now it was Sunday. I still hadn't heard from Clay, which told me he hadn't yet come to his senses.

He also hadn't been at school, so I couldn't see for myself whether he was miserable or flourishing. Meanwhile, I was there every day, sulking with my crappy school coffee.

And the longer he went without talking to me, the less I believed he ever would. I didn't blame myself for it, not at all. I still believed in the fairy-tale stories of romance novels, even as I began to accept that Clay wouldn't be my prince. Someone would.

My art students had gone all out, making vintage-looking wooden signs for every game booth, painting the booths in multicolor with vivid images on each one.

The dunk tank had a cartoon of someone who looked an awful lot like Principal Pindich in pineapple shorts riding on a surfboard over the cliff of a wave.

On the kissing booth, they'd painted swans with intertwined necks, beaks together forming a heart. Game booths with bottles and basketballs were similarly painted, and everything looked fresh and festive. Thanks to the big fundraising push the Parent-Teacher Association gave—some of us suspected they were making amends after the chicken salad incident—we had sold more tickets and raised more money for the school than ever before.

I'd spent the past two days working nearly around the clock with the art students, getting everything finished and hung, and I could barely stand up. Not to mention the past week when my thoughts kept returning to the look on Clay's face when he told me he couldn't be a better man.

He hadn't reached out, and I'd given him the space he asked for. I'd hoped he'd hear my words, even if it took him a week. It was the hardest thing I'd ever had to do because I hated to leave someone who was hurting alone.

But the longer he went without a word, the sadder I got. I remembered what he'd said to me: *The point isn't to be so self-sufficient that you don't need anyone else. The point is to be vulnerable around the right person. To need that person enough to feel something.*

To need that person enough to feel something.

Like a heart breaking.

Crushed into pieces so tiny it can't possibly be restored.

Vulnerable and utterly defenseless.

He'd gotten me here, and now all I could do was feel.

And somehow I had to put on clothes and come help the seniors fundraise for all their end-of-year festivities. I'd made them a promise and I couldn't let them down.

I had to go work the goddamn kissing booth.

———

My shift started at noon and I got to the carnival at exactly noon. I didn't want to chance running into anyone who might want to get into a long conversation about Clay and our failed relationship.

The gossip mill had already taken on a life of its own and there were so many versions of the story about Clay's supposed bet and the new Green Valley Spinster moniker I'd probably never shake. I'd gone to the school board and filed a formal complaint against Pindich, but he always managed to charm someone into letting him skate through his troubles.

So I'd left my house with exactly twelve minutes to spare, knowing I could make the drive, park, and find my way to my booth without having time to chat with anyone. So far, so good.

It shouldn't have made me so nervous to stand in a kissing booth. After all, I knew most of the folks in the Parent-Teacher Association. They were the main people who'd show up at a school fundraiser, right?

Nevertheless, I spent a little extra time getting dressed, curling my hair, and putting on makeup, notably a lip stain that wouldn't be kissed off. Then I thought about Clay and wondered if he'd even show up at the carnival for the second shift in the kissing booth. Probably not, especially not if he was worried about a confrontation with me.

We all got a short lunch break during each shift, and I'd planned to take mine sometime close to two, after a couple hours of kissing. Seemed like I might need some hydration by then, or at least some sustenance.

But when I saw Principal Pin Dick's soggy form making a beeline toward my corner of the carnival, I quickly put the Closed for Lunch placard out in an obvious place where he could see it from thirty feet away.

Exhaling a grateful breath, I wondered if I could make my break last long enough to avoid the principal completely, or if he'd somehow manage to find me.

"Closed for lunch, eh?" The deep baritone set my heart on a collision course with my chest. My face heated and I broke out in a nervous sweat, and that was all before I looked up into Clay's beautiful face, which then sent goose bumps racing across my skin and a plunge of heat from my chest to my core.

"Yes. We get an hour." Why did I tell him that? He didn't care about the rules and regulations of the carnival. Besides, his kissing booth shift started after mine.

So why was he here early? Why was he here now, when I could do nothing to escape? Whatever this was, whatever he wanted to say to me, I had to listen to it here in public. And then get kissed by a hundred strangers.

People were starting to watch us, and the good school teacher in me knew I needed to put a pin in our conversation until after the carnival. But those lips, that hard jaw dusted with a few days' worth of scruff, and those lazy hazel eyes begged me to stay right where I was.

He held up a fistful of tickets, all hot pink. All for my booth.

"You want to kiss me here?" I couldn't help asking.

I was all for spending the rest of the weekend in Clay's bedroom, but the current situation with its array of noisy game booths, petting zoo smells, and most of Green Valley High's student body didn't spark the romance I wanted.

He nodded, all of his normal swagger back in action. He wore dark jeans that hugged his hips, and I knew without him turning around what kind of treatment they'd give his perfectly formed ass. I felt a little torn. I did want him to turn around for my own gawking pleasure, but I also wanted him to stay.

If he'd come here to talk to me—or to kiss me—I wanted to hear what he had to say.

He tore off one ticket and held it up. "So what's the deal? What does one ticket entitle me to?"

Was this how we were going to function now? Him mocking my participation in a school carnival by trying to make me uncomfortable?

Fine. If he wanted to play this game, I'd play.

"Yes, it entitles you to one kiss. One very quick kiss."

"What if I want more?"

I rolled my eyes. "Then you can get back in line behind everyone else and take another turn."

He shook his head. "There won't be anyone else. I bought all the tickets."

Now I was confused.

"Wait, *what?*"

He pulled a wad of pink tickets from his back pocket. There were easily a hundred hot-pink tickets, all marked for the kissing booth. He moved closer and cupped my jaw with one hand. He didn't lean in right away, instead letting himself gaze at me with a look of such adoration that my stomach dropped and my heart squeezed inside my chest. To say nothing about the deep pink invading my cheeks.

Nothing had changed one bit in the way I reacted to him. But something was different in the way he was staring at me now. Possessive. Feral. Hungry.

Shoving the wad of hot-pink paper toward the ticket box, Clay took a step back and nodded at me to deposit them.

"Clay, what are you doing?"

He looked at his watch. "Four-hour shift. Ten seconds a kiss plus twenty seconds or so in between them, though I'd be happy to keep right on going without a break." He winked and his smile turned to a full-on smirk. "Equals four hundred eighty kisses. And I bought five hundred tickets. Every last one of 'em."

"But why?"

"Because I'm not going to let another fucking man kiss you. Not today, not ever."

My breath caught in my throat. My vision went fuzzy. My heart kicked up to a frantic pace. And none of that mattered because Clay's lips were on mine and the world disappeared.

Except for the cheering. Loud, raucous cheering. And when we came up for air, I saw that half the student body and their parents were watching us and cheering us on.

"Let's go." He grabbed my hand and guided me away from the booth. I didn't have time to ask where he wanted to go or why. Maybe it didn't matter. As he intertwined our fingers, I felt the stress and tension of the past few weeks fall away. All the wondering about what Clay would decide for himself finally had an endpoint.

The fact that he'd come here to talk was progress. I knew it cost him a piece of the security he clung to. We were alike in that way. It gave me faith.

"Oh, hi, you two. I see you're exhibiting some PDA in front of our impressionable youth?" Pindich appeared in a fresh, dry tank top that showed a bit too much of his spray tan for my liking. As usual, his smile when his eyes roamed over my cutoff denim shorts was a bit too close to a leer.

I expected Clay to drop my hand. A rule-follower, he would heed the reminder that we shouldn't be holding hands at a school-wide event. But his grip tightened possessively. Looking down, I saw a vein in his forearm bulge. His skin was tanned from afternoons on the track, unlike Pindich's orangey hue.

"Don't fucking look at her like that," Clay said, pinning Pindich with a glare.

Our principal, unaccustomed to being spoken to like that—by Clay of all people—did a double take. His eyes got a little buggy and he tilted his head as though deciding whether he'd heard correctly.

"Did you just . . . threaten the head of school?" Pindich asked, his lips curling.

"I did not," Clay replied calmly. "A threat would imply some form of retribution levied against you if you don't do what I want. I'm just telling you straight. Quit looking at Alexandra like she's some sort of snack. In fact, don't look at her at all."

Pindich turned to me as if to ascertain whether I was on board with Clay's request. "Works for me," I replied.

I barely registered the conversation, still so focused on the feel of Clay's hand wrapped around mine. I hadn't fully allowed myself to accept how much I'd missed him until now. And now, I just wanted to be alone with him.

"I hope you won't mind the lost income when we're forced to downsize the English department next year. I've been thinking that these senior seminars are pulling too much from the budget." Pindich feigned sadness, pulling his lips into an upside-down smile.

Clay took a step closer to Pindich, which highlighted how much taller and more fit he was. He pointed a finger at the principal. "See, now that sounds like a threat."

Pindich remained calm. "Not at all. Just a fact."

"A fact. Yeah, okay, I can handle facts." Clay angled himself so that Pindich was in the shade produced by his towering form. "I've collected a few myself from the Hart Law Firm in Knoxville, where the court just unsealed some documents. Seems there were some inappropriate documents with forged signatures passed off as real. In fact, I believe you knew my grandmother, and her estate plan was rewritten several times—I didn't know you were so tight with her that she almost left you money . . ."

Pindich paled slightly, but it was barely visible beneath the spray tan. When he swallowed like he was choking down a rock, however, that was abundantly visible. "I don't know anything about that."

"You may not, but other people may find it suspicious if they're pointed to the documents."

Pindich pressed his lips together and swayed on his feet. "Again, I have no—"

"Give up the fight. Or I will find every woman you made feel the least bit uncomfortable in the entire county and file a class action lawsuit against you so large it will make your head spin. Starting with the teachers at this school."

I'd never heard Clay talk to anyone that way, and hearing him level Pindich with those words brought me halfway to orgasm.

"You think you could maybe talk to some folks, find some money in the budget so I can keep my classes going?"

When Pindich found his voice, it was small and raspy. "I know it's a student favorite." He turned and made his way back to the dunk tank where I saw the baseball team lining up and ready to bean him.

When I looked back at Clay, he didn't look smug. He didn't look broken. He looked calm. "I heard everything you said to me that day on the track. Loud and clear. And now I have something to say to you. You're mine. You have been from the day we met. I just waited a long fucking time to do something about it. Tell me I didn't wait too long, Alexandra."

And that melted my heart.

"You didn't."

His eyes went soft, that deeper color that was full of passion and heat, but he said nothing.

"Talk to me, greyhound. What are you thinking?"

His lips quirked to the side in that way I loved. Like they couldn't help themselves because something brought on some unexpected joy.

"This. You. It's you."

"What? What's me?"

"Everything. The reason I do . . . everything. The reason it's worth getting up every day and living."

My heart flooded with warmth. I hoped he meant that he was starting to believe all the things I'd tried to convince him of and failed.

"It's not about meds or no meds. It's about finding something that makes me feel like my true self, and you're it, Alexandra. You're my reason."

And there it was. My fairy tale.

I felt tears prick the corners of my eyes for reasons that had nothing to do with my mom or my dad or my own self-sufficiency. I'd held out for what I wanted and he was standing here in front of me telling me what I wanted to hear—that he believed. Not in me, but in himself. And that made me whole.

"You were right. This version of me—if he's good enough to love you—he's good enough."

I shook my head. "No, that's not true. You are more than good enough, Clay. You're the best. Every day. Toward your students, toward me. The only one who hasn't been getting the benefit of the tremendous gifts you put out into the world is you. You've been denying yourself that, and you need to stop."

He nodded slowly, his eyes drifting shut. "I know." When he opened them, they were soft. Determined but with grace. "I know. I'm working on that."

"I think you're already there," I whispered.

CHAPTER
THIRTY-THREE

ALLY

ll I'd told Clay about our date was that it would be outdoors. "Bring a fleece. And a blanket."

His knowing grin when he came to pick me up said I'd sufficiently fooled him. He thought we were going camping.

As much as I'd grown to love the wilderness, especially with him by my side, today's activity would feature no unexpected animals popping up and threatening to eat our picnic lunch, which I carried in a backpack. There would, however, be bears.

"Okay, take this exit," I instructed Clay, pointing to the Cherry Street exit in East Knoxville, where I was on a date. With my boyfriend.

"Turn in here." I watched Clay's face as he recognized the entrance to the Knoxville Zoological Gardens and cast a quizzical look my way. "I know. It will all become clear."

We parked the truck in the lot, and Clay insisted on carrying my backpack, which I allowed as long as he promised not to peek inside. As it was, I was pretty sure he could tell from the weight and the sloshing noise there was a large thermos in there. But he didn't know it contained homemade lemonade with mint springs floating in it.

I paid our entrance fee and felt Clay's hand slip into mine as we walked along the path at the zoo's entrance. He gamely allowed me to lead, never asking where I was taking us or why I'd chosen the zoo.

We walked past the red panda enclosure where I was tempted to stop, but I stayed focused on my destination, which was just a bit farther into the zoo.

Clay saw it before I did. "No, really?" The sheer delight in his voice confirmed I'd made the right choice. Black Bear Falls, the bear habitat in the zoo, was one of the nation's best. When we neared, we could see two bears wrestling with each other in a puddle of water, rolling around to the delight of the kids with their faces pressed up against the outside of the enclosure.

One bear was biting at a stream of water cascading from a rock, and another one was biting its bear companion.

"Perfect spot for us to camp with bears and not worry about getting eaten," I said, pointing at the backpack. "Though we're not spending the night here, in case you're scared."

"Honestly, spending the night inside a zoo freaks me out more than being in the wilderness," Clay admitted.

I thought about that for a moment, and after seeing the outdoors the way Clay did, I had to agree.

We stood and watched the bears for a while, marveling at how much energy they had and how playful they were. "I almost want to meet a bear in the woods now because they seem pretty fun," I said.

"Ha. Still not going to happen, at least not in the places where I'm planning on taking you camping."

"Oh, so you have more camping plans for me, do you?"

"I have a lot more plans for nights inside a tent. Can you blame me?"

God, I loved this man.

Nudging him with my elbow, I pointed to a pristine stretch of grass next to a picnic area. "Let's sit over there. That way we can still watch these guys while we have lunch."

He carried the backpack over to the grass and we unpacked the wooly plaid picnic blanket, the thermos of lemonade, various cups, plates, and utensils, and the mammoth sandwiches I'd picked up at Daisy's early this morning. "And also, there's pie."

He grimaced. "Pie kind of makes me think of that awful dinner at my parents' house."

"That's why I brought it. Figured we needed to reimagine pie."

Clay liked that idea, but even more, he liked the idea of lying down on the blanket with me curled up by his side. As he held one of my hands against his heart, he ran his other hand through my hair. I tipped my head against his shoulder and closed my eyes against the sun, but every time I opened them, Clay looked content.

"This is good, Alexandra. Perfect day."

"Hey, I've always meant to ask you, why do you call me Alexandra?"

"It's your name."

"Yes, but everyone calls me Ally."

He shrugged. "I've always preferred Alexandra."

That made me smile. "She prefers you too."

We stayed like that for half the day, eventually digging into the picnic, but mostly content to lie around lazily and talk. About our parents and the way they'd done a number on us in their own ways. About our students who we'd miss next year when they all scattered for college. About us—hopes and plans, dreams for a future neither one of us had imagined when we first met as teenagers.

Well, maybe we each had hoped for it a little bit.

"This is what we should have done from the beginning, instead of breaking up," Clay said, gesturing around us.

"What, having a picnic with bears?"

"No, talking. And I take full responsibility for that. I panicked and I left the table. That's on me."

I hated that he continued beating himself up over it. "Bygones," I said. When he opened his mouth to argue, I covered it with mine. He didn't resist, instead gripping my shoulders and gently pulling me down onto the blanket. I curled up on my side and wrapped my arms around his neck, giving myself just enough distance so I could look at him but not an inch more.

Our bodies connected in so many places—my knees curled in against his stomach, his hand on my cheek, mine behind his neck, one of his legs draped lazily over mine. Our hearts intertwined. Like they were meant to be.

Like they called the shots and we just needed to wake up and realize it.

EPILOGUE

ALLY

Three Months Later

The bright yellow glare of sun glinting off of Bandit Lake hurt my eyes but I couldn't stop staring in the direction of where Clay was rigging up a rowboat. He'd given me a sincere, well-reasoned speech about why I'd love fishing, soft-pedaling the part about rigging up a fishing pole with worms or chunks of raw fish and sitting in a cold boat for hours waiting for something to bite.

The hopeful glint in his eyes was tempered by the hesitancy in his voice while he waited for me to object. I did not. Yet.

"You know, fishing should've been an early part of your plan," Clay called from the boat, a dozen yards away. As though he could read my mind. "If you wanted to be sure you could survive on your own, finding a food source was probably more important than learning to put a tourniquet around a tree," he observed. Even though his face was lost to the glare of sunlight, I knew he was smiling.

"Maybe I never really wanted to be the kind of self-sufficient that involves worms," I called back, a smile equally evident in my voice. There were still a few things he didn't know about me, my ability to catch a fish being one of them.

A second later, he pulled me against him. With the sunlight and all, I didn't see him coming, but I wasn't about to send him away. "Oh. Hi," I said, wrapping my arms around his waist.

"Hi." He nuzzled my neck and kissed me there. Then he moved along my jaw and over to my mouth. His preferred destination. And mine.

But we risked never making it onto the lake if we didn't stay focused, and realizing this, he tore himself away. But his eyes never left me as he walked backward to the boat.

Meantime, I busied myself checking our cooler to make sure it had wine chilling over ice and the charcuterie platter I'd pulled together yesterday when Clay proposed the idea of taking a late-summer boat ride on the lake.

Now, tucking a container of fried chicken in next to the various meats and cheeses, I had to admit our basket was photo-worthy. Even the green checkered tablecloth that lined the accompanying picnic basket felt perfect amid the pine trees. The basket contained plates and utensils, along with a loaf of Donner Bakery's finest French bread and enough dried fruit, brownies, and cookies to keep Clay and me well-fed for a week, just in case our boat sprung a leak or something and we ended up stranded.

Finally, Clay finished wiping down the interior of the rowboat and set up the oars on either side. When he beckoned me over, I noticed orange life jackets splayed out over the bench seats in the silver metal boat. "Oh, I'm good. I know how to swim," I said.

"Safety first," he said, giving me a stern teacher scowl that I didn't buy for a minute.

"Don't you think you're going a little overboard?"

"Haha."

"No. Seriously. Do you really want me to wear a life jacket?"

His serious expression told me he did. Well, fine. I'd kiss that look right off his face. I walked over to the boat, where Clay held up the orange flotation device. Slinging it over my head, he used the webbed straps to tug me closer to him. His lips found mine as he tightened the straps.

"You think you can distract me from what you're doing that easily, sailor?" I mumbled when he broke the dizzying kiss.

"I think I want you to come back from our little outing alive, that's what I think."

"But a rowboat barely moves. I don't see myself falling out of a stationary boat and getting swallowed by Jaws."

But there was no dissuading Captain Clay. He tightened the straps a bit more and I sucked in a breath. "Too. Tight. Can't. Breathe . . . ," I gasped.

He loosened them only slightly before tossing his own life vest over his head. Somehow, he managed to make a traffic-cone-orange flotation device look sexy as hell on his tall, muscular frame. Catching me ogling him, he gave me the crooked, smiling-despite-himself grin that I loved.

"Okay, ready to take this baby for a spin?" He pointed at the silver boat bobbing in the water, still tied to a post with a long rope. The simplest of boats, it had three faded wooden benches inside the metal shell and two oars resting on top of those. Clay rolled up his pants and kicked off his tennis shoes, before tossing them into the boat. I was about to do the same, reaching down to untie my shoes, when Clay scooped me up with a strong hand beneath my legs. "Allow me," he said.

I wrapped my arms around his neck as he waded into the water beside the boat and deposited me over the side on one of the bench seats. The boat tipped to the side, so I scooted toward the middle of the bench to right it. Instantly, I realized that this boat could, in fact, dump me into the lake without much trouble, so I straightened out my life vest and turned to watch Clay behind the boat.

He swept the rope over the top of the post and rolled it up as he walked back to the boat. With one hand on the side of the boat and a skilled hop, he hefted himself inside the shell and settled himself on the bench facing me. Then he handed me one of the oars.

"Ready?"

I was too busy marveling at how he did everything with such easy grace. If I hadn't fallen for him already, I'd have yet a new reason.

"I feel like I should be wearing a frilly dress, and holding a parasol," I said in a coquettish Southern accent. "Like we're a scene in a Monet painting." Except that we weren't. Not in casual clothes and orange life vests.

Clay chuckled and started rowing, his back facing the lake. His body moved with easy grace, those well-defined arms working the oars. No wonder I couldn't concentrate on my own rowing. I gave it my best effort, but I was barely moving the boat compared to Clay's strong strokes. "If I'm about to hit the Loch Ness monster or something, you'll let me know, okay?"

I looked over his shoulder and confirmed, "Nessie must still be sleeping."

His smirk let me know he expected me to have a similar fear of water creatures as I'd once had of bears. But he didn't know everything about me, especially some of the lengths I'd gone to in order to feel self-sufficient.

Over the past several months with Clay, I'd come to realize that being truly self-sufficient meant knowing what I needed in order to be happy. And he was sitting in front of me, rowing backward, knowing he could trust me to guide him in the right direction. The feeling was mutual.

The lake was calm and still in the late morning. A couple other boats bobbed in the distance, but out here, surrounded by water, we were alone. Soft ripples in the water lapped at the sides of the boat and rocked it gently beneath us.

Once we'd rowed far enough from shore to reach the sunny part of the lake, Clay pulled in the oars and handed me a fishing pole. I examined the fishing pole while he opened the container of bait. It was a Quest spin rod, which made sense for fishing off a boat for medium-sized fish, the type stocked in Bandit Lake each summer. We'd catch mainly striped bass or trout, and I'd had experience with both. The fishing course I'd taken a couple years back required me to learn a list of over three hundred species of fish that could be found in Tennessee. This little outing on the lake was going to be a snap.

"It takes a bit of getting used to. The bait smells awful, but it's part of the fun." Clay winked and it was all I could do not to yank his face into my hands and kiss the smirk from it, but I waited patiently for the rest of his explanation.

I held the hook steady as Clay opened a container of tiny crawfish. The sight of them made me squirm, even if I knew they made the best bait. Bravely, I reached for one and skewered it on the hook, making sure it was good and stuck so it wouldn't drop off when it hit the water.

Clay took me through the basics, pulling me onto the middle bench where he sat and wrapping his arms around me tighter than they needed to be for a fishing lesson. As I let my head fall back against his chest, I decided that fishing was my new favorite hobby. "I don't care if we catch any fish. Can we just stay here like this?"

Leaning in to kiss my neck . . . my cheek . . . my temple . . . he nodded. "As long as you want."

Being careful not to tip the boat too much to either side, I turned so our lips met more squarely and Clay let the pole fall to the floor of the boat. The little craft had a nice wide bottom, so I wasn't overly worried about tipping as I pressed against Clay's hard chest and our kiss grew heated and deep within seconds.

The *thwack, thwack* of canoe oars in the near distance stopped us from testing the balance of the boat under very different conditions. Clay's cheeks were pink as he backed away and gave the paddler a wave.

"Okay, I think I'm ready to give it a go." Still sitting beside Clay, I brought the pole up at an angle, gave it a sharp toss, and let the line go. The lure and hook went sailing out over the water and dropped cleanly in a few dozen yards away.

"That look okay?"

Clay's head whipped around and he caught my smug expression before his smile broke wide open. He wagged a finger at me. "You've been holding out on me, honey."

"I know how to fish," I admitted.

I'd never seen such a big smile on Clay's face. "You know how to fish," he confirmed.

Nodding, I reeled my line in taut and gave it a little tug.

"What else do you know how to do?" he asked, hanging his arm around my shoulder and leaning back on his other hand to take in the view around us.

I didn't want to admit that I hadn't ever really thought about all that I'd learned to do in service of being self-sufficient, which didn't feel any more like code for being alone. I'd simply done it because each new thing was a step in front of the one behind it. And here I was, self-sufficient and relaxing in the arms of someone who loved me for it.

I shrugged and planted a kiss on the warm skin of his shoulder. "All to be revealed in time."

Pulling away so he could look at me, Clay gazed at my sun-heated face like I was a marvel or just very interesting. "You never cease to surprise me, Alexandra Dalbotten, and I will never stop loving that about you." I tipped my head against his shoulder, so content as our little boat bobbed on the water, my fishing line glinting in the sun. "I'll never stop loving *you*," he said, more quietly, almost like it was a thought he didn't realize he was speaking out loud.

That's how it had become between us—a shorthand of thoughts and words that all pointed in the same direction. Me toward him, him back toward me. I couldn't imagine a life apart from Clay, and it astounded me every day to be able to affirm that thought.

"I love you too, Clay. So, so much."

I'd spent so much time thinking about how to surprise Clay with my fishing abilities that it never occurred to me he planned to surprise me with something himself. So even when he moved off the bench to kneel in front of me, I still wasn't getting it.

The boat drifted and turned, which caused the sun to hit my eyes, so I couldn't quite see what Clay was doing, except that I had a vague sense of him reaching for something in the pocket of his shirt.

"You have a fish in there? Planning to slip it onto your line when I wasn't looking and claim you caught something?" I teased.

"Exactly right. Gotta have a fish story to tell the grandkids."

"Grandkids?" It was then that the boat turned enough that I could fully see Clay, who was holding out a ring box with a beautiful solitaire diamond ring that made my eyes bug right out of my head.

"Clay . . ."

He nodded. "Alexandra. I knew that once I had you, I wouldn't be able to let you go. I knew it when I was seventeen. And I knew it when you walked into my yard with fourteen jackets. You're my forever."

After all the hours and hours I'd spent reading romance novels, soaking up every storybook proposal, dreaming of a moment like this, and never quite believing it could happen to me, I needed a moment to take it in.

And yet . . .

That was one moment too long. That was the moment a rather large fish took the bait off my line and began swimming away with the hook. My line whizzed from the rod, and on instinct, I let it race for a moment before rapidly cranking the spindle and fighting to reel the fish in. Standing up, I braced myself against the center bench, but the boat lurched to the side.

Clay jumped up to help, but that unsteadied us further. As I grabbed on to him, he caught the fishing pole falling from my hands and took over reeling the fish in as the boat listed even more to the side.

I'll always see what happened next as if it played out in slow motion. The boat tipping farther. Me crying out and gripping Clay's arm. Clay leaning toward the center of the boat to steady it. Me watching the ring box fly out of his hand and leaning toward it. The boat tipping the rest of the way and landing both of us in the water.

The moments after that were a blur. Kicking, swimming, bumping my head on the shell of the boat, worrying because Clay was underwater for what seemed like way too long.

And then he emerged. I'd never been so relieved to see a person's face. He flipped water from his hair and looked me over. "You okay?"

"Yeah," I panted, treading water. Clay tugged on my life vest, pulling me closer. In between us, his other hand emerged from the water holding the ring. "Oh my God, I thought it went overboard!"

"It did. But the box had foam in the lid, so it didn't sink," he said, going with the flow as though this was part of his plan to begin with. For all I knew, maybe it was.

Sliding the ring onto my finger, he asked me again to be his forever. His wife.

"Yes. Yes, greyhound. I'm yours."

The fishing pole and the fish long gone, we stayed in the water, allowing the life vests to do the work while Clay held my face in his hands and kissed me until we were chilled through from the lake water. And then a little bit longer.

When he leaned away to look at me, he chuckled and tipped his head against mine. "Guess I was incorrect."

"Why?"

"Because *this* is the story we'll tell our grandkids."

Indeed.

ABOUT THE AUTHOR

Stacy Travis writes charming, spicy romance about bookish, sassy women and the hot alphas who fall for them.

Writing makes her infinitely happy, but that might be the coffee talking.

She's worked as a journalist, camp counselor, TV writer, SAT tutor, corporate finance researcher, education technology editor, and non-fiction author. When she's not on a deadline, she's in running shoes complaining that all roads seem to go uphill. Or on the couch with a margarita. Or fangirling at a soccer game.

She's never met a dog she didn't want to hug. And if you have no plans for Thanksgiving, she'll probably invite you to dinner.

Stacy lives in Los Angeles with her very tall sons and a poorly-trained rescue dog who hoards socks. And she's serious about the Thanksgiving thing.

Find Stacy Travis online:
Facebook: https://www.facebook.com/stacytravisromance
Facebook Reader Group: https://bit.ly/2B1psS4fbgroup
Instagram: https://www.instagram.com/stacytravisauthor
TikTok: https://www.tiktok.com/@stacytravisauthor

Find Smartypants Romance online:
Website: www.smartypantsromance.com
Facebook: https://www.facebook.com/smartypantsromance
Twitter: @smartypantsrom
Instagram: @smartypantsromance
Newsletter: https://smartypantsromance.com/newsletter/

ALSO BY STACY TRAVIS

The Summer Heat Duet

1. The Summer of Him: A Mistaken Identity Celebrity Romance

2. Forever with Him: An Opposites Attract Contemporary Romance

The Berkeley Hills Series – small-town romance series of standalone novels

1. In Trouble with Him: A Forbidden Love Contemporary Romance (Finn and Annie's story)

2. Second Chance at Us: A Second Chance Romance (Becca and Blake)

3. Falling for You: A Friends to Lovers Romance (Isla and Owen)

4. The Spark Between Us: A Grumpy-Sunshine, Brother's Best Friend Romance (Sarah and Braden)

5. Playing for You: A Sports Romance (Tatum and Donovan)

6. No Match for Her - an Opposites-Attract Friends-to-Lovers Romance (Cherry and Charlie)

San Francisco Strikers Series – sports series of standalone novels

1. He's a Keeper: A Grumpy-Sunshine Sports Romance (Molly and Holden)

2. He's a Player: A Second Chance Sports Romance (Jordan and Tim)

3. He's a Charmer: A Brother's Best Friend Sports Romance (Linnie and Weston)

ALSO BY SMARTYPANTS ROMANCE

<u>Green Valley Chronicles</u>

<u>The Love at First Sight Series</u>

<u>Baking Me Crazy by Karla Sorensen (#1)</u>

<u>Batter of Wits by Karla Sorensen (#2)</u>

<u>Steal My Magnolia by Karla Sorensen (#3)</u>

<u>Worth the Wait by Karla Sorensen (#4)</u>

<u>Fighting For Love Series</u>

<u>Stud Muffin by Jiffy Kate (#1)</u>

<u>Beef Cake by Jiffy Kate (#2)</u>

<u>Eye Candy by Jiffy Kate (#3)</u>

<u>Knock Out by Jiffy Kate (#4)</u>

<u>The Donner Bakery Series</u>

<u>No Whisk, No Reward by Ellie Kay (#1)</u>

<u>Dough You Love Me? By Stacy Travis (#2)</u>

<u>Tough Cookie by Talia Hunter (#3)</u>

<u>Muffin But Trouble by Talia Hunter (#4)</u>

<u>*Oh Brother! Series*</u>

<u>Crime and Periodicals by Nora Everly (#1)</u>

<u>Carpentry and Cocktails by Nora Everly (#2)</u>

<u>Hotshot and Hospitality by Nora Everly (#3)</u>

<u>Architecture and Artistry by Nora Everly (#4)</u>

<u>*Small Town Silver Fox Series*</u>

<u>Love in Due Time by L.B. Dunbar (#1)</u>

<u>Love in Deed by L.B. Dunbar (#2)</u>

<u>Love in a Pickle by L.B. Dunbar (#3)</u>

<u>The Green Valley Library Series</u>

<u>Prose Before Bros by Cathy Yardley (#1)</u>

<u>**Story of Us Collection**</u>

My Story of Us: Zach by Chris Brinkley (#1)

My Story of Us: Thomas by Chris Brinkley (#2)

My Story of Us: Grayson by Chris Brinkley (#3)

Seduction in the City

<u>Cipher Security Series</u>

Code of Conduct by April White (#1)

Code of Honor by April White (#2)

Code of Matrimony by April White (#2.5)

Code of Ethics by April White (#3)

<u>Cipher Office Series</u>

Weight Expectations by M.E. Carter (#1)

Sticking to the Script by Stella Weaver (#2)

Cutie and the Beast by M.E. Carter (#3)

Weights of Wrath by M.E. Carter (#4)

<u>Common Threads Series</u>

Mad About Ewe by Susannah Nix (#1)

Give Love a Chai by Nanxi Wen (#2)

Key Change by Heidi Hutchinson (#3)

Not Since Ewe by Susannah Nix (#4)

Lost Track by Heidi Hutchinson (#5)

Ewe Complete Me by Susannah Nix (#6)

Meet Your Matcha by Nanxi Wen (#7)

All Mixed Up by Heidi Hutchinson (#8)

Write or Wrong by Heidi Hutchinson (#9)

<u>Bad Habit Book Club Series</u>

Nun Too Soon by Lissa Sharpe (#1)

<u>Educated Romance</u>

<u>Work For It Series</u>

Street Smart by Aly Stiles (#1)

Heart Smart by Emma Lee Jayne (#2)

Book Smart by Amanda Pennington (#3)

Smart Mouth by Emma Lee Jayne (#4)

Play Smart by Aly Stiles (#5)

Look Smart by Aly Stiles (#6)

Smart Move by Amanda Pennington (#7)

Stage Smart by Aly Stiles (#8)

Lessons Learned Series

Under Pressure by Allie Winters (#1)

Not Fooling Anyone by Allie Winters (#2)

Can't Fight It by Allie Winters (#3)

The Vinyl Frontier by Lola West (#4)

Out of this World

London Ladies Embroidery Series

Neanderthal Seeks Duchess by Laney Hatcher (#1)

Well Acquainted by Laney Hatcher (#2)

Love Matched by Laney Hatcher (#3)

Wolf Brothers Series

Truth or Wolf by Anne Marsh (#1)

Wolf and Bare It by Anne Marsh (#2)